The
Heretic's
Apprentice

The Sixteenth Chronicle
of Brother Cadfael

Ellis Peters

Futura

A Futura Book

First published in Great Britain in 1989 by
Headline Book Publishing plc

This edition published in 1990 by
Futura Publications, a Division of
Macdonald & Co (Publishers) Ltd
London & Sydney

ISBN 0 7088 4410 8

Printed in Great Britain by
BPCC Hazell Books
Aylesbury, Bucks, England
Member of BPCC Ltd.

Futura Publications
A Division of
Macdonald & Co (Publishers) Ltd
Orbit House
1 New Fetter Lane
London EC4A 1AR
A member of Maxwell Macmillan Pergamon Publishing Corporation

The Heretic's Apprentice

By the same author

The Heretic's Apprentice

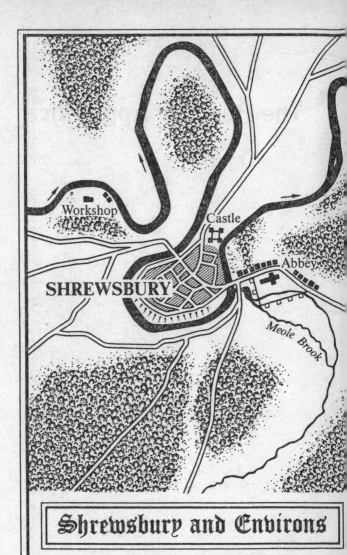

Workshop

Castle

Abbey

SHREWSBURY

Meole Brook

𝕾𝖍𝖗𝖊𝖜𝖘𝖇𝖚𝖗𝖞 𝖆𝖓𝖉 𝕰𝖓𝖛𝖎𝖗𝖔𝖓𝖘

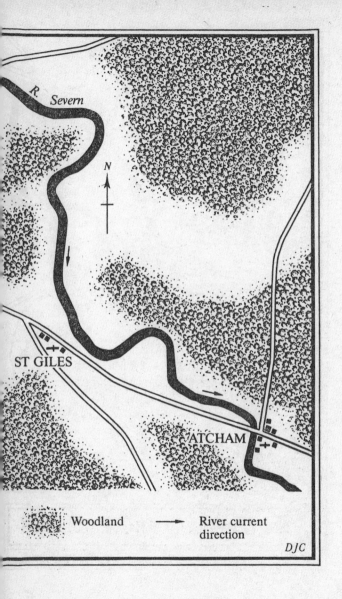

R. *Severn*

N

ST GILES

ATCHAM

Woodland   → River current direction

DJC

Chapter One

N THE nineteenth day of June, when the eminent visitor arrived, Brother Cadfael was in the abbot's garden, trimming off dead roses. It was a task Abbot Radulfus kept jealously to himself in the ordinary way, for he was proud of his roses, and valued the brief moments he could spend with them, but in three more days the house would be celebrating the anniversary of the translation of Saint Winifred to her shrine in the church, and the preparations for the annual influx of pilgrims and patrons were occupying all his time, and keeping all his obedientiaries busy into the bargain. Brother Cadfael, who had no official function, was for once allowed to take over the dead-heading in his place, the only brother privileged to be trusted with the abbatial blossoms, which must be immaculate and bright for the saint's festival, like everything else within the enclave.

This year there would be no ceremonial procession all the way from Saint Giles, at the edge of the town, as there had been two years previously, in 1141. There her relics had rested while proper preparation was made to receive them, and on the great day, Cadfael remembered, the threatened rain had fallen all around, yet never a drop had spattered her reliquary or its attendants, or doused the candles that accompanied her erect as lances,

1

undisturbed by the wind. Small miracles following wherever Winifred passed, as flowers sprang in the footsteps of Welsh Olwen in the legend. Great miracles came more rarely, but Winifred could manifest her power where it was deserved. They had good reason to know and be glad of that, both far away in Gwytherin, the scene of her ministry, and here in Shrewsbury. This year the celebrations would remain within the enclave, but there would still be room enough for wonders, if the saint had a mind to it.

The pilgrims were already arriving for the festival, in such numbers that Cadfael hardly spared a look or an ear for the steady bustle far up the great court, round the gatehouse and the guest-hall, or the sound of hooves on the cobbles, as grooms led the horses down into the stable-yard. Brother Denis the hospitaller would have a full house to accommodate and feed, even before the festival day itself, when the townsfolk and the villagers from miles around would flood in for worship.

It was only when Prior Robert was seen to round the corner of the cloister at the briskest walk his dignity would permit, and head purposefully for the abbot's lodging, that Cadfael paused in his leisurely trimming of spent flowers to note the event, and speculate. Robert's austere long visage had the look of an angel sent on an errand of cosmic importance, and endowed with the authority of the superb being who had sent him. His silver tonsure shone in the sun of early afternoon, and his thin patrician nose probed ahead, sniffing glory.

'We have a more than ordinarily important visitor,' thought Cadfael. And he followed the prior's progress into the doorway of the abbot's lodging with interest, not greatly surprised to see the abbot himself issue forth a few minutes later, and set off up the court with Robert striding at his side. Two tall men, much of a height, the one all smooth, willowy elegance, carefully cultivated, the other all bone and sinew and hard, undemonstrative intelligence. It had been a severe blow to Prior Robert when he was passed over in favour of a stranger, to fill the vacancy left by the deposition of Abbot Heribert, but he had not given up hope. And he was durable, he might even outlive Radulfus and come into his own at last. Not, prayed Cadfael devoutly, for many years yet.

He had not long to wait before Abbot Radulfus and his visitor came down the court together, in the courteous and wary conversation of strangers measuring each other at first meeting. Here was a guest of too great and probably too private significance to be housed in the guest-hall, even among the nobility. A man almost as tall as Radulfus, and in all but the shoulders twice his width, well-fleshed and portly almost to fat, and yet it was powerful and muscular flesh, too. At first glance his was a face rounded and glossy with good living, full-lipped, full-cheeked and self-indulgent. At second glance the lips set into a formidable and intolerant strength, the fleshy chin was seen to clothe a determined jaw, and the eyes in their slightly puffy settings had nevertheless a sharp and critical intelligence. His head was uncovered, and wore the tonsure, otherwise Cadfael, who had never seen him before, would have taken him for some baron or earl of the king's court, for his clothing, but for its sombre colours of dark crimson and black, had a lordly splendour about its cut and its ornament, a long, rich gown, full-skirted but slashed almost to the waist before and behind for riding, its gold-hemmed collar open in the summer weather upon a fine linen shirt, and a gold-linked chain and cross that circled a thick, muscular throat. Doubtless there was a body-servant or a groom somewhere at hand to relieve him of the necessity of carrying cloak or baggage of any kind, even the gloves he had probably stripped off on dismounting. The pitch of his voice, heard distantly as the two prelates entered the lodging and vanished from sight, was low and measured, and yet held a suggestion of current displeasure.

In a few moments Cadfael saw the possible reason for that. A groom came down the court from the gatehouse

3

leading two horses to the stables, a solid brown cob, most likely his own mount, and a big, handsome black beast with white stockings, richly caparisoned. No need to ask whose. The impressive harness, scarlet saddle-cloth and ornamented bridle made all plain. Two more men followed with their less decorated horseflesh in hand, and a packhorse into the bargain, well loaded. This was a cleric who did not travel without the comforts to which he was accustomed. But what might well have brought that note of measured irritation into his voice was that the black horse, the only one of the party worthy to do justice to his rider's state, if not the only one fitted to carry his weight, went lame in the left foreleg. Whatever his errand and destination, the abbot's guest would be forced to prolong his stay here for a few days, until that injury healed.

Cadfael finished his clipping and carried away the basket of fading heads into the garden, leaving the hum and activity of the great court behind. The roses had begun to bloom early, by reason of fine, warm weather. Spring rains had brought a good hay crop, and June ideal conditions for gathering it. The shearing was almost finished, and the wool dealers were reckoning up hopefully the value of their clips. Saint Winifred's modest pilgrims, coming on foot, would have dry travelling and warm lying, even out of doors. Her doing, perhaps? Cadfael could well believe that if the Welsh girl smiled, the sun would shine on the borders.

The earlier sown of the two pease fields that sloped down from the rim of the garden to the Meole brook had already ripened and been harvested, ten days of sun bringing on the pods very quickly. Brother Winfrid, a hefty, blue-eyed young giant, was busy digging in the roots to feed the soil, while the haulms, cropped with sickles, lay piled at the edge of the field, drying for fodder and bedding. The hands that wielded the spade were huge and brown, and looked as if they should have been clumsy, but in fact were as deft and delicate in

4

handling Cadfael's precious glass vessels and brittle dried herbs as they were powerful and effective with mattock and spade.

Within the walled herb-garden the drowning sweetness hung heavy, spiced and warm. Weeds can enjoy good growing weather no less than the herbs on which they encroach, and there was always work to be done at this season. Cadfael tucked up his habit and set to work on his knees, close to the warm earth, with the heady fragrance disturbed and quivering round him like invisible wings, and the sun caressing his back.

He was still at it, though in a happy languor that made no haste, rather luxuriating in the touch of leaf and root and soil, when Hugh Beringar came looking for him two hours later. Cadfael heard the light, springy step on the gravel, and sat back on his heels to watch his friend's approach. Hugh smiled at seeing him on his knees.

'Am I in your prayers?'

'Constantly,' said Cadfael gravely. 'A man has to work at it in so stubborn a case.'

He crumbled a handful of warm, dark earth between his hands, dusted his palms, and Hugh gave him a hand to help him rise. There was a good deal more steel in the young sheriff's slight body and slender wrist than anyone would suppose. Cadfael had known him for five years only, but drawn nearer to him than to many he had rubbed shoulders with all the twenty-three years of his monastic life. 'And what are you doing here?' he demanded briskly. 'I thought you were north among your own lands, getting in the hay.'

'So I was, until yesterday. The hay's in, the shearing's done, and I've brought Aline and Giles back to the town. Just in time to be summoned to pay my respects to some grand magnate who's visiting here, and is none too pleased about it. If his horse hadn't fallen lame he'd still be on his way to Chester. Have you not a drink, Cadfael, for a thirsty man? Though why I should be parched,' he added absently, 'when he did all the talking, is more than I know.'

Cadfael had a wine of his own within the workshop, new but fit to drink. He brought a jug of it out into the sunshine, and they sat down together on the bench against the north wall of the garden, to sun themselves in unashamed idleness.

'I saw the horse,' said Cadfael. 'He'll be days yet before he's fit to take the road to Chester. I saw the man, too, if it's he the abbot made haste to welcome. By the sound of it he was not expected. If he's in haste to get to Chester he'll need a fresh horse, or more patience than I fancy he possesses.'

'Oh, he's reconciled. Radulfus may have him on his hands a week or more yet. If he made for Chester now he wouldn't find his man there, there's no haste. Earl Ranulf is on the Welsh border, fending off another raid from Gwynedd. Owain will keep him busy a while.'

'And who is this cleric on his way to Chester?' asked Cadfael curiously. 'And what did he want with you?'

'Well, being frustrated himself – until I told him there was no hurry, for the earl was away riding his borders – he had a mind to be as busy a nuisance to all about him as possible. Send for the sheriff, at least exact the reverence due! But there is a grain of purpose in it, too. He wanted whatever information I had about the whereabouts and intentions of Owain Gwynedd, and especially he wished to know how big a threat our Welsh prince is being to Earl Ranulf, how glad the earl might be to have some help in the matter, and how willing he might be to pay for it in kind.'

'In the king's interests,' Cadfael deduced, after a moment of frowning thought. 'Is he one of Bishop Henry's familiars, then?'

'Not he! Stephen's making wise use of the archbishop for once, instead of his brother of Winchester. Henry's busy elsewhere. No, your guest is one Gerbert, of the Augustinian canons of Canterbury, a big man in the household of Archbishop Theobald. His errand is to make a cautious gesture of peace and goodwill to Earl

6

Ranulf, whose loyalty – to Stephen's or any side! – is never better than shaky, but might be secured – or Stephen hopes it might! – on terms of mutual gain. You give me full and fair support there in the north, and I'll help you hold off Owain Gwynedd and his Welshmen. Stronger together than apart!'

Cadfael's bushy eyebrows were arched towards his grizzled tonsure. 'What, when Ranulf is still holding Lincoln castle, in Stephen's despite? Yes, and other royal castles he holds illegally? Has Stephen shut his eyes to that fashion of support and friendship?'

'Stephen has forgotten nothing. But he's willing to dissemble if it will keep Ranulf quiet and complacent for a few months. There's more than one unchancy ally getting too big for his boots,' said Hugh. 'I fancy Stephen has it in mind to deal with one at a time, and there's one at least is a bigger threat than Ranulf of Chester. He'll get his due, all in good time, but there's one Stephen has more against than a few purloined castles, and it's worth buying Chester's complacence until Essex is dealt with.'

'You sound certain of what's in the king's mind,' said Cadfael mildly.

'As good as certain, yes. I saw how the man bore himself at court, last Christmas. A stranger might have doubted which among us was the king. Easy going Stephen may be, meek he is not. And there were rumours that the earl of Essex was bargaining again with the empress while she was in Oxford, but changed his mind when the siege went against her. He's been back and forth between the two of them times enough already. I think he's near the end of his rope.'

'And Ranulf is to be placated until his fellow-earl has been dealt with.' Cadfael rubbed dubiously at his blunt brown nose, and thought that over for a moment in silence. 'That seems to me more like the bishop of Winchester's way of thinking than King Stephen's,' he said warily.

'So it may be. And perhaps that's why the king is

using one of Canterbury's household for this errand, and not Winchester's. Who's to suspect any motion of Henry's mind could be lurking behind Archbishop Theobald's hand? There isn't a man in the policies of king or empress who doesn't know how little love's lost between the two.'

Cadfael could not well deny the truth of that. The enmity dated back five years, to the time when the archbishopric of Canterbury had been vacant, after William of Corbeil's death, and King Stephen's younger brother, Henry, had cherished confident pretensions to the office, which he certainly regarded as no more than his due. His disappointment was acute when Pope Innocent gave the appointment instead to Theobald of Bec, and Henry made his displeasure so clear and the influence he could bring to bear so obvious that Innocent, either in a genuine wish to recognise his undoubted ability, or in pure exasperation and malice, had given him, by way of consolation, the papal legateship in England, thus making him in fact superior to the archbishop, a measure hardly calculated to endear either of them to the other. Five years of dignified but fierce contention had banked the fires. No, no suspect earl approached by an intimate of Theobald's was likely to look behind the proposition for any trace of Henry of Winchester's devious manipulations.

'Well,' allowed Cadfael cautiously, 'it may suit Ranulf to be civil, seeing his hands are full with the Welsh of Gwynedd. Though what Stephen can offer him by way of help is hard to see.'

'Nothing,' agreed Hugh with a short bark of laughter, 'and Ranulf will know that as well as we do. Nothing but his forbearance, but that will be worth welcoming, in the circumstances. Oh, they'll understand each other well enough, and no trust on either side, but either one of them will see that the other will keep to his part for the present, out of self-interest. An agreement to put off contention to a more convenient time is better at this moment than no agreement at all, and the need to look over a shoulder every hour or so. Ranulf can give all his mind to Owain Gwynedd, and Stephen can give all his to the matter of Geoffrey de Mandeville in Essex.'

'And in the meantime we must entertain Canon Gerbert until his horse is fit to bear him.'

'And his body-servant and his two grooms, and one of Bishop de Clinton's deacons, lent as his guide here through the diocese. A meek little fellow called Serlo, who goes in trembling awe of the man. I doubt if he'd ever heard of Saint Winifred, for that matter – Gerbert, I mean, not Serlo – but he'll be wanting to direct her festival for you, now that he's halted here.'

'He had that look about him.' Cadfael admitted. 'And what have you told him about the small matter of Owain Gwynedd?'

'The truth, if not the whole truth. That Owain is able to keep Ranulf so busy on his own border that he'll have no time to make trouble elsewhere. No need to make any real concessions to keep him quiet, but sweet talk can do no harm.'

'And no need to mention that you have an arrangement with Owain,' agreed Cadfael placidly, 'to leave us alone here, and keep the earl of Chester off your back. It may not restore any of Stephen's purloined castles in the north, but at least it keeps the earl's greedy hands off any more of them. And what's the news from the west? This uneasy quietness down there in Gloucester's country has me wondering what's afoot. Have you any word of what he's up to?'

The desultory and exhausting civil war between cousins for the throne of England had been going on for more than five years, in spasmodic motion about the south and west, seldom reaching as far north as Shrewsbury. The Empress Maud, with her devoted champion and illegitimate half-brother Earl Robert of Gloucester, held almost undisputed sway now in the south-west, based on Bristol and Gloucester, King Stephen held the rest of the country, but with a shaky and tenuous grip in those parts most remote from his base in London and the southern counties. In such disturbed conditions every baron and earl was liable to look to his own ambitions and opportunities, and set out to secure a little kingdom for himself rather than devote his energies to supporting king or empress. Earl Ranulf of Chester felt himself distant enough from either rival's power to feather his own nest while fortune favoured the bold, and it was becoming all too plain that his professed loyalty to King Stephen took second place to the establishment of a realm of his own spanning the north from Chester to Lincoln. Canon Gerbert's errand certainly implied no confidence in the earl's word, however piously pledged, but was meant to hold him quiescent for a time for his own interests, until the king was ready to deal with him. So, at least, Hugh judged the matter.

'Robert,' said Hugh, 'is busy strengthening all his defences and turning the south-west into a fortress. And he and his sister between them are bringing up the lad she hopes to make king some day. Oh, yes, young Henry is still there in Bristol, but Stephen has no chance in the world of carrying his war that far, and even if he could, he would not know what to do with the boy when he had him. But neither can she get more good out of the child than the pleasure of his presence, though perhaps that's benefit enough. In the end they'll have to send him home again. The next time he comes – the next time it may be in earnest and in arms. Who knows?'

The empress had sent over into France, less than a year ago, to plead for help from her husband, but Count Geoffrey of Anjou, whether he believed in his wife's claim to the throne of England or not, had no intentions of sending over to her aid forces he himself was busy using adroitly and successfully in the conquest of Normandy, an enterprise which interested him much more than Maud's pretensions. He had sent over, instead of the knights and arms she needed, their ten-year-old son.

What sort of father, Cadfael wondered, could this Count of Anjou be? It was said that he set determined store upon the fortunes of his house and his successors, and gave his children a good education, and certainly he had every confidence, justifiably, in Earl Robert's devotion to the child placed in his charge. But still, to send a boy so young into a country disrupted by civil war! No doubt he had Stephen's measure, of course, and knew him incapable of harming the child even if he got him into his hands. And what if the child himself had a will of his own, even at so tender an age, and had urged the venture in his own right?

Yes, an audacious father might well respect audacity in his son. No doubt, thought Cadfael, we shall hear more of this Henry Plantagenet who's minding his lessons and biding his time in Bristol.

'I must be off,' said Hugh, rising and stretching lazily in the warmth of the sun. 'I've had my fill of clerics for today – no offence to present company, but then, you're no cleric. Did you never fancy taking minor orders, Cadfael? Just far enough to claim the benefit if ever one of your less seemly exploits came to light? Better the abbot's court than mine, if ever it came to it!'

'If ever it came to it,' said Cadfael sedately, rising with him, 'the likelihood is you'd need to keep your mouth tight shut, for you'd be in it with me nine times out of ten. Do you remember the horses you hid from the king's round-up when –'

Hugh flung an arm round his friend's shoulders, laughing. 'Oh, if you're to start remembering, I can more than match you. Better agree to let old deeds rest. We were always the most reasonable of men. Come on, bear me company as far as the gatehouse. It must be getting round towards Vespers.'

They made their way along the gravel path together without haste, beside the box hedge and through the vegetable garden to where the rose beds began. Brother Winfrid was just coming over the crest from the slope of the pease-field, striding springily with his spade over his shoulder.

'Get leave soon, and come up and see your godson,' said Hugh as they rounded the box hedge, and the hum and bustle of the court reached out to surround them like the busy sound of bees in swarm. 'As soon as we reach town Giles begins asking for you.'

'I will, gladly. I miss him when you go north, but he's better there through the summer than here shut within walls. And Aline's well?' He asked it serenely, well aware that he would have heard of it at once if there had been anything amiss.

'Blooming like a rose. But come and see for yourself. She'll be expecting you.'

They came round the corner of the guest-hall into the court, still almost as lively as a town square. One more horse was being led down to the stables, Brother Denis was receiving the arriving guest, dusty from the road, at the door of his domain; two or three attendant novices were running to and fro with brychans and candles and pitchers of water; visitors already settled stood watching the newcomers throng in at the gatehouse, greeting friends among them, renewing old acquaintances and embarking on new; while the children of the cloister, oblates and schoolboys alike, gathered in little groups, all eyes and ears, bouncing and shrilling like crickets, and darting about among the pilgrims as excitedly as dogs at a fair. The passing of Brother Jerome, scuttling up the court from the cloister towards the infirmary, would normally have subdued the boys into demure silence, but in this cheerful turmoil it was easy to avoid him.

'You'll have your house full for the festival,' said Hugh, halting to watch the coloured chaos, and taking pleasure in it as candidly as did the children.

In the group gathered just within the gate there was a sudden ripple of movement. The porter drew back towards the doorway of his lodge, and on either side people recoiled as if to allow passage to horsemen, but there was no sharp rapping of hooves striking the cobbles under the arch of the gateway. Those who entered came on foot, and as they emerged into the court the reason for making such generous way for them became apparent. A long, flat handcart came creaking in, towed by a thickset, grizzled countryman before, and pushed by a lean and travel-stained young man behind. The load it carried was covered by a dun-coloured cloak, and topped with a bundle wrapped in sacking, but by the way the two men leaned and strained at it it was seen to be heavy, and the shape of it, a man's height long and shoulder-wide, brought mortality to mind. A ripple of silence washed outward from it, and by degrees reached the spot where Hugh and Cadfael stood watching. The children looked on great-eyed, ears pricked, at once awestricken and inquisitive, intent on missing nothing.

'I think,' said Hugh quietly, 'you have a guest who'll need a bed somewhere else than in the guest-hall.'

The young man had straightened up wincingly from stooping into the weight of the cart, and looked round him for the nearest authority. The porter came towards him, circling the cart and coffin with the circumspect bearing of one accustomed to everything, and not to be put out of countenance even by the apparition of death intruding like a morality play into the preparations for a festival. What passed between them was too soft, too earnest and private to be heard beyond the two of them, but it seemed that the stranger was asking lodging for both himself and his charge. His bearing was reverent and courteous, as was due in these surroundings, but also quietly confident. He turned his head and gestured with his hand towards the church. A young fellow of perhaps twenty-six or twenty-seven years, in clothes sun-faded and very dusty from the roads. Above average tall, thin and sinewy, large-boned and broad-shouldered, with a tangle of straw-coloured hair somewhat fairer than the deep tan of his forehead and cheeks, and a good, bold prow of a nose, thin and straight. A proud face, somewhat drawn with effort just now, and earnest with the gravity of his errand, but by nature, Cadfael thought, studying him across the width of the court, it should be an open, hopeful, good-natured countenance, ready to smile, and a wide-lipped mouth ready to confide at the first friendly invitation.

'One of your flock from here in the Foregate?' asked Hugh, viewing him with interest. 'But no, by the look of him he's been on the roads from somewhere a good deal more distant.'

'But for all that,' said Cadfael, shaking his head over an elusive likeness, 'it seems to me I've seen that face before, somewhere, at some time. Or else he reminds me of some other lad I've known.'

'The lads you've known in your time could come from half the world over. Well, you'll find out, all in good time,' said Hugh, 'for it seems Brother Denis is giving his attention to the matter, and one of your youngsters is off into the cloister in haste to fetch somebody else.'

The somebody else proved to be no less than Prior Robert himself, with Brother Jerome trotting dutifully at his heels. The length of Robert's stride and the shortness of Jerome's legs turned what should have been a busy, self-important bustle into a hasty shamble, but it would always get Jerome in time to any spot where there was something happening that might provide him with occasion for curiosity, censure or sanctimony.

'Your strange visitors are acceptable,' observed Hugh, seeing how the conference was proceeding, 'if only on probation. I suppose he could hardly turn away a dead man.'

'The fellow with the cart I do know,' said Cadfael. 'He comes from close under the Wrekin, I've seen him bringing goods in to market. Cart and man must be hired for this delivery. But the other has come from far beyond that, for sure. Now I wonder how far he's brought his charge, hiring help along the way. And whether he's reached the end of his journey here.'

It was by no means certain that Prior Robert welcomed the sudden appearance of a coffin in the centre of a court thronged with pilgrims hoping for good omens and pleasurable excitement. In fact Prior.Robert never showed an approving face to anything that in any way disrupted the smooth and orthodox course of events within the enclave. But clearly he could find no reason to refuse whatever was being requested here with due deference. If only on probation, as Hugh had said, they were to be permitted to remain. Jerome ran officiously to round up four sturdy brothers and novices, to hoist the coffin from the cart and bear it away towards the cloister, bound, no doubt, for the mortuary chapel within the church. The young man lifted the modest roll of his possessions, and trudged somewhat wearily along behind the cortège, to vanish into the south archway of the cloister. He walked as if he were stiff and footsore, but bore himself erect and steadily, with no studied show of grief, though his face remained thoughtfully solemn, preoccupied rather with what went on in his own mind than what those around him here might be thinking.

Brother Denis came down the steps from the guest-hall and walked briskly down the court after this funereal procession, presumably to retrieve and house with decent friendliness the living guest. The onlookers stared after for a moment, and then returned to their interrupted occasions, and the hum and motion of activity resumed, at first softly and hesitantly, but very soon more vociferously than before, since they had now something pleasurably strange to talk about, once the moment of awe was over.

Hugh and Cadfael crossed the court to the gatehouse in considering silence. The carter had taken the shafts of his lightened cart and hauled it back through the arch of the gatehouse into the Foregate. Evidently he had been paid for his trouble in advance, and was content with his hire.

'It seems that one's job is done,' said Hugh, watching

15

him turn into the street. 'No doubt you'll soon hear what's afoot from Brother Denis.'

Hugh's horse, the tall grey he perversely favoured, was tethered at the gatehouse; no great beauty in looks or temperament, hard-mouthed, strong-willed and obstinate, with a profound contempt for all humanity except his master, and nothing more than the tolerant respect of an equal even for Hugh.

'Come up soon,' said Hugh with his toe in the stirrup and the reins gathered in his hand, 'and bring me all the gossip. Who knows, in a day or so, you may be able to fit a name to the face.'

Chapter Two

ADFAEL CAME out from the refectory after supper into a light, warm evening, radiant with reflected brightness from a rosy sunset. The readings during the meal, probably chosen by Prior Robert in compliment to Canon Gerbert, had been from the writings of Saint Augustine, of whom Cadfael was not as fond as he might have been. There is a certain unbending rigidity about Augustine that offers little compassion to anyone with whom he disagrees. Cadfael was never going to surrender his private reservations about any reputed saint who could describe humankind as a mass of corruption and sin proceeding inevitably towards death, or one who could look upon the world, for all its imperfections, and find it irredeemably evil. In this glowing evening light Cadfael looked upon the world, from the roses in the garden to the wrought stones of the cloister walls, and found it unquestionably beautiful. Nor could he accept that the number of those predestined to salvation was fixed, limited and immutable, as Augustine proclaimed, nor indeed that the fate of any man was sealed and hopeless from his birth, or why not throw away all regard for others and rob and murder and lay waste, and indulge every anarchic appetite in this world, having nothing beyond to look forward to?

In this undisciplined mood Cadfael proceeded to the infirmary, instead of to Collations, where the pursuit of Saint Augustine's ferocious righteousness would certainly continue. Much better to go and check the contents of Brother Edmund's medicine cupboard, and sit and gossip a little while with the few old brothers now too feeble to play a full part in the order of the monastic day.

Edmund, a child of the cloister from his fourth year and meticulous in observation, had gone dutifully to the chapter-house to listen to Jerome's reading. He came back to make his nightly rounds just as Cadfael was closing the doors of the medicine-cupboard, and memorising with silently moving lips the three items that needed replenishment.

'So this is where you got to,' said Edmund, unsurprised. 'That's fortunate, for I've brought with me someone who needs to borrow a sharp eye and a steady hand. I was going to try it myself, but your eyes are better than mine.'

Cadfael turned to see who this late evening patient might be. The light within there was none too good, and the man who came in on Edmund's heels was hesitant in entering, and hung back shyly in the doorway. Young, thin, and about Edmund's own height which was above the average.

'Come in to the lamp,' said Edmund, 'and show Brother Cadfael your hand.' And to Cadfael, as the young man drew near in silence: 'Our guest is newly come today, and has had a long journey. He must be in good need of his sleep, but he'll sleep the better if you can get the splinters out of his flesh, before they fester. Here, let me steady the lamp.'

The rising light cast the young man's face into sharp and craggy relief, fine, jutting nose, strong bones of cheek and jaw, deep shadows emphasising the set of the mouth and the hollows of the eyes under the high forehead. He had washed off the dust of travel and brushed

18

into severe order the tangle of fair, waving hair. The colour of his eyes could not be determined at this moment, for they were cast down beneath large, arched lids at the right hand he was obediently holding close to the lamp, palm upturned. The young man who had brought with him into the abbey a dead companion, and asked shelter for them both.

The hand he proffered deprecatingly for inspection was large and sinewy, with long, broad-jointed fingers. The damage was at once apparent. In the heel of his palm, in the flesh at the base of the thumb, two or three ragged punctures had been aggravated by pressure into a small inflamed wound. If it was not already festering, without attention it very soon would be.

'Your porter keeps his cart in very poor shape,' said Cadfael. 'How did you impale yourself like this? Pushing it out of a ditch? Or was he leaving you more than your share of the work to do, safe with his harness in front there? And what have you been using to try and dig out the splinters? A dirty knife?'

'It's nothing,' said the young man. 'I didn't want to bother you with it. It was a new shaft he'd just fitted, not yet smoothed off properly. And it did make a very heavy load, what with having to line and seal it with lead. The slivers have run in deep, there's wood still in there, though I did prick out some.'

There were tweezers in the medicine cupboard. Cadfael probed carefully in the inflamed flesh, narrowing his eyes over the young man's palm. His sight was excellent, and his touch, when necessary, relentless. The rough wood had gone deep, and splintered further in the flesh. He coaxed out fragment after fragment, and flexed and pressed the place to discover if any still remained. There was no telling from the demeanour of his patient, who stood placid and unflinching, taciturn by nature, or else shy and withdrawn here in a place still strange to him.

'Do you still feel anything there within?'

19

'No, only the soreness, no pricking,' said the youth, experimenting.

The path of the longest splinter showed dark under the skin. Cadfael reached into the cupboard for a lotion to cleanse the wound, comfrey and cleavers and woundwort, which had got its name for good reason. 'To keep it from taking bad ways. If it's still angry tomorrow, come to me and we'll bathe it again, but I think you have good healing flesh.'

Edmund had left them, to make the round of his elders, and refill the little constant lamp in their chapel. Cadfael closed the cupboard, and took up the lamp by which he had been working, to restore it to its usual place. It showed him his patient's face fully lit from before, close and clear. The deep-set eyes, fixed unwaveringly on Cadfael, must surely be a dark but brilliant blue by daylight; now they looked almost black. The long mouth with its obstinate set suddenly relaxed into a wide boyish smile.

'Now I do know you!' said Cadfael, startled and pleased. 'I thought when I saw you come in at the gatehouse I'd seen that face somewhere before. Not your name! If ever I knew that, I've forgotten it years since. But you're the boy who was clerk to old William of Lythwood, and went off on pilgrimage with him, long ago now.'

'Seven years,' said the boy, flashing into animation at being remembered. 'And my name's Elave.'

'Well, well, so you're safe home after your wanderings! No wonder you had the look of having come half across the world. I remember William bringing his last gift to the church here, before he set out. He was bent on getting to Jerusalem, I recall at the time I half wished I could go with him. Did he reach the city indeed?'

'He did,' said Elave, growing ever brighter. 'We did! Lucky I was that ever I took service with him, I had the best master a man could have. Even before he took the notion to take me with him on his journey, not having a son of his own.'

'No, no more he had,' agreed Cadfael, looking back through seven years. 'It's his nephews took over his business. A shrewd man he was, and a good patron to our house. There are many here among the brothers will remember his benefits . . .'

He caught himself up abruptly there. In the flush of recollection of the past he had lost sight for a while of the present. He came back to it with a sudden recoil into gravity. This boy had departed with a single companion, and with a single companion he now returned.

'Do you tell me,' Cadfael asked soberly, 'that it's William of Lythwood you've brought home in a coffin?'

'It is,' said Elave. 'He died at Valognes, before we could reach Barfleur. He'd kept money by to pay his score if it happened, and get us both home. He'd been ill since we started north through France, sometimes we had to halt a month or more along the way till he could go again. He knew he was for dying, he made no great trouble about it. And the monks were good to us. I write a good hand, I worked when I could. We did what we wanted to do.' He told it quite simply and tranquilly; having been so long with a master content in himself and his faith, and unafraid of his end, the boy had grown into the same practical and cheerful acceptance. 'I have messages to deliver for him to his kin. And I'm charged to ask a bed for him here.'

'Here in abbey ground?' asked Cadfael.

'Yes. I've asked to be heard tomorrow at chapter. He was a good patron to this house for all his life, the lord abbot will remember that.'

'It's a different abbot we have now, but Prior Robert will know, and many others among us. And Abbot Radulfus will listen, you need not fear a refusal from him. William will have witnesses enough. But I'm sorry he could not come home alive to tell us of it.' He eyed the lanky young man before him with considered respect. 'You've done well by him, and a hard road you must have had of it, these last miles. You must have been

21

barely a grown man when he took you off overseas.'

'I was nearly nineteen,' said Elave, smiling. 'Nineteen and hardy enough, strong as a horse I was. I'm twenty-six now, I can make my own way.' He was studying Cadfael as intently as he was being studied. 'I remember you, Brother. You were the one who soldiered in the east once, years ago.'

'So I did,' acknowledged Cadfael, almost fondly. Confronted with this young traveller from places once well known, and sharp with memories for him, he felt the old longings quickening again within him, and the old ghosts stirring. 'When you have time, you and I could have things to talk about. But not now! If you're not worn out with journeying, you should be, and there'll be a moment or two to spare tomorrow. Better go and get your sleep now. I'm bound for Compline.'

'It's true,' owned Elave, heaving a long, fulfilled sigh at having reached the end of his charge. 'I'm main glad to be here, and have done with what I promised him. I'll bid you goodnight, then, Brother, and thanks.'

Cadfael watched him cross the width of the court to the steps of the guest-hall, a tough, durable young man who had packed into seven years more journeying than most men saw in a lifetime. No one else within these walls could follow in spirit where he had been, no one but Cadfael. The old appetite stirred ravenously, after contented years of stability and peace.

'Would you have known him again?' asked Edmund, emerging at Cadfael's shoulder. 'He came one or twice on his master's errands, I remember, but between eighteen or so and his middle twenties a man can change past recognition, especially a man who's made his way to the ends of the earth and back. I wonder sometimes, Cadfael, I even glimpse sometimes, what I may have missed.'

'And do you thank your father for giving you to God,' wondered Cadfael, 'or wish he'd left you your chances among men?' They had been friends long enough and closely enough to permit such a question.

Brother Edmund smiled his quiet, composed smile. 'You at least can question no one's act but your own. I am of a past order, Cadfael, there'll be no more of me, not under Radulfus, at any rate. Come to Compline, and pray for the constancy we promised.'

The young man Elave was admitted to chapter next morning, as soon as the immediate household affairs had been dealt with.

The numbers at chapter were swelled that day by the visiting clerics. Canon Gerbert, his mission necessarily delayed for a while, could not but turn his frustrated energies to meddling in whatever came to hand, and sat enthroned beside Abbot Radulfus throughout the session, and the bishop's deacon, committed to faithful attendance on this formidable prelate, hovered anxiously at his elbow. This Serlo was, as Hugh had said, a meek little fellow with a soft, round, ingenuous face, much in awe of Gerbert. He might have been in his forties, smooth-cheeked and pink and wholesome, with a thin, greying ring of fair hair, erased here and there by incipient baldness. No doubt he had suffered from his over-powering companion along the road, and was intent simply on completing his errand as soon and as peaceably as possible. It might seem a very long way to Chester, if he was instructed to go so far.

Into this augmented and august assembly Elave came when he was bidden, refreshed and bright with the relief of reaching his goal and shedding his burden of responsibility. His face was open and confident, even joyful. He had no reason to expect anything but acceptance.

'My lord,' said Elave, 'I have brought back from the Holy Land the body of my master, William of Lythwood, who was well known in this town, and has been in his time a benefactor to the abbey and the church. Sir, you will not have known him, for he left on his pilgrimage seven years ago, but there are brothers here who will remember his gifts and charities, and bear witness for him. It was his wish to be buried in the cemetery here at the abbey, and I ask for him, with all respect, his funeral and grave within these walls.'

Probably he had rehearsed that speech many times, Cadfael thought, and shaped and reshaped it doubtfully, for he did not seem like a man of many or ready words, unless, perhaps, he was roused in defence of something he valued. However that might be, he delivered it from the heart. He had a pleasant voice, pitched agreeably low, and travel had taught him how to bear himself among men of all kinds and all fortunes.

Radulfus nodded acknowledgement, and turned to Prior Robert. 'You were here, Robert, seven years ago and more, as I was not. Tell me of this man as you remember him. He was a merchant of Shrewsbury?'

'A much respected merchant,' said the prior readily. 'He kept a flock folded and grazed on the Welsh side of the town, and acted as agent for a number of other sheep-farmers of the middle kind, to sell their clips together to the best advantage. He also had a workshop preparing vellum from the skins. Of good repute, very fine white vellum. We have bought from him in the past. So do other monastic houses. His nephews have the business now. Their family house is near Saint Alkmund's church in the town.'

'And he has been a patron of our house?'

Brother Benedict the sacristan detailed the many gifts William had made over the years, both to the choir and the parish of Holy Cross. 'He was a close friend of Abbot Heribert, who died here among us three years ago.' Heribert, too gentle and mild for the taste of Bishop Henry of Winchester, then papal legate, had been demoted to give place to Radulfus, and had ended his days quite happily as a simple choir-monk, without regrets.

'William also gave freely in winter for the poor,' added Brother Oswald the almoner.

'It seems that William has well deserved to have what he asks,' said the abbot and looked up encouragingly at his petitioner. 'I understand you went with him on pilgrimage. You have done well by your master, I commend your loyalty, and I trust the journey has done great good to you, living, as to your master, who died still a pilgrim. There could be no more blessed death. Leave us now. I will speak with you again very soon.'

Elave made him a deep reverence, and went out from the chapter-house with a buoyant step, like a man going to a festival.

Canon Gerbert had refrained from comment while the petitioner was present, but he cleared his throat vociferously as soon as Elave had vanished, and said with weighty gravity: 'My lord abbot, it is a great privilege to be buried within the walls. It must not be granted lightly. Is it certain that this is a fit case for such an honour? There must be many men, above the rank of merchant, who would wish to achieve such a resting-place. It behoves your house to consider very gravely before admitting anyone, however charitable, who may fall short of worthiness.'

'I have never held,' said Radulfus, unperturbed, 'that rank or trade is valued before God. We have heard an impressive list of this man's gifts to our church, let alone those to his fellow-men. And bear in mind that he undertook, and accomplished, the pilgrimage to Jerusalem, an act of devotion that testifies to his quality and courage.'

It was characteristic of Serlo, that harmless and guileless soul – so Cadfael thought long afterwards, when the dust had settled – to speak up with the best of intentions at the wrong moment, and in disastrously wrong words.

'So good counsel prevailed,' he said, beaming. 'A timely word of admonishment and warning has had this blessed effect. Truly a priest should never be silent when he hears doctrine misread. His words may turn a soul astray into the right path.'

His childlike gratification faded slowly into the heavy silence he had provoked. He looked about him without immediate understanding, and gradually perceived how most eyes avoided him, looking studiously far into distance or down into folded hands, while Abbot Radulfus viewed him steadily and hard but without expression, and Canon Gerbert turned on him a cold, transfixing glare. The beaming smile faded sickly from Serlo's round and innocent face. 'To pay good heed to stricture and obey instruction atones for all errors,' he ventured, trying to edge away whatever in his words had caused this consternation, and failing. His voice ebbed feebly into silence.

'What doctrine,' demanded Gerbert with black deliberation, 'had this man misread? What occasion had his priest had to admonish him? Are you saying that he was *ordered* to go on pilgrimage, to purge some mortal error?'

'No, no, not ordered,' said Serlo faintly. 'It was suggested to him that his soul would benefit by such a reparation.'

'Reparation for what gross offence?' pursued the canon relentlessly.

'Oh, none, none that did harm to any, no act of violence or dishonesty. It is long past,' said Serlo gallantly, digging in his heels with unaccustomed bravery to retrieve what he had launched. 'It was nine years ago, when Archbishop William of Corbeil, of blessed memory, sent out a preaching mission to many of the towns in England. As papal legate he was concerned for the wellbeing of the Church, and thought fit to use preaching canons from his own house at St. Osyth's. I was sent to attend on the reverend Father who came into our diocese, and I was with him when he preached here at the High Cross. William of Lythwood entertained us to supper afterwards, and there was much earnest talk. He was not contumacious, he did but enquire and question, and in all solemnity. A courteous, hospitable man.

But even in thought – for want of proper instruction . . .'

'What you are saying,' pronounced Gerbert menacingly, 'is that a man who was reproved for heretical views is now asking for burial within these walls.'

'Oh, I would not say heretical,' babbled Serlo in haste. 'Misguided views, perhaps, but I would not say heretical. There was no complaint ever made of him to the bishop. And you have seen that he did as he was counselled, for two years later he set out on this pilgrimage.'

'Many men undertake pilgrimages for their own pleasure,' said Gerbert grimly, 'rather than for the proper purpose. Some even for trade, like hucksters. The act is no absolution for error, it is the sincere intent that delivers.'

'We have no reason,' Abbot Radulfus pointed out drily, 'to conclude that William's intent was less than sincere. These are judgements which are out of our hands, we should have the humility to acknowledge as much.'

'Nevertheless, we have a duty under God, and cannot evade it. What proof have we that the man ever changed those suspect beliefs he held? We have not examined as to what they were, how grave, and whether they were ever repented and discarded. Because there is here in England a healthy and vigorous Church, we must not think that the peril of false belief belongs only to the past. Have you not heard that there are loose preachers abroad in France who draw the credulous after them, reviling their own priests as greedy and corrupt, and the rites of the Church as meaningless? In the south the abbot of Clairvaux is grown much concerned about such false prophets.'

'Though the abbot of Clairvaux has himself warned,' interjected Radulfus briskly, 'that the failure of the priesthood to set an example of piety and simplicity helps to turn people to these dissenting sects. The Church has a duty also to purge its own shortcomings.'

Cadfael listened, as all the brothers were listening,

with pricked ears and alert eyes, hoping that this sudden squall would slacken and blow over just as nimbly. Radulfus would not allow any prelate to usurp his authority in his own chapter-house, but not even he could forbid an envoy of the archbishop to assert his rights of speech and judgement in a matter of doctrine. The very mention of Bernard of Clairvaux, the apostle of austerity, was a reminder of the rising influence of the Cistercians, to which order Archbishop Theobald was sympathetically inclined. And though Bernard might put in a word for popular criticism of the worldliness of many high churchmen, and yearn for a return to the poverty and simplicity of the Apostles, by all accounts he would have small mercy on anyone who diverged from the strictly orthodox where dogma was concerned. Radulfus might sidestep one citation of Bernard by countering with another, but he was quick to change the subject before he risked losing the exchange.

'Here is Serlo,' he said simply, 'who remembers whatever contention the archbishop's missioner had with William. He may also recall whatever points of belief had arisen between them.'

Serlo, by the dubious look on his face, hardly knew whether to be glad of such an opportunity or sorry. He opened his mouth hesitantly, but Radulfus stopped him with a raised hand.

'Wait! It is also only fair that the one man who can truly testify to his master's mind and observance before death should be present to hear what is said of him, and answer it on his behalf. We have no right to exclude a man from the favour he has asked without a just hearing. Denis, will you go and ask the young man Elave to come back into council?'

'Very gladly,' said Brother Denis, and went out with such indignant alacrity that it was not difficult to read his mind.

Elave came back into chapter in all innocence, expecting

his formal answer and in no doubt what it would be. His alert step and confident face spoke for him. He had no warning of what was to come, even when the abbot spoke up, choosing his words with careful moderation.

'Young sir, there is here some debate concerning your master's request. It has been said that before he departed on his pilgrimage he had been in some dispute with a priest sent by the archbishop to preach here in Shrewsbury, and had been reproved for certain beliefs he held, which were not altogether in accord with Church doctrine. It is even suggested that his pilgrimage was enjoined upon him almost as penance. Do you know anything of this? It may well be that it never came to your ears at all.'

Elave's level brows, thick and russet, darker than his hair, drew together in doubt and bewilderment, but not yet disquiet.

'I knew he had given much thought to some articles of faith, but no more than that. He *wanted* his pilgrimage. He was growing old but still hearty, there were others and younger could manage here in his stead. He asked me if I would go with him, and I went. There was never any dispute between him and Father Elias that I know of. Father Elias knew him for a good man.'

'The good who go astray into wrong paths do more harm than the evil, who are our open enemies,' said Canon Gerbert sharply. 'It is the enemy within who betrays the fortress.'

Now that, thought Cadfael, rings true of Church thinking. A Seljuk Turk or a Saracen can cut down Christians in battle or throw stray pilgrims into dungeons, and still be tolerated and respected, even if he's held to be already damned. But if a Christian steps a little aside in his beliefs he becomes anathema. He had seen it years ago in the east, in the admittedly beleaguered Christian churches. Hardpressed by enemies, it was on their own they turned most savagely. Here at home he had never before encountered it, but it might yet come to be as common as in Antioch or Alexandria. Not, however, if Radulfus could rein it in.

'His own priest does not seem to have regarded William as an enemy, either within or without,' said the abbot mildly. 'But Deacon Serlo here is about to tell us what he recalls of the contention, and it is only just that you should afterwards speak as to your master's mind before his death, in assurance that he is worthy to be buried here within the precinct.'

'Speak up!' said Gerbert as Serlo hesitated, dismayed and unhappy at what he had set in motion. 'And be precise! On what heads was fault found with the man's beliefs?'

'There were certain small points at issue,' Serlo said submissively, 'as I remember it. Two in particular, besides his doubts concerning the baptism of infants. He had difficulty in comprehending the Trinity . . .'

Who does not! though Cadfael. If it were comprehensible, all these interpreters of the good God would be out of an occupation. And every one of those denies the interpretation set up by every other.

'He said if the first was Father, and the second Son, how could they be co-eternal and co-equal? And as to the Spirit, he could not see how it could be equal with either Father or Son if it emanated from them. Moreover, he saw no need for a third, creation, salvation and all things being complete in Father and Son. Thus the third served only to satisfy the vision of those who think in threes, as the song-makers and the soothsayers do, and all those who deal with enchantment.'

'He said that of the Church?' Gerbert's countenance was stiff and brow black.

'Not of the Church, no, that I do not believe he ever said. And the Trinity is a most high mystery, many have difficulty with it.'

'It is not for them to question or reason with inadequate minds, but to accept with unquestioning faith. Truth is set before them, they have only to believe. It is the perverse and perilous who have the arrogance to bring mere fallible reason to bear on what is ineffable. Go on! Two points, you said. What is the second?'

Serlo cast an almost apologetic glance at Radulfus, and an even more rapid and uneasy one at Elave, who all this time was staring upon him with knotted brows and thrusting jaw, not yet committed to fear or anger or any other emotion, simply waiting and listening.

'It arose out of this same matter of the Father and the Son. He said that if they were of one and the same substance, as the creed calls them consubstantial, then the entry of the Son into humankind must mean also the entry of the Father, taking to himself and making divine that which he had united with the godhead. And therefore the Father and the Son alike knew the suffering and the death and the resurrection, and as one partake in our redemption.' .

'It is the Patripassian heresy!' cried Gerbert, outraged. 'Sabellius was excommunicated for it, and for other his errors. Noetus of Smyrna preached it to his ruin. This is indeed a dangerous venture. No wonder the priest warned him of the pit he was digging for his own soul.'

'Howbeit,' Radulfus reminded the assembly firmly, 'the man, it seems, listened to counsel and undertook the pilgrimage, and as to the probity of his life, nothing has been alleged against it. We are concerned, not with what he speculated upon seven years and more ago, but with his spiritual wellbeing at his death. There is but one witness here who can testify as to that. Now let us hear from his servant and companion.' He turned to look closely at Elave, whose face had set into controlled and conscious awareness, not of danger, but of deep offence. 'Speak for your master,' said Radulfus quietly, 'for you knew him to the end. What was his manner of life in all that long journey?'

'He was regular in observance everywhere,' said Elave, 'and made his confession where he could. There was no fault found with him in any land. In the Holy City we visited all the most sacred places, and going and returning we lodged whenever we could in abbeys and priories, and everywhere my master was accepted for a good and pious man, and paid his way honestly, and was well regarded.'

'But had he renounced his views,' demanded Gerbert, 'and recanted his heresy? Or did he still adhere secretly to his former errors?'

'Did he ever speak with you about these things?' the abbot asked, overriding the intervention.

'Very seldom, my lord, and I did not well understand such deep matters. I cannot answer for another man's mind, only for his conduct, which I knew to be virtuous.' Elave's face had set into contained and guarded calm. He did not look like a man who would fall short in understanding of deep matters, or lack the interest to consider them.

'And in his last illness,' Radulfus pursued mildly, 'he asked for a priest?'

'He did, Father, and made his confession and received absolution without question. He died with all the due rites of the Church. Wherever there was place and time along the way he made his confession, especially after he first fell ill, and we were forced to stay a whole month in the monastery at Saint Marcel before he was fit to continue the journey home. And there he often spoke with the brothers, and all these matters of faith and doubt were understood and tolerated among them. I know he spoke openly of things that troubled him, and they found no fault there with debating all manner of questions concerning holy things.'

Canon Gerbert stared cold suspicion. 'And where was this place, this Saint Marcel? And when was it you spent a month there? How recently?'

'It was in the spring of last year. We left early in the May, and made the pilgrimage from there to Saint James at Compostela with a party from Cluny, to give thanks that my master was restored to health. Or so we thought then, but he was never in real health again, and we had many halts thereafter. Saint Marcel is close by Chalons on the Saône. It is a daughter house of Cluny.'

Gerbert sniffed loudly and turned up his masterful nose at the mention of Cluny. That great house had taken seriously to the pilgrim traffic and had given aid and support, protection along the roads and shelter in their houses to many hundreds not only from France, but of recent years from England, too. But for the close dependants of Archbishop Theobald it was first and foremost the mother-house of that difficult colleague and ambitious and arrogant rival, Bishop Henry of Winchester.

'There was one of the brothers died there,' said Elave, standing up sturdily for the sanctity and wisdom of Cluny, 'who had written on all these things, and taught in his young days, and he was revered beyond any other among the brothers, and had the most saintly name among them. He saw no wrong in pondering all these difficult matters by the test of reason, and neither did his abbot, who had sent him there from Cluny for his health. I heard him read once from Saint John's Gospel, and speak on what he read. It was wonderful to hear. And that was but a short time before he died.'

'It is presumption to play human reason like a false light upon divine mysteries,' warned Gerbert sourly. 'Faith is to be received, not taken apart by the wit of a mere man. Who was this brother?'

'He was called Pierre Abelard, a Breton. He died in the April, before we set out for Compostela in the May.'

The name had meant nothing to Elave beyond what he had seen and heard for himself, and kept wonderingly in his mind ever since. But it meant a great deal to Gerbert. He stiffened in his stall, flaring up half a head taller, as a candle suddenly rears pale and lofty as the wick flares.

'That man? Foolish, gullible soul, do you not know the man himself was twice charged and convicted of heresy? Long ago his writings on the Trinity were burned, and the writer imprisoned. And only three years ago at the Council of Sens he was again convicted of heretical writings, and condemned to have his works destroyed and end his life in perpetual imprisonment.'

It seemed that Abbot Radulfus, though less exclamatory, was equally well informed, if not better.

'A sentence which was very quickly revoked,' he remarked drily, 'and the author allowed to retire peacefully into Cluny at the request of the abbot.'

Unwarily Gerbert was provoked into snapping back without due thought. 'In my view no such revocation should have been granted. It was not deserved. The sentence should have stood.'

'It was issued by the Holy Father,' said the abbot gently, 'who cannot err.' Whether his tongue was in his cheek at that moment Cadfael could not be sure, but the tone, though soft and reverent, stung, and was meant to sting.

'So was the sentence!' Gerbert snapped back even more unwisely. 'His Holiness surely had misleading information when he withdrew it. Doubtless he made a right judgement upon such truth as was presented to him.'

Elave spoke up as if to himself, but loudly enough to carry to all ears, and with a brilliance of eye and a jut of jaw that spoke more loudly still. 'Yet by very definition a thing cannot be its opposite, therefore one judgement or the other must be error. It could as well be the former as the latter.'

Who was it claimed, Cadfael reflected, startled and pleased, that he could not understand the arguments of the philosophers? This lad had kept his ears open and his mind alert all those miles to Jerusalem and back, and learned more than he's telling. At least he's turned Gerbert purple and closed his mouth for a moment.

A moment was enough for the abbot. This dangerous line of talk was getting out of hand. He cut it short with decision.

'The Holy Father has authority both to bind and to loose, and the same infallible will that can condemn can also with equal right absolve. There is here, it seems to me, no contradiction at all. Whatever views he may have held seven years ago, William of Lythwood died on pilgrimage, confessed and shriven, in a state of grace. There is no bar to his burial within this enclave, and he shall have what he has asked of us.'

Chapter Three

AS CADFAEL came through the court after dinner, to return to his labours in the herb-garden, he encountered Elave. The young man was just coming down the steps from the guest-hall, in movement and countenance bright and vehement, like a tool honed for fine use. He was still roused and ready to be aggressive after the rough passage of his master's body to its desired resting-place, the bones of his face showed polished with tension, and his prow of a nose quested belligerently on the summer air.

'You look ready to bite,' said Cadfael, coming by design face to face with him.

The boy looked back at him for a moment uncertain how to respond, where even this unalarming presence was still an unknown quantity. Then he grinned, and the sharp tension eased.

'Not you, at any rate, Brother! If I showed my teeth, did I not have cause?'

'Well, at least you know our abbot all the better for it. You have what you asked. But as well keep a lock on your lips until the other one is gone. One way to be sure of saying nothing that can be taken amiss is to say nothing at all. Another is to agree with whatever the prelates say. But I doubt that would have much appeal for you.'

'It's like threading a way between archers in ambush,' said Elave, relaxing. 'For a cloistered man, Brother, you say things aside from the ordinary yourself.'

'We're none of us as ordinary as all that. What I feel, when the divines begin talking doctrine, is that God speaks all languages, and whatever is said to him or of him in any tongue will need no interpreter. And if it's devoutly meant, no apology. How is that hand of yours? No inflammation?'

Elave shifted the box he was carrying to his other arm, and showed the faded scar in his palm, still slightly puffed and pink round the healed punctures.

'Come round with me to my workshop, if you've the time to spare,' Cadfael invited, 'and let me dress that again for you. And that will be the last you need think of it.' He cast a glance at the box tucked under the young man's arm. 'But you have errands to do in the town? You'll be off to visit William's kinsfolk.'

'They'll need to know of his burying, tomorrow,' said Elave. 'They'll be here. There was always a good feeling among them all, never bad blood. It was Girard's wife who kept the house for the whole family. I must go and tell them what's arranged. But there's no haste, I daresay once I'm up there it will be for the rest of the day and into the evening.'

They fell in amicably together, side by side, out of the court and through the rose garden, rounding the thick hedge. As soon as they entered the walled garden the sun-warmed scent of the herbs rose to enfold them in a cloud of fragrance, every step along the gravel path between the beds stirring wave on wave of sweetness.

'Shame to go withindoors on such a day,' said Cadfael. 'Sit down here in the sun, I'll bring the lotion out to you.'

Elave sat down willingly on the bench by the north wall, tilting his face up to the sun, and laid his burden down beside him. Cadfael eyed it with interest, but went first to bring out the cleansing lotion, and anoint the fading wound once again.

'You'll feel no more of that now, it's clean enough. Young flesh heals well, and you've surely been through more risks crossing the world and back than you should be meeting here in Shrewsbury.' He stoppered the flask, and sat down beside his guest. 'I suppose they won't even know yet, that you're back and their kinsman dead – the family there in the town?'

'Not yet, no. There was barely time last night to get my master well bestowed, and what with the dispute in chapter this morning, I've had no chance yet to get word to them. You know them – his nephews? Girard sees to the flock and the sales, and fetches in the wool clips from the others he deals for. Jevan always managed the vellum making, even in William's day. Come to think of it, for all I know things may be changed there since we left.'

'You'll find them all living,' said Cadfael reassuringly, 'that I do know. Not that we see much of them down here in the Foregate. They come sometimes on festival days, but they have their own church at Saint Alkmund's.' He eyed the box Elave had laid down on the bench between them. 'Something William was bringing back to them? May I look? Faith, I own I'm looking already, I can't take my eyes from it. That's a wonderful piece of carving. And old, surely.'

Elave looked down at it with the critical appreciation and indifferent detachment of one to whom it meant simply an errand to be discharged, something he would be glad to hand over and be rid of. But he took it up readily and placed it in Cadfael's hands to be examined closely.

'I have to take it by way of a dowry for the girl. When he grew too ill to go on he thought of her, seeing he'd taken her into his household from the day she was born. So he gave me this to bring to Girard, to be used for her when she marries. It's a poor lookout for a girl with no dowry when it comes to getting a husband.'

'I remember there was a little girl,' said Cadfael, turning the box in his hands with admiration. It was enough to excite the artist in any man. Fashioned from some dark eastern wood, about a foot long by eight inches wide and four deep, the lid flawlessly fitted, with a small, gilded lock. The under surface was plain, polished to a lustrous darkness almost black, the upper surface and the edges of the lid beautifully and intricately carved in a tracery of vine leaves and grapes, and in the centre of the lid a lozenge containing an ivory plaque, an aureoled head, full-face, with great Byzantine eyes. It was so old that the sharp edges had been slightly smoothed and rounded by handling, but the lines of the carving were still picked out in gold.

'Fine work!' said Cadfael, handling it reverently. He balanced it in his hands, and it hung like a solid mass of wood, nothing shifting within. 'You never wondered what was in it?'

Elave looked faintly surprised, and hoisted indifferent shoulders. 'It was packed away, and I had other things to think about. I've only this past half-hour got it out of the baggage-roll. No, I never did wonder. I took it he'd saved up some money for her. I'm just handing it over to Girard as I was told to do. It's the girl's, not mine.'

'You don't know where he got it?'

'Oh, yes, I know where he bought it. From a poor deacon in the market in Tripoli, just before we took ship for Cyprus and Thessalonika on our way home. There were Christian fugitives beginning to drift in then from beyond Edessa, turned out of their monasteries by mamluk raiders from Mosul. They came with next to nothing, they had to sell whatever they'd contrived to bring with them in order to live. William drove shrewd bargains among the merchants, but he dealt fairly with those poor souls. They said life was becoming hard and dangerous in those parts. The journey out we made the slow way, by land. William wanted to see the great collection of relics in Constantinople. But coming home we started by sea. There are plenty of Greek and Italian merchant ships plying as far as Thessalonika, some even all the way to Bari and Venice.'

'There was a time,' mused Cadfael, drawn back through the years, 'when I knew those seas very well. How did you fare for lodging on the way out, all those miles afoot?'

'Now and then we went a piece in company, but mostly it was we two alone. The monks of Cluny have hospices all across France and down through Italy, even close by the emperor's city they have a house for pilgrims. And as soon as you reach the Holy Land the Knights of Saint John provide shelter everywhere. It's a great thing to have done,' said Elave, looking back in awe and wonder. 'Along the way a man lives a day at a time, and looks no further ahead than the next day, and no further behind than the day just passed. Now I see it whole, and it is wonderful.'

'But not all good,' said Cadfael. 'That couldn't be, we couldn't ask it. Remember the cold and the rain and the hunger at times, and losses by thieves now and then, and a few knocks from those who prey on travellers – oh, never tell me you met none! And the weariness, and the times when William fell ill, the bad food, the sour water, the stones of the road. You've met all that. Every man who travels that far across the world has met it all.'

'I do remember all that,' said Elave sturdily, 'but it is still wonderful.'

'Good! So it should be,' said Cadfael, sighing. 'Lad, I should be glad to sit and talk with you about every step of the way, when your time's free. You go and deliver your box to Master Girard, and that's your duty done. And what will you do now? Go back to work for them as before?'

'No, not that. It was for William I worked. They have their own clerk, I wouldn't wish to displace him, and they don't need two. Besides, I want more, and different. I'll take time to look about me. I've come back with more skills than when I went, I'd like to use them.' He rose, and tucked the carved box securely under his arm.

'I've forgotten,' said Cadfael, following the gesture thoughtfully, 'if indeed I ever knew – how did he come by the child? He had none of his own, and as far as I know, Girard has none, and the other brother has never married. Where did the girl come from? Some foundling he took in?'

'You could say so. They had a serving maid, a simple soul, who fell foul of a small huckster at the fair one year, and brought forth a daughter. William gave houseroom to the pair of them, and Margaret cared for the baby like her own child, and when the mother died they simply kept the girl. A pretty little thing she was. She had more wit than her mother. It was William named her Fortunata, for he said she'd come into the world with nothing, not even a father, and still found herself a home and a family, and so she'd still fall on her feet lifelong. She was eleven, rising twelve,' said Elave, 'when we set out, and grown into a skinny, awkward little thing all teeth and elbows. They say the prettiest pups make the ugliest dogs. She'll need a decent dowry to make up for her gawky looks.'

He stretched his long person, hoisted his box more firmly under his arm, dipped his fair head in a small, friendly reverence, and was off along the path, his haste to discharge all the final duties with which he had been entrusted tempered somewhat by a sense of the seven years since he had seen William's family, and the inevitable estrangement time must have brought about, until now scarcely realised. What had once been familiar was now alien, and it would take time to edge his way back to it. Cadfael watched him disappear round the corner of the box hedge, torn between sympathy and envy.

The house of Girard of Lythwood, like so many of the merchant burgages of Shrewsbury, was in the shape of an

L, the short base directly on the street, and pierced by an arched entry leading through to the yard and garden behind. The base of the L was of only one storey, and provided the shop where Jevan, the younger brother, stored and sold his finished leaves and gatherings of vellum and the cured skins from which they were folded and cut to order. The upright of the L showed its gable end to the street, and consisted of a low undercroft and the living floor above, with a loft in the steep roof that provided extra sleeping quarters. The entire burgage was not large, space being valuable within so enclosed a town, in its tight noose of river. Outside the loop, in the suburbs of Frankwell on one side and the Foregate on the other, there was room to expand, but within the wall every inch of ground had to be used to the best advantage.

Elave halted before the house, and stood a moment to take in the strangeness of what he felt, a sudden warmth of homecoming, an almost panic reluctance to go in and declare himself, a mute wonder at the smallness of the house that had been his home for a number of years. In the overwhelming basilicas of Constantinople, as in the profound isolation of deserts, a man grows used to immensity.

He went in slowly through the narrow entry and into the yard. On his right the stables, the byre for the cow, the store shed and low coop for the chickens were just as he remembered them, and on his left the house door stood wide open, as it always had on such summer days. A woman was just coming up from the garden that stretched away beyond the house, with a basket of clothes in her arms, crisp washing just gathered from the hedge. She observed the stranger entering, and quickened her step to meet him.

'Goodday, sir! If you're wanting my husband . . .' She halted there, astonished, recognising but not believing at first what she saw. Between eighteen and twenty-five a young man does not change so much as to be unrecog-

42

nisable to his own family, however he may have filled out and matured during that time. It was simply that she had had no warning, no word to indicate that he was within five hundred miles of her.

'Mistress Margaret,' said Elave, 'you've not forgotten me?'

The voice completed what his face had begun. She flushed bright with acceptance and evident pleasure. 'Dear, now, and it *is* you! Just for a moment there you had me struck out of my wits, thinking I was seeing visions, and you still half the world away, in some outlandish place. Well, now, and here you are safe and sound, after all that journeying. Glad I am to see you again, boy, and so will Girard and Jevan be. Who'd have thought you'd spring out of nowhere like this, all in a moment, and just in time for Saint Winifred's festival. Come within, come, let me put this laundry down and get you a draught to drink, and tell me how you've fared all this long time.'

She freed a hand to take him warmly by the arm and usher him within, to a bench by the unshuttered window of the hall, with such voluble goodwill that his silence passed unnoticed. She was a neat, brown-haired, bustling woman in her middle forties, healthy and hardworking and a good and discreet neighbour, and her shining housekeeping reflected her own strong-willed brightness.

'Girard's away making up the wool clip, he'll be a day or so yet. His face will be a sight to see when he comes in and sees Uncle William sitting here at the table like in the old days. Where is he? Is he following you up now, or had he business below at the abbey?'

Elave drew breath and said what had to be said. 'He'll not be coming, Mistress.'

'Not coming?' she said, astonished, turning sharply in the doorway of her larder.

'Sorry I am to have no better word to bring you. Master William died in France, before we could embark for home. But I've brought him home, as I promised him

43

I would. He lies at the abbey now, and tomorrow he's to be buried there, in the cemetery among the patrons of the house.'

She stood motionless, staring at him with pitcher and cup forgotten in her hands, and for a long moment she was silent.

'It was what he wanted,' said Elave. 'He did what he set out to do, and he has what he wanted.'

'Not everyone can say as much,' said Margaret slowly. 'So Uncle William's gone! Business below at the abbey, did I say? And so he has, but not as I supposed. And you left to bring him over the sea alone! And Girard away, and who's to tell where at this moment? It will grieve him if he's not here to pay the last dues to a good man.' She shook herself, and stirred out of her brief stillness, practical always. 'Well, now, no fault of yours, you did well by him, and have no need to look back. Sit you down and be easy. You're home, at least, done your wanderings for the time being, you can do with a rest.'

She brought him ale, and sat down beside him, considering without distress all that was now needful. A competent woman, she would have everything ordered and seemly whether her husband returned in time or not.

'He was nearing eighty years old,' she said, 'by my reckoning. He had a good life, and was a good kinsman and a good neighbour, and he ended doing a blessed thing, and one that he wanted with all his heart, once that old preacher from St. Osyth's put the thought in his mind. There,' said Margaret, shaking her head with a sigh, 'here I am harking back like a fool, and I never meant to. Time's short! I should have thought the abbot could have sent us word of the need as soon as you came in at the gatehouse.'

'He knew nothing of it until this morning at chapter. He's been here only four years, and we've been gone seven. But everything is in hand now.'

'Maybe it is, down there, but I must see to it that all's ready up here, for there'll be all the neighbours in to join us, and I hope you'll come back with us, after the funeral. Conan's here, that's lucky, I'll send him west to see if he can find Girard in time, though there's no knowing just where he'll be. There are six flocks he has to deal with out there. Sit you here quietly, while I go and bring Jevan from the shop, and Aldwin from his books, and you can tell us all how it was with the old man. Fortunata's off in the town marketing, but she'll surely be back soon.'

She was off on the instant, bustling out to fetch Jevan out of his shop, and Elave was left breathless and mute with her ready volubility, having had no chance as yet to mention the charge he had still to deliver. In a few minutes she was back with the vellum-maker, the clerk, and the shepherd Conan hard on her heels, the entire core of the household but for the absent fosterchild. All these Elave knew well from his former service, and only one was much changed. Conan had been a youngster of twenty when last seen, slender and willowy, now he had broadened out and put on flesh and muscle, swelling into gross good looks, ruddy and strong with outdoor living. Aldwin had entered the household in Girard's service, and stepped into Elave's shoes when William took his own boy with him on pilgrimage. A man of past forty at that time, barely literate but quick with numbers as a gift of nature, Aldwin looked much the same now at nearing fifty, but that his hair had rather more grey in it, and was thinning on the crown. He had had to work hard to earn his place and hold it, and his long face had set into defensive lines of effort and anxiety. Elave had got his letters early, from a priest who had seen his small parishioner's promise and taken pains to bring it to fruit, and the boy had shamelessly enjoyed his superiority when he had worked in Aldwin's company. He remembered now how he had happily passed on his own skills to the much older man, not out of any genuine wish to help him, but rather to impress and dazzle both Aldwin and the observers with his own cleverness. He was older and wiser now, he had discovered how great was the world and how small his own person. He was glad that Aldwin should have this secure place, this sound roof over his head, and no one now to threaten his tenure.

Jevan of Lythwood was just past forty, seven years younger than his brother, tall, erect and lightly built, with a cleanshaven, scholarly face. He had not been formally educated in boyhood, but by reason of taking early to the craft of vellum-making he had come to the notice of lettered men who bought from him, monastics, clerks, even a few among the lords of local manors who had some learning, and being of very quick and eager intelligence he had set himself to learn from them, aroused their interest to help him forward, and turned himself into a scholar, the only person in this house who could read Latin, or more than a few words of English. It was good for business that the seller of parchments should measure up to the quality of his work, and understand the uses the cultured world made of it.

All these came hurrying in on Margaret's heels to gather familiarly around the table, and welcome back the traveller and his news. The loss of William, old, fulfilled, and delivered from this world in a state of grace and to the resting-place he had desired, was not a tragedy, but the completion of an altogether satisfactory life, the more easily and readily accepted because he had been gone from this household for seven years, and the gap he had left had closed gently, and had not now been torn open again by his recovered presence. Elave told what he could of the journey home, of the recurring bouts of illness, and the death, a gentle death in a clean bed and with a soul confessed and shriven, at Valognes, not far from the port where he should have embarked for home.

'And his funeral is to be tomorrow,' said Jevan. 'At what hour?'

'After the Mass at ten. The abbot is to take the office himself. He stood by my master's claim for admittance,' said Elave by way of explanation, 'against some visiting canon there from Canterbury. One of the bishop's deacons is travelling with him, and let out like a fool some old business of falling out with a travelling preacher, years ago, and this Gerbert would have every word dragged out again, and wanted to call William a heretic and refuse him entry, but the abbot set his foot firmly on that and let him in. I came close,' admitted Elave, roused to recollection, 'to sticking my own neck in a heretic's collar, arguing with the man. And he's one who doesn't take kindly to being opposed. He could hardly turn on the abbot in his own house, but I doubt he feels much love for me. I'd better keep my head low till he moves on.'

'You did quite right,' said Margaret warmly, 'to stand by your master. I hope it's done you no harm.'

'Oh, surely not! It's all past now. You'll be at the Mass tomorrow?'

'Every man of us,' said Jevan, 'and the women, too. And Girard, if we can find him in time, but he's on the move, and may be near the border by now. He meant to come back for Saint Winifred's feast, but there's always the chance of delays among the border flocks.'

Elave had left the wooden box lying on the bench under the window. He rose to fetch it to the table. All eyes settled upon it with interest.

'This I was ordered to deliver into Master Girard's hands. Master William sent it to him to be held in trust for Fortunata until her marriage. It's her dowry. When he was so ill he thought of her, and said she must have a dowry. And this is what he sent.'

Jevan was the first to reach out to touch and handle it, fascinated by the beauty of the carving.

'This is rare work. Somewhere in the east he found this?' He took it up, surprised at the weight. 'It makes a handsome treasury. What's within it?'

'That I don't know. It was near his death when he gave it to me and told me what he wanted. Nothing more, and I never questioned him. I had enough to do, then and afterwards.'

'So you did,' said Margaret, 'and you did it very well, and we owe you thanks, for he was our kin, and a good man, and I'm glad he had so good a lad to see him safely all that way and back again home.' She took up to the box from the table, where Jevan had laid it down, and was fingering the gilded carving with evident admiration. 'Well, if it was sent to Girard, I'll keep it aside until Girard comes home. This is the business of the man of the house.'

'Even the key,' said Jevan, 'is a piece of art. So our Fortunata lives up to her name, as Uncle William always said she would. And the lucky girl still out marketing, and doesn't yet know of her fortune!'

Margaret opened the tall press in a corner of the room, and laid both box and key on an upper shelf within. 'There it stays until my husband comes home, and he'll take good care of it until my girl shows a fancy to get wed, and maybe sets eyes on the lad she wants for husband.'

All eyes had followed William's gift to its hiding-place. Aldwin said sourly: 'There'll be aplenty will fancy her for wife, if they get wind she has goods to bring with her. She'll have need of your good counsel, Mistress.'

Conan had said nothing at all. He had never been a talker. His eyes followed the box until the door of the press closed on it, but all he had to say throughout was said at the last, when Elave rose to take his leave. The shepherd rose with him.

'I'll be off, then, and take the pony, and see if I can find where the master is. But whether or not, I'll be back by nightfall.'

They were all dispersing to their various occupations when Margaret drew Elave back by the sleeve, delaying him until the rest had gone.

'You'll understand, I'm sure, how it is,' she said confidingly. 'I wouldn't say anything but just to you, Elave. You were always a good lad with the accounts,

48

and worked hard, and to tell the honest truth, Aldwin is no match for you, though he does his best, and can manage well enough all that's required of him. But he's getting older, and has no home or folks of his own, and what would he do if we parted with him now? You're young, there's many a merchant would be glad to hire you, with your knowledge of the world. You won't take it amiss . . .'

Elave had caught her drift long before this, and broke in hastily to reassure her. 'No, no, never think of it! I never expected to have my old place back. I wouldn't for the world put Aldwin's nose out of joint. I'm glad he should be secure the rest of his life. Never trouble for me, I shall look about me and find work to do. And as for bearing any grudge that I'm not asked back, I never so much as thought of it. Nothing but good have I had from this house, and I shan't forget it. No, Aldwin can go on with his labours with all my goodwill.'

'That's like the lad I remember!' she said with hearty relief. 'I knew you'd take it as it's meant. I hope you may get good service with some travelling merchant, one that trades oversea, that would suit you, after all you've seen and done. But you will come up with us tomorrow after Uncle William's burial, and take meat with us?'

He promised readily, glad to have their relationship established and understood. To tell the truth, he thought he might have felt confined and restricted here now, dealing with the buying of stock and paying of wages, the weighing and marketing of wool, and the small profits and expenses of a good but limited business. He was not yet sure what he did want, he could afford to spend a little while looking round before committing himself. Going out at the hall door he came shoulder to shoulder with Conan, on his way out to the stable, and dropped back to let Margaret's messenger go first.

A young woman with a basket on her arm had just emerged from the narrow entry that led to the street, and was crossing the yard towards them. She was not over-tall, but looked tall by reason of her erect bearing and long, free step, light and springy from the ground like the gait of a mettlesome colt. Her plain grey gown swayed with the lissom movement of a trim body, and the well-poised head on her long neck was crowned with a great coiled braid of dark hair lit with shadowy gleams of red. Halfway across the yard towards them she halted abruptly, gazing open-mouthed and wide-eyed, and suddenly she laughed aloud, a joyous, silver sound of pleasurable amazement.

'You!' she said, in a soft, delighted cry. 'Is it truth? I am not dreaming?'

She stopped them both on the instant, brought up short by the warmth of her greeting, Elave gaping like an idiot at this unknown girl who yet appeared not only to recognise him, but to take pleasure in the recognition, Conan fallen warily silent beside him, his face expressionless, his eyes roving from one face to the other, narrowed and intent.

'Do you not know me?' cried the girl's clear bell of a voice, through the bubbling spring of her laughter.

Fool that he was, who else could she be, coming in thus bare-headed from the shops of the town? But it was true, he would not have known her. The thin little pointed face had filled out into a smooth ivory oval, the teeth that had looked far too many and too large for her mouth shone now even and white between dark-rose lips that smiled at his astonishment and confusion. All the sharp little bones had rounded into grace. The long hair that had hung in elflocks round scrawny childish shoulders looked like a crown, thus braided and coiled upon her head, and the greenish hazel eyes whose stare he had found disconcerting seven years ago now sparkled and glowed with pleasure at seeing him again, a very arresting flattery.

'I know you now,' he said, fumbling for words. 'But you're changed!'

'You are not,' she said. 'Browner, perhaps, and your

hair's even fairer than it used to be, but I'd have known you anywhere. And you turn up like this without a word of warning, and they were letting you go without waiting for me?'

'I'm coming again tomorrow,' he said, and hesitated to attempt the explanation, here in the yard, with Conan still lingering on the borders of their meeting. 'Mistress Margaret will tell you about it. I had messages to bring . . .'

'If you knew' said Fortunata, 'how often and how long we've talked of you both, and wondered how you were faring in those far places. It's not every day we have kinsfolk setting out on such an adventure, do you think we never gave you a thought?'

Hardly once in all those years had it entered his mind to wonder about any of those left behind. Closest to him in this house, and alone significant, had been William, and with William he had gone, blithely, without a thought for anyone left to continue life here, least of all a leggy little girl of eleven with a spotty skin and a disconcerting stare.

'I doubt,' he said, abashed, 'that I ever deserved you should.'

'What has desert to do with it?' she said. 'And you were leaving now until tomorrow? No, that you can't! Come back with me into the house, if only for an hour. Why must I wait until tomorrow to get used to seeing you again?'

She had him by the hand, turning him back towards the open door, and though he knew it was no more than the open and gallant friendliness of one who had known him from her childhood, and wished him well in absence as she wished well to all men of goodwill – nothing more than that, not yet! – he went with her like a bidden child, silenced and charmed. He would have gone wherever she led him. He had that to tell her that would cloud her brightness for a while, and afterwards no rights in her or in this house, no reason to believe she would ever be

51

more to him than she was now, or he to her. But he went with her, and the warm dimness of the hall received them.

Conan looked after them for a long moment, before he went on towards the stable, his thick brows drawn together, and his wits very busy in his head.

Chapter Four

IT WAS FULLY dark when Conan came home again, and he came alone.

'I went as far as Forton, but he'd gone on to Nesse early in the day, likely he'd have finished there and moved on before night. I thought it best to come back. He'll not be home tomorrow, not until too late to see old William to his grave, not knowing the need.'

'He'll be sorry to let the old man go without him,' said Margaret, shaking her head, 'but there's nothing to be done about it now. Well, we'll have to manage everything properly on his behalf. I suppose it would have been a pity to fetch him back so far and lose two days or more in the middle of the shearing time. Perhaps it's just as well he was out of reach.'

'Uncle William will sleep just as well,' said Jevan, unperturbed. 'He had an eye to business in his day, he wouldn't favour waste of time, or risk of another dealer picking up one of his customers while his back was turned. Never fret, we'll make a good family showing tomorrow. And if you want to be up early to prepare your table, Meg, you'd best be off to bed and get your rest.'

'Yes,' she said, sighing, and braced her hands on the table to rise. 'Never mind, Conan, you did what you could. There's meat and bread and ale in the kitchen for you, as soon as you've stabled the pony. Goodnight to you both! Jevan, you'll put out the lamp and see the door bolted?'

'I will. When did you know me to forget? Goodnight, Meg!'

The master bedchamber was the only one on this main floor. Fortunata had a small room above, closed off from the larger part of the loft where the menservants had their beds, and Jevan slept in a small chamber over the entry from the street into the yard, where he kept his choicest wares and his chest of books.

Margaret's door closed behind her. Conan had turned to go out to the kitchen, but in the doorway he looked back, and asked: 'Did he stay long? The young fellow? He was for going, the same time I left, but we met with Fortunata in the yard, and he turned back with her.'

Jevan looked up in tolerant surprise. 'He stayed and ate with us. He's bidden back with us tomorrow, too. Our girl seemed pleased to see him.' His grave, long face, very solemn in repose, was nevertheless lit by a pair of glittering black eyes that missed very little, and seemed to be seeing too far into Conan at this moment for Conan's comfort, and finding what they saw mildly amusing. 'Nothing to fret you,' said Jevan. 'He's no shepherd, to put a spoke in your wheel. Go and get your supper, and let Aldwin do the fretting, if there's any to be done.'

It was a thought which had not been in Conan's mind until that moment, but it had its validity, just as surely as the other possibility which had really been preoccupying him. He went off to the kitchen with the two considerations churning in his brain, to find the meal left for him, and Aldwin sitting morosely at the trestle table with a half empty mug of ale.

'I never thought,' said Conan, spreading his elbows on the other side of the table, 'we should ever see that young spark again. All those perils by land and sea that we hear about, cutthroats and robbers by land, storm and shipwreck and pirates on the sea, and he has to wriggle his way between the lot of them and come safe home. More than his master did!'

'Did you find Girard?' asked Aldwin.

'No, he's too far west. There was no time to go farther after him, they'll have to bury the old man without him. Small grief to me,' said Conan candidly, 'if it was Elave we were burying.'

'He'll be off again,' Aldwin said, strenuously hoping so. 'He'll be too big for us now, he won't stay.'

Conan gave vent to a laugh that held no amusement. 'Go, will he? He was for going this afternoon until he set eyes on Fortunata. He came back fast enough when she took him by the hand and bade him in again. And by what I saw of the looks between them, she'll have no eyes for another man while he's around.'

Aldwin gave him a wary and disbelieving look. 'Are you taking a fancy to get the girl for yourself? I never saw sign of it before.'

'I like her well enough, always have. But for all they treat her like a daughter, she's none of their kind, just a foundling taken in for pity. And when it's money, it sticks close in the blood, and mostly to the men, and Dame Margaret has nephews if Girard has none on his side. Like or not like, a man has to think of his prospects.'

'And now you think better of the girl because she has a dowry from old William,' Aldwin guessed shrewdly, 'and want the other fellow out of sight and mind. For all he brought her the dowry! And how do you know but what's in it may be worth nothing to boast of?'

'In a fine carved casket like that? You saw how it was ornamented, all tendrils and ivory.'

'A box is a box. It's what it holds that counts.'

'No man would put rubbish in a box like that. But little value or great, it's worth the wager. For I do like the girl, and I think it only good sense and no shame,' vowed

Conan roundly, 'to like her the better for having possessions. And you'd do well,' he added seriously, 'to think on your own case if that youngster comes to Fortunata's lure and stays here, where he was taught his clerking.'

He was giving words to what had been eating away at Aldwin's always tenuous peace of mind ever since Elave had showed his face. But he made one feeble effort to stand it off. 'I've seen no sign he'd be wanted back here.'

'For one not wanted he was made strangely welcome, then,' retorted Conan. 'And didn't I just say something to Jevan, that made him answer how *I* had nothing to fret about, seeing Elave was no shepherd, to threaten me. Let Aldwin do the fretting, says he, if there's any to be done.'

Aldwin had been doing the fretting all the evening, and it was made manifest by the tight clenching of his hands, white at the knuckle, and the sour set of his mouth, as though it were full of gall. He sat mute, seething in his fears and suspicions, and this light pronouncement of Jevan's, all the confirmation they needed.

'Why did he have to come safe out of a mad journey that's killed its thousands before now?' wondered Conan, brooding. 'I wish the man no great harm, God knows, but I wish him elsewhere. I'd wish him well, if only he'd make off somewhere else to enjoy it. But he'd be a fool not to see that he can do very well for himself here. I can't see him taking to his heels.'

'Not,' agreed Aldwin malevolently, 'unless the hounds were snapping at them.'

Aldwin sat for some while after Conan had gone off to his bed. By the time he rose from the table the hall would certainly be in darkness, the outer door barred, and Jevan already in his own chamber. Aldwin lit an end of candle from the last flicker of the saucer lamp, to light him through the hall to the wooden stairway to the loft, before he blew out the dwindling flame.

In the hall it was silent and still, no movement but the

very slight creak of a shutter in the night breeze. Aldwin's candle made a minute point of light in the darkness, enough to show him his way the width of a familiar room. He was halfway to the foot of the stair when he halted, stood hesitating for a moment, and listening to the reassuring silence, and then turned and made straight for the corner press.

The key was always in the lock, but seldom turned. Such valuables as the house contained were kept in the coffer in Girard's bedchamber. Aldwin carefully opened the long door, set his candle to stand steady on a shelf at breast-level, and reached up to the higher shelf where Margaret had placed Fortunata's box. Even when he had it set down beside his light he wavered. How if the key turned creakingly instead of silently, or would not yield at all? He could not have said what impelled him to meddle, but curiosity was strong and constant in him, as if he had to know the ins and outs of everything in the household, in case some overlooked detail might be held in store to be used against him. He turned the little key, and it revolved sweetly and silently, well made like the lock it operated and the box it adorned and guarded. With his left hand he raised the lid, and with his right lifted the candle to cast its light directly within.

'What are you doing there?' demanded Jevan's voice, sharp and irritable from the top of the stairway.

Aldwin started violently, shaking drops of hot wax on to his hand. He had the lid closed and the key turned in an instant, and thrust the box back on to its upper shelf in panic haste. The open door of the press screened what he was about. From where Jevan came surging down the first few treads of the stairs, a moving shadow among shadows, he would see the light, though not its source, a segment of the open cupboard, and Aldwin's body in sharp silhouette, but could not have seen what his hands were up to, apart, perhaps, from that movement of reaching up to replace the violated treasure. Aldwin clawed along the shelf and turned with the candle in one hand, and the small knife he had just palmed from his own belt in the other.

'I left my penknife here yesterday, when I cut a new peg to fasten the handle of the small bucket. I shall need it in the morning.'

Jevan had come the rest of the way down the staircase, and advanced upon him in resigned irritation, brushing him aside to close the door of the press.

'Take it, then, and get to bed, and give over disturbing the household at this hour.'

Aldwin departed with what was for him unusual alacrity and docility, only too pleased to have come so well out of what might have been an awkward encounter. He did not so much as look round, but carried his guttering candle-end up the stairs and into the loft with a shaking hand. But behind him he heard the small, grating sound of a large key turning, and knew that Jevan had locked the press. His clerk's furtive foragings might be tolerated and passed over as annoying but harmless, but they were not to be encouraged. Aldwin had best walk warily with Jevan for a while, until the incident was forgotten.

The vexing thing was that it had all been for nothing. He had never had time to examine what was in the box, but had had to close the lid hastily in the same moment as opening it, with no time to get a glimpse within. He was not going to try that again. The contents of Fortunata's box would have to remain a secret until Girard came home.

On the twenty-first day of June, after mid-morning Mass, William of Lythwood was buried in a modest corner of the graveyard east of the abbey church, where good patrons of the house found a final resting-place. So he had what he wanted, and slept content.

Among those attending, Brother Cadfael could discern certain currents of discontent. He knew the clerk Aldwin much as he had known Elave in his day, as an occasional messenger on behalf of his master, and to tell truth, had never yet seen him looking content, but his bearing on this day seemed more abstracted and morose than usual, and he and the shepherd had their heads together in a conspiratorial manner, and their eyes narrowed and sharp upon the returned pilgrim in a manner which suggested that he was by no means welcome to them, however amiably the rest of the household behaved to him. And the young man himself seemed preoccupied with his own thoughts, and for all his concentration upon the office, his eyes strayed several times towards the young woman who stood modestly a pace behind Dame Margaret, earnestly attentive and very solemn beside the grave of the man who had given her a home and a name. And a dowry!

She was well worth looking at. Possibly Elave was debating reconsidering his determination to look about him for something more and better than could be found in his old employment. The skinny little thing all teeth and elbows had grown into a very attractive woman. One, however, who showed no sign at this moment of finding the young man as disturbing as he obviously found her. She had devoted herself wholly to her benefactor's funeral rites, and had no attention to spare for anything else.

Before the company dispersed there were civilities to be exchanged, condolences to be dispensed by the clerics and gracefully received by the family. In the sunlit court the company sorted itself, for the decent while required, into little groups, kind with kind, Abbot Radulfus and Prior Robert paying due attentions to Margaret and Jevan of Lythwood before withdrawing, Brother Jerome, as the prior's chaplain, making it his business to spend some minutes with the lesser members of the bereaved household. A few words had to be said to the girl, before he moved on to the menservants. The pious platitudes he first offered to Conan and Aldwin showed signs of developing into something much more voluble and interesting, and at the same time more confidential, for now there were three heads together instead of two, and still the occasional narrowed glance darted in Elave's direction.

Well, the young man had behaved impeccably throughout, and since the confrontation with Canon Gerbert had kept a guard on his tongue. Small bait for Brother Jerome there, though the very hint of unorthodoxy, especially when frowned upon by so eminent a prelate, was enough to cause Jerome's little nose to sniff the air like a meagre hound on a scent. The canon himself had not chosen to grace William's obsequies with his presence, but he would probably receive a full account from Prior Robert, who also knew how to value the opportunity to cultivate a close confidant and agent of the archbishop.

Howbeit, this minor matter, which had briefly threatened to blaze up into a dangerous heat, must surely be over now. William had his wish, Elave had done his loyal duty in securing it for him, and Radulfus had maintained the petitioner's right. And once tomorrow's festivities were over, Gerbert would soon be on his way, and without his exalted rigidity, almost certainly sincere, and probably excited by recent embassages to France and Rome, there would be an end here in Shrewsbury of these arid measurings and probings of every word a man spoke.

Cadfael watched the household of William of Lythwood muster its funeral guests and sally forth from the gatehouse towards the town, and went off to dinner in the refectory with the easy mind of a man who believes himself to have seen an important matter satisfactorily settled.

William's wake was well supplied with ale, wine and mead, and went the way of most wakes, from dignified solemnity and pious remembrance to sentimental and increasingly elaborated reminiscence, while discreet voices grew louder and anecdotes borrowed as much from imagination as from memory. And since Elave had been his companion for seven years while he had been out of sight and often out of mind of these old neighbours of his, the young man found himself being plied with the best ale in the house, in exchange for the stories he had to tell of the long journey and the wonders seen along the way, and of William's dignified farewell to the world.

If he had not drunk considerably more than he was accustomed to, he might not have given direct and open answers to oblique and insinuating questions. On the other hand, in view of his habitual and belligerent honesty, and the fact that he had no reason to suppose he had need of caution in this company, it is at least equally probable that he would.

It did not begin until all the visitors were leaving, or already gone, and Jevan was out in the street taking slow and pleasurable leave of the last of them, and being a comfortable, neighbourly time about it. Margaret was in the kitchen with Fortunata, clearing away the remains of the feast and supervising the washing of the pots that had provided it. Elave was left sitting at the table in the hall with Conan and Aldwin, and when most of the work in the kitchen was done, Fortunata came in quietly and sat down with them.

They were talking of the next day's festival. It was only seemly that a funeral should be fittingly observed and tidied away before the day of Saint Winifred's translation, so that everything on the morrow could be festive and auspicious, like the unclouded weather they hoped for. From the efficacy of the relics of saints and the validity of their miracles it was no long way to the matter of William. It was, after all, William's day, and fitting that they should be remembering him well into the dusk.

'According to one of the brothers down there,' said Aldwin earnestly, 'the little anxious grey fellow that runs so busy about the prior, it was a question whether the old man would be let in at all. Somebody there was for digging up that old scuffle he had with the missioner, to deny him a place.'

'It's a grave matter to disagree with the Church,' agreed Conan, shaking his head. 'It's not for us to know better than the priests, not where faith's concerned. Listen and say Amen, that's my advice. Did ever William talk to you about such things, Elave? You travelled a long way and a good many years with him, did he try to take you along with him down that road, too?'

'He never made any secret of what he thought,' said Elave. 'He'd argue his point, and with good sense, too, even to priests, but there was none of them found any great fault with him for thinking about such things. What are wits for unless a man uses them?'

'That's presumption,' said Aldwin, 'in simple folk like us, who haven't the learning or the calling of the churchmen. As the king and the sheriff have power over us in their field, so has the priest in his. It's not for us to meddle with matters beyond us. Conan's right, listen and say Amen!'

'How can you say Amen to damning a newborn child to hell because the little thing died before it could be baptised?' Elave asked reasonably. 'It was one of the things that bothered him. He used to argue not even the worst of men could throw a child into the fire, so how could the good God? It's against his nature.'

'And you,' said Aldwin, staring curiosity and concern, 'did you agree with him? Do you say so, too?'

'Yes, I do say so. I can't believe the reason they give us, that babes are born into the world already rotten with sin. How can that be true? A creature new and helpless, barely into this world, how can it ever have done wrong?'

'They say,' ventured Conan cautiously, 'even babes unborn are rotten with the sin of Adam, and fallen with him.'

'And I say that it's only his own deeds, bad and good, that a man will have to answer for in the judgement, and that's what will save or damn him. Though it's not often I've known a man so bad as to make me believe in damnation,' said Elave, still absorbed into his own reasoning, and intent only on expressing himself clearly and simply, without suspicion of hostility or danger. 'There was a father of the Church, once, as I heard tell, in Alexandria, who held that in the end everyone would find salvation. Even the fallen angels would return to their fealty, even the devil would repent and make his way back to God.'

He felt the chill and the shiver that went through his audience, but thought no more of it than that his travelled wisdom, small as it still was, had carried him out of the reach of their parochial innocence. Even Fortunata, listening silently to the talk of the menfolk, had stiffened and opened her eyes wide and round at such an utterance, startled and perhaps shocked. She said nothing in this company, but she followed every word that was spoken, and the colour ebbed and flowed in her cheeks as she glanced attentively from face to face.

'That's blasphemous!' said Aldwin in an awed whisper. 'The Church tells us there's no salvation but by grace, not by works. A man can do nothing to save himself, being born sinful.'

'I don't believe that,' said Elave stubbornly. 'Would the good God have made a creature so imperfect that he can have no free will of his own to choose between right and wrong? We can make our own way towards salvation, or down into the muck, and at the last we must every one stand by his own acts in the judgement. If we are men we ought to make our own way towards grace, not sit on our hams and wait for it to lift us up.'

'No, no, we're taught differently,' insisted Conan doggedly. 'Men are fallen by the first fall, and incline towards evil. They can never do good but by the grace of God.'

'And I say they *can* and do! A man *can* choose to avoid sin and do justly, of his own will, and his own will *is* the gift of God, and meant to be used. Why should a man get credit for leaving it all to God?' said Elave, roused but reasonable. 'We think about what we're doing daily with our hands, to earn a living. What fools we should be not to give a thought to what we're doing with our souls, to earn an eternal life. *Earn* it,' said Elave with emphasis, 'not wait to be given it unearned.'

'It's against the Church fathers,' objected Aldwin just as strongly. 'Our priest here preached a sermon once about Saint Augustine, how he wrote that the number of the elect is fixed and not to be changed, and all the rest are lost and damned, so how can their free will and their own acts help them? Only God's grace can save, everything else is vain and sinful.'

'I don't believe it,' said Elave loudly and firmly. 'Or why should we even try to deal justly? These very priests urge us to do right, and demand of us confession and penance if we fall short. Why, if the roll is already made up? Where is the sense of it? No, I do not believe it!'

Aldwin was looking at him in awed solemnity. 'You do not believe even Saint Augustine?'

'If he wrote that, no, I do not believe him.'

There was a sudden heavy silence, as though this blunt statement had knocked both his interrogators out of words. Aldwin, looking sidewise with narrowed and solemn eyes, drew furtively along the bench, removing even his sleeve from compromising contact with so perilous a neighbour.

'Well,' said Conan at length, too cheerfully and too loudly, shifting briskly on his side of the table as though time had suddenly nudged him in the ribs, 'I suppose we'd best be stirring, or we'll none of us be up in time to get the work done tomorrow before Mass. Straight from a wake to a wedding, as the saying goes! Let's hope the weather still holds.' And he rose, thrusting back his end of the bench, and stood stretching his thick, long limbs.

'It will,' said Aldwin confidently, recovering from his wary stillness with a great intake of breath. 'The saint had the sun shine on her procession when they brought her here from Saint Giles, while it rained all around. She won't fail us tomorrow,' And he, too, rose, with every appearance of relief. Plainly the convivial evening was over, and two, at least, were glad of it.

Elave sat still until they were gone, with loud and over-amiable goodnights, about their last tasks before bed. The house had fallen silent. Margaret was sitting in the kitchen, going over the day's events for flaws and compensations with the neighbour who came in to help her on such special occasions. Fortunata had not moved or spoken. Elave turned to face her, doubtfully eyeing her stillness, and the intent gravity of her face. Silence and solemnity seemed alien in her, and perhaps really were, but when they took possession of her they were entire and impressive.

'You are so quiet,' said Elave doubtfully. 'Have I offended you in anything I've said? I know I've talked too much, and too presumptuously.'

'No,' she said, her voice measured and low, 'nothing has offended me. I never thought about such things before, that's all. I was too young, when you went away, for William ever to talk so to me. He was very good to me, and I'm glad you spoke up boldly for him. So would I have done.'

But she had no more to say, not then. Whatever she was thinking now about such things she was not yet ready to say, and perhaps by tomorrow she would have abandoned the consideration of what was difficult even for the world's philosophers and theologians, and would come down with Margaret and Jevan to Saint Winifred's festival content to enjoy the music and excitement and worship without questioning, to listen and say Amen.

She went out with him across the yard and through the entry into the street when he left, and gave him her hand at parting, still in a silence that was composed and withdrawn.

'I shall see you at church tomorrow?' said Elave,

belatedly afraid that he had indeed alienated her, for she confronted him with so wide and thoughtful a stare of her unwavering hazel eyes that he could not even guess at what went on in the mind behind them.

'Yes,' said Fortunata simply, 'I shall be there.' And she smiled, briefly and abstractedly, withdrew her hand gently from his, and turned back to return to the house, leaving him to walk back through the town to the bridge still unhappily in doubt whether he had not talked a great deal too much and too rashly, and injured himself in her eyes.

The sun duly shone for Saint Winifred on her festival day, as it had on the day of her first coming to the abbey of Saint Peter and Saint Paul. The gardens overflowed with blossom, the eager pilgrims housed by Brother Denis put on their best and came forth like so many more gaily coloured flowers, the burgesses of Shrewsbury flocked down from the town, and the parishioners of Holy Cross in from the Foregate and the scattered villages of Father Boniface's extensive parish. The new priest had only recently been inducted after a lengthy interregnum, and his flock were still carefully taking his measure, after their unhappy experience with the late Father Ailnoth. But first reactions were entirely favourable. Cynric the verger acted as a kind of touchstone for Foregate opinion. His views, so seldom expressed in words, but so easy for the simple and direct to interpret by intuition, would be accepted without question by most of those who worshipped at Holy Cross, and it was already clear to the children. Cynric's closest cronies in spite of his taciturnity, that their long, bony, silent friend liked and approved of Father Boniface. That was enough for them. They approached their new priest with candour and confidence, secure in Cynric's recommendation.

Boniface was young, not much past thirty, of unassuming appearance and modest bearing, no scholar like his predecessor, but earnestly cheerful about his duties.

The deference he showed to his monastic neighbours disposed even Prior Robert to approve of him, though with some condescension in view of the young man's humble birth and scanty Latin. Abbot Radulfus, conscious of one disastrous mistake in the previous appointment, had taken his time over this one, and studied the candidates with care. Did the Foregate really need a learned theologian? Craftsmen, small merchants, husbandmen, cottars and hardworking villeins from the villages and manors, they were better off with one of their own kind, aware of their needs and troubles, not stooping to them but climbing laboriously with them, elbow to elbow. It seemed that Father Boniface had energy and determination for the climb, force enough to urge a few others upward with him, and the stubborn loyalty not to leave them behind if they tired. In Latin or in the vernacular, that was language the people could understand.

This was a day on which secular and monastic clergy united to do honour to their saint, and chapter was postponed until after High Mass, when the church was open to all the pilgrims who wished to bring their private petitions to her altar, to touch her silver reliquary and offer prayers and gifts in the hope of engaging her gentle attention and benevolence for their illnesses, burdens and anxieties. All day long they would be coming and going, kneeling and rising in the pale, resplendent light of the scented candles Brother Rhun made in her honour. Ever since she had visited Rhun, himself a pilgrim, with her secret counsel, and lifted him out of lameness in her arms, to the bodily perfection of his present radiance, Rhun had made himself her page and squire, and his beauty reflected and testified to hers. For everyone knew that Winifred had been, as her legend said, the fairest maiden in the world in her day.

Everything, in fact, seemed to Brother Cadfael to be working together in perfect accord to make this what it should be, a day of supreme content, without blemish.

He went to his stall in the chapter-house well satisfied with the world in general, and composed himself to sit through the day's business, even the most uninteresting details, with commendable attention. Some of the obedientiaries could be tedious enough on their own subjects to send a tired man to sleep, but today he was determined to extend virtuous tolerance even to the dullest of them.

Even to Canon Gerbert, he resolved, watching that superb cleric sail into the chapter-house and appropriate the stall beside the abbot, he would attribute only the most sanctified of motives, whatever fault the visitor might find with the discipline here, and however supercilious his behaviour towards Abbot Radulfus. Today nothing must ruffle the summer tranquillity.

Into this admirable mood a sudden disagreeable wind blew, driven before the billowing skirts of Prior Robert's habit as he strode in with aristocratic nose aloft and nostrils distended, as though someone had thrust an evil-smelling obscenity under them. Such sweeping speed in one so dedicated to preserving his own dignity sent an ominous shiver along the ranks of the brothers, all the more as Brother Jerome was disclosed scuttling in the prior's shadow. His narrow, pallid face proclaimed an excitement half horrified, half gratified.

'Father Abbot,' declaimed Robert, trumpeting outrage loud and clear, 'I have a most grave matter to bring before you. Brother Jerome here brought it to my notice, as I must in conscience bring it to yours. There is one waiting outside who has brought a terrible charge against William of Lythwood's apprentice, Elave. You recall how suspect the master's faith was once shown to be; now it seems the servant may outdo the master. One of the same household bears witness that last night, before other witnesses also, this man gave voice to views utterly opposed to the Church's teaching. Girard of Lythwood's clerk, Aldwin, denounces Elave for abominable heresies, and stands ready to maintain the charge against him before this assembly, as is his bounden duty.'

Chapter Five

T WAS SAID, and could not be unsaid. The word, once launched, has a deadly permanence. This word brought with it a total stillness and silence, as though a killing frost had settled on the chapter-house. The paralysis lasted for some moments before even the eyes moved, swerving from the righteous indignation of the prior's countenance to glide sidelong over Brother Jerome and peer through the open doorway in search of the accuser, who had not yet shown himself, but waited humbly somewhere out of sight.

Cadfael's first thought was that this was no more than another of Jerome's acidities, impulsive, ill-founded and certain to be refuted as soon as enquiry was made. Most of Jerome's mountains turned out molehills on examination. Then he looked round to read Canon Gerbert's austere face, and knew that this was a far graver matter, and could not be lightly set aside. Even if the archbishop's envoy had not been present to hear, Abbot Radulfus himself could not have ignored such a charge. He could bring reason to bear on the proceedings that must follow, but he could not halt them.

Gerbert would clench his teeth into any such deviation, that much was certain from the set of his lips and the wide, predatory stare of his eyes, but at least he had the courtesy to leave the first initiative here to the abbot.

'I trust,' said Radulfus, in the dry, deliberate voice that indicated his controlled displeasure, 'that you have satisfied yourself, Robert, that this accusation is seriously meant, and not a gesture of personal animosity? It might be well, before we proceed further, to warn the accuser of the gravity of what he is doing. If he speaks out of some private spite, he should be given the opportunity to think better of his own position, and withdraw the charge. Men are fallible, and may say on impulse things quickly regretted.'

'I have so warned him,' said the prior firmly. 'He answers that there are two others who heard what he heard, and can bear witness as he can. This does not rest simply on a dispute between two men. Also, as you know, Father, this Elave returned here only a few days ago, the clerk Aldwin can have no grudge against him, surely, in so short a time.'

'And this is the same who brought home his master's body,' Canon Gerbert cut in sharply, 'and showed even then, I must say, certain rebellious and most questionable tendencies. This charge must not pass as leniently as the lingering suspicions against the dead man.'

'The charge has been made, and apparently is persisted in,' agreed Radulfus coldly. 'It must certainly be brought to question, but not here, not now. This is a matter for the seniors only, not for novices and the younger brothers among us. Am I to understand, Robert, that the accused man as yet knows nothing of what is charged against him?'

'No, Father, not from me, and certainly not from the man Aldwin, he came secretly to Brother Jerome to tell what he had heard.'

'The young man is a guest in our house,' said the abbot. 'He has a right to know what is said of him, and to answer it fully. And the other two witnesses of whom the accuser speaks, who are they?'

'They belong to the same household, and were present

in the hall when these things were spoken. The girl Fortunata is a fosterchild to Girard of Lythwood, and Conan is his head shepherd.'

'They are both still here within the enclave,' put in Brother Jerome, eagerly helpful. 'They attended Mass, and are still in the church.'

'This matter should be dealt with at once,' urged Canon Gerbert, stiff with zeal. 'Delay can only dim the memories of the witnesses, and give the offender time to consider his interests and run from trial. It is for you to direct, Father Abbot, but I would recommend you to do so immediately, boldly, while you have all these people here within your gates. Dismiss your novices now, and send word and summon those witnesses and the man accused. And I would give orders to the porters to see that the accused does not pass through the gates.'

Canon Gerbert was accustomed to instant compliance with even his suggestions, let alone his orders, however obliquely expressed, but in his own house Abbot Radulfus went his own way.

'I would remind this chapter,' he said shortly, 'that while we of the Order certainly have a duty to serve and defend the faith, every man has also his parish priest, and every parish priest has his bishop. We have here with us the representative of Bishop de Clinton, in whose diocese of Lichfield and Coventry we dwell, and in whose cure accused, accuser and witnesses rest.' Serlo was certainly present, but had said not a word until now. In Gerbert's presence he went in awe and silence. 'I am sure,' said Radulfus with emphasis, 'that he will hold, as I do, that though we may be justified in making a first enquiry into the charge made, we cannot proceed further without referring the case to the bishop, within whose discipline it falls. If we find upon examination that the charge is groundless, that can be the end of the matter. If we feel there is need to proceed further with it, then it must be referred to the man's own bishop, who has the right to deal with it by whatever tribunal he sees fit to appoint.'

'That is truth,' said Serlo gallantly, thus encouraged to follow where he might have hesitated to lead. 'My bishop would certainly wish to exercise his writ in such a case.'

A judgement of Solomon, thought Cadfael, well content with his abbot. Roger de Clinton will be no better pleased to have another cleric usurping his authority in his diocese than Radulfus is to see any man, were it the archbishop himself, leave alone his envoy, twitching the reins away from him here. And young Elave will probably have good reason to be glad of it before all's done. Now how did he come to let down his guard so rashly with witnesses by, after one fright already past?

'I would not for the world trespass upon the ground of Bishop de Clinton,' said Gerbert, hastily jealous for his own good repute, but not sounding at all pleased about it. 'Certainly he must be informed if this matter proves to be true substance. But it is we who are faced with the need to probe the facts, while memories are fresh, and put on record what we discover. No time should be lost. Father Abbot, in my view we should hold a hearing now, at once.'

'I am inclined to the same opinion,' said the abbot drily. 'In the event of the charge turning out to be malicious or trivial, or untrue, or simply mistaken, it need then go no further, and the bishop will be spared a grief and an aggravation, no less than the waste of his time. I think we are competent to probe out the difference between harmless speculation and wilful perversion.'

It seemed to Cadfael that that indicated pretty clearly the abbot's view of the whole unfortunate affair, and though Canon Gerbert had opened his mouth, most probably to proclaim that even speculation among the laity was itself harm enough, he thought better of it, and clenched his teeth again grimly on the undoubted reserve he felt about the abbot's attitude, character and fitness for his office. Men of the cloth are as liable to instant antipathies as are ordinary folk, and these two were as far apart as east from west.

'Very well,' said Radulfus, running a long, command-ing glance round the assembly, 'let us proceed. This chapter is suspended. We will summon it again when time permits. Brother Richard and Brother Anselm, will you see all the juniors set to useful service, and then seek out those three people named? The young woman Fortunata, the shepherd Conan, and the accused man. Bring them here, and say nothing as to the cause until they come before us. The accuser, I take it,' he said, turning upon Jerome, 'is already here without.'

Jerome had lingered in the shadow of the prior's skirts all this time, sure of his righteousness but not quite sure of the abbot's recognition of it. This was the first encour-agement he had received, or so he read it, and visibly brightened.

'He is, Father. Shall I bring him in?'

'No,' said the abbot, 'not until the accused is here to confront him. Let him say what he has to say face to face with the man he denounces.'

Elave and Fortunata entered the chaper-house together, open of face, puzzled and curious at being summoned thus, but plainly innocent of all foreboding. Whatever had been said unwisely at last night's gathering, whatever she was expected to confirm against the speaker, it was perfectly clear to Cadfael that the girl had no reser-vations about her companion, indeed the very fact that they came in together, and had obviously been found together when the summons was delivered, spoke for itself. The expectancy in their faces was wondering but unthreatened, and Aldwin's accusation, when it was uttered, would come as a shattering blow not to the young man only, but to the girl as well. Gerbert would certainly have one reluctant witness, if not a hostile one, Cadfael reflected, conscious of his own heart's alerted and partisan sympathy. Conscious, too, that Abbot Radulfus had noted, as he had, the significance of their trusting entrance, and the wondering look they exchanged, smiling, before they made their reverence to the array of prelates and monastics before them, and waited to be enlightened.

'You sent for us, Father Abbot,' said Elave, since no one else broke the silence. 'We are here.'

The 'we' says it all, thought Cadfael. If she had any doubts of him last night, she has forgotten them this morning, or thought them over and rejected them. And that is valid evidence, too, whatever she may be forced to say later.

'I sent for you, Elave,' said the abbot with deliberation, 'to help us in a certain matter which has arisen here this morning. Wait but a moment, there is one more has been summoned to attend.'

He came in at that moment, circumspectly and in some awe of the tribunal before him, but not, Cadfael thought, ignorant of its purpose. There was no open-eyed but unintimidated wonder in Conan's weathered, wary, rosily comely face, and noticeably he kept his eyes respectfully upon the abbot, and never cast a glance aside at Elave. He knew what was in the wind, he came prepared for it. And this one, if he discreetly showed no eagerness displayed no reluctance, either.

'My lord, they told me Conan is wanted here. That's my name.'

'Are we now ready to proceed?' demanded Canon Gerbert impatiently, stirring irritably in his stall.

'We are,' said Radulfus. 'Well, Jerome, bring in the man Aldwin. And Elave, stand forward in the centre. This man has somewhat to say of you that should be said only in your presence.'

The name alone had jolted both Fortunata and Elave, even before Aldwin showed his face in the doorway, and came in with a resolution and belligerence that were not native to him, and probably cost him an effort to maintain. His long face was set in lines of arduous determination, a man naturally resigned and timorous bent on going through with an enterprise that called for courage.

He took his stand almost within arm's length of Elave, and jutted an aggressive jaw at the young man's shocked stare, but there were drops of sweat on his own balding forehead. He spread his feet to take firm grip on the stones of the floor, and stared back at Elave without blinking. Elave had already begun to understand. By her bewildered face Fortunata had not. She drew back a pace or two, looking searchingly from one man's face to the other, her lips parted on quickened breath.

'This man,' said the abbot evenly, 'has made certain charges against you, Elave. He says that last night, in his master's house, you gave voice to views on matters of religion that run counter to the teachings of the Church, and bring you into grave danger of heresy. He cites these witnesses present in support of what he urges against you. How do you say, was there indeed such talk between you? You were there to speak, and they to hear?'

'Father,' said Elave, grown very pale and quiet, 'I was there in the house. I did have speech with them. The talk did turn on matters of faith. We had only yesterday buried a good master, it was natural we should give thought to his soul and our own.'

'And do you yourself, in good conscience, believe that you said nothing that could run counter to true belief?' asked Radufus mildly.

'To the best that I know and understand, Father, I never did.'

'You, fellow, Aldwin,' ordered Canon Gerbert, leaning forward in his stall, 'repeat those things of which you complained to Brother Jerome. Let us hear them all, and in the words you heard spoken, so far as you can recall them. Change nothing!'

'My lords, as we sat together, we were speaking of William who was newly buried, and Conan asked if he had ever taken Elave with him down the same road that got him into straits with the priest, those years ago. And Elave said William never made any secret of what he thought, and on his travels no one ever found fault with him for thinking about such matters. What are wits for, he said, unless a man uses them. And we said that it was presumption in us simple folk, that we should listen and say Amen to what the Church tells us, for in that field the priests have authority over us.'

'A very proper saying,' said Gerbert roundly. 'And how did he reply?'

'Sir, he said how could a man say Amen to damning a child unchristened to hell? The worst of men, he said, could not cast an infant into the fire, so how could God, being goodness itself, do so? It would be against God's very nature, he said.'

'That is to argue,' said Gerbert, 'that infant baptism is unneeded, and of no virtue. There can be no other logical end of such reasoning. If they are in no need of redemption by baptism, to be spared inevitable reprobation, then the sacrament is brought into contempt.'

'Did you say the words Aldwin reports of you?' asked Radulfus quietly, his eyes on Elave's roused and indignant face.

'Father, I did. I do not believe such innocent children, just because baptism does not reach them in time before they die, can possibly fall through God's hands. Surely his hold is more secure than that.'

'You persist in a deadly error,' insisted Gerbert. 'It is as I have said, such a belief casts out and debases the sacrament of baptism, which is the only deliverance from mortal sin. If one sacrament is brought into derision, then all are denied. On this count alone you stand in danger of judgement.'

'Sir,' Aldwin took him up eagerly, 'he said also that he did not believe in the need because he did not believe that children are born into the world rotten with sin. How could that be, he said, of a little thing newly come into being, helpless to do anything of itself, good or evil. Is not that indeed to make an empty mockery of baptism? And we said that we are taught and must believe

76

that even the babes yet unborn are rotten with the sin of Adam, and fallen with him. But he said no, it is only his own deeds, bad and good, that a man must answer for in the judgement, and his own deeds will save or damn him.'

'To deny original sin is to degrade every sacrament,' Gerbert repeated forcibly.

'No, I never thought of it so,' protested Elave hotly. 'I did say a helpless newborn child cannot be a sinner. But surely baptism is to welcome him into the world and into the Church, and help him to keep his innocence. I never said it was useless or a light thing.'

'But you do deny original sin?' Gerbert pressed him hard.

'Yes,' said Elave after a long pause. 'I do deny it.' His face had sharpened into icy whiteness, but his jaw was set and his eyes had begun to burn with a deep, still anger.

Abbot Radulfus eyed him steadily and asked in a mild and reasonable voice: 'What, then, do you believe to be the state of the child on entering this world? A child the son of Adam, as are we all.'

Elave looked back at him as gravely, arrested by the serenity of the voice that questioned him. 'His state is the same,' he said slowly, 'as the state of Adam before his fall. For even Adam had his innocence once.'

'So others before you have argued,' said Radulfus, 'and have not inevitably been called heretical. Much has been written on the subject, in good faith and in deep concern for the good of the Church. Is this the worst you have to urge, Aldwin, against this man?'

'No, Father,' Aldwin said in haste, 'there is more. He said it is a man's own acts that will save or damn him, but that he had not often met a man so bad as to make him believe in eternal damnation. And then he said that there was a father of the Church once, in Alexandria, who held that in the end everyone would find salvation, even the fallen angels, even the devil himself.'

In the shudder of unease that passed along the ranks

of the brothers the abbot remarked simply: 'So there was. His name was Origen. It was his theme that all things came from God, and will return to God. As I recall, it was an enemy of his who brought the devil into it, though I grant the implication is there. I gather that Elave merely cited what Origen is said to have written and believed. He did not say that he himself believed it? Well, Aldwin?'

Aldwin drew in his chin cautiously at that, and gave some thought to the possibility that he himself was edging his way through quicksands. 'No, Father, that is true. He said only that there was a father of the Church who spoke so. But we said that was blasphemy, for the teaching of the Church is that salvation comes by the grace of God, and no other way, and a man's works can avail him not at all. But then he said outright: I do not believe that!'

'Did you so?' asked Radulfus.

'I did,' Elave's blood was up, the pallor of his face had burned into a sharp-edged brightness that was almost dazzling. Cadfael at once despaired of him and exulted in him. The abbot had done his best to temper all this fermenting doubt and malice and fear that had gathered in the chapter-house like a bitter cloud, making it hard to breathe, and here was this stubborn creature accepting all challenges, and digging in his heels to resist even his friends. Now that he was embattled he would do battle. He would not give back one pace out of regard for his skin. 'I did say so. I say it again. I said that we have the power in ourselves to make our own way towards salvation. I said we have free will to choose between right and wrong, to labour upwards or to dive down and wallow in the muck, and at the last we must every one answer for our own acts in the judgement. I said if we are men, and not beasts, we ought to make our own way towards grace, not sit on our hams and wait for it to lift us up, unworthy.'

'By such arrogance,' trumpeted Canon Gerbert,

offended as much by the flashing eyes and obdurate voice as by what was said, 'by such pride as yours the rebel angels fell. So you would do without God, and repudiate his divine grace, the only means to salve your insolent soul –'

'You wrong me,' flashed back Elave. 'I do not deny divine grace. The grace is in the gifts he has given us, free will to choose good and refuse evil, and mount towards our own salvation, yes, and the strength to choose rightly. If we do our part, God will do the rest.'

Abbot Radulfus tapped sharply with his ring on the arm of his stall, and called the assembly to order with unshaken authority. 'For my part,' he said as they quieted, 'I find no fault with a man for holding that he can and should aspire to grace by right use of grace. But we are straying from what we are here to do. Let us by all means listen scrupulously to all that Elave is alleged to have said, and let him admit what he admits and deny what he denies of it, and let these witnesses confirm or refute. Have you yet more to add, Aldwin?'

By this time Aldwin had learned to be careful how he trod with the abbot, and add nothing to the bare words he had memorised overnight.

'Father, but one more thing. I said I had heard a preacher tell how Saint Augustine wrote that the number of the elect is already fixed and cannot be changed, and all the rest are doomed to reprobation. And he said that he did not believe it. And I could not keep from asking again, did he not believe even Saint Augustine? And he said again, no, he did not.'

'I said,' cried Elave hotly, 'that I could not believe the roll was already made up, for why then should we even try to deal justly or pay God worship, or give any heed to the priests who urge us to keep from sin, and demand of us confession and penance if we trespass? To what end, if we are damned whatever we do? And when he asked again, did I not believe even Saint Augustine, I said that *if he wrote that*, no, I did not believe him. For I have no knowledge else that he ever did write such a thing.'

'Is that truth?' demanded Radulfus, before Gerbert could speak. 'Aldwin, do you bear out those were the actual words spoken?'

'It may be so,' agreed Aldwin cautiously. 'Yes, I think he did say *if* the saint had so written. I saw no difference there, but your lordships will better judge than I.'

'And that is all? You have nothing more to add?'

'No, Father, that's all. After that we let him lie, we wanted no more of him.'

'You were wise,' said Canon Gerbert grimly. 'Well, Father Abbot, can we now hear if the witnesses confirm all that has been said? It seems to me there is substance enough in what we have heard, if these two persons also can verify it.'

Conan gave his own account of the evening's talk so fluently and willingly that Cadfael could not resist the feeling that he had learned his speech by heart, and the impression of a small conspiracy emerged, for Cadfael at least, so clearly that he wondered it was not obvious to all. To the abbot, he thought, studying the controlled, ascetic face, it almost certainly was, and yet even if these two had connived for their own ends, yet the fact remained that these things had been said, and Elave, even if he corrected or enlarged here and there, did not deny them. How had they contrived to get him to talk so openly? And more important still, how had they ensured that the girl should also be present? For it became increasingly plain that on her evidence everything depended. The more Abbot Radulfus might suspect Aldwin and Conan of malice against Elave, the more important was what Fortunata might have to say about it.

She had listened intently to all that passed. Belated understanding had paled her oval face and dilated her eyes into glittering green anxiety, flashing from face to face as question and answer flew and the tension in the chapter-house mounted. When the abbot turned to look at her she stiffened, and the set of her lips tightened nervously.

'And you, child? You also were present and heard what passed?'

She said carefully: 'I was not present throughout. I was helping my mother in the kitchen when these three were left together.'

'But you joined them later,' said Gerbert. 'At what stage? Did you hear him say that infant baptism was needless and useless?'

At that she spoke up boldly: 'No, sir, for he never did say that.'

'Oh, if you stick upon the wording ... Did you hear him say, then, that he did not believe unbaptised children suffered damnation? For that leads to the same end.'

'No,' said Fortunata. 'He never did say what his own belief was in that matter. He was speaking of his master, who is dead. He said that William used to say not even the worst of men could throw a child into the fire, so how could God do so? When he said this,' said Fortunata firmly, 'he was telling us what William had said, not what he himself thought.'

'That is true, but only half the truth,' cried Aldwin, 'for the next moment I asked him plainly: Do you also hold that belief? And he said: Yes, I do say so.'

'Is that true, girl?' demanded Gerbert, turning upon Fortunata a black and threatening scowl. And when she faced him with eyes flashing but lips tight shut: 'It seems to me that this witness has no devout wish to help us. We should have done better to take all testimony under oath, it seems. Let us at least make sure in this woman's case.' He turned his forbidding gaze hard and long upon the obdurately silent girl. 'Woman, do you know in what suspicion you place yourself if you do not speak truth? Father Prior, bring her a Bible. Let her swear upon the Gospels and imperil her soul if she lies.'

Fortunata laid her hand upon the proffered book which Prior Robert solemnly opened before her, and took the oath in a voice so low as to be barely audible. Elave had opened his mouth and taken a step towards her in helpless anger at the aspersion cast upon her, but stopped himself as quickly and stood mute, his teeth clenched upon his rage, and his face soured with the bitter taste of it.

'Now,' said the abbot, with such quiet but formidable authority that even Gerbert made no further attempt to wrest the initiative from him, 'let us leave questioning until you have told us yourself, without haste or fear, all you recall of what went on in that meeting. Speak freely, and I believe we shall hear truth.'

She took heart and drew steady breath, and told it carefully, as best she remembered it. Once or twice she hesitated, sorely tempted to omit or explain, but Cadfael noticed how her left hand clasped and wrung the right hand that had been laid upon the open Gospel, as though it burned, and impelled her past the momentary silence.

'With your leave, Father Abbot,' said Gerbert grimly when she ended, 'when you have put such questions as you see fit to this witness, I have three to put to her, and they encompass the heart of the matter. But first do you proceed.'

'I have no questions,' said Radulfus. 'The lady has given us her full account on oath, and I accept it. Ask what you have to ask.'

'First,' said Gerbert, leaning forward in his stall with thick brown brows drawn down over his sharp, intimidating stare, 'did you hear the accused say, when asked pointblank if he agreed with his master in denying that unbaptised children were doomed to reprobation, that yes, he did so agree?'

She turned her head aside for an instant, and wrung at her hand for reminder, and in a very low voice she said: 'Yes, I heard him say so.'

'That is to repudiate the sacrament of baptism. Second, did you hear him deny that all the children of men are rotten with the sin of Adam? Did you hear him say that only a man's own deeds will save or damn him?'

With a flash of spirit she said, louder than before: 'Yes, but he was not denying grace, the grace is in the gift of choice –'

Gerbert cut her off there with uplifted hand and flashing eyes. 'He said it. That is enough. It is the claim that grace is unneeded, that salvation is in a man's own hands. Thirdly, did you hear him say, and repeat, that he did not believe what Saint Augustine wrote of the elect and the rejected?'

'Yes,' she said, this time slowly and carefully. '*If* the saint so wrote, he said, he did not believe him. No one has ever told me, and I cannot read or write, beyond my name and some small things. Did Saint Augustine say what the preacher reported of him?'

'That is enough!' snapped Gerbert. 'This girl bears out all that has been charged against the accused. The proceedings are in your hands.'

'It is my judgement,' said Radulfus, 'that we should adjourn, and deliberate in private. The witnesses are dismissed. Go home, daughter, and be assured you have told truth, and need trouble not at all what follows, for the truth cannot but be good. Go, all of you, but hold yourselves ready should you be needed again and recalled. And you, Elave . . .' He sat studying the young man's face, which was raised to him pale, resolute and irate, with set mouth and wide and brilliant eyes, still burning for Fortunata's distress. 'You are a guest in our house. I have seen no cause why any man of us should not take your word.' He was aware of Gerbert stiffening with disapproval beside him, but swept on with raised voice, overriding protest. 'If you promise not to leave here until this matter is resolved, then you are free in the meantime to go back and forth here as you will.'

For a moment Elave's attention wavered. Fortunata had turned in the doorway to look back, then she was gone. Conan and Aldwin had left hastily on their dismissal, and vanished before her, eager to escape while their case was surely safe in the hands of the visiting prelate, whose nose for unorthodoxy was shown to be so keen and his zeal so relentless. Accuser and witnesses were gone. Elave returned his obdurate but respectful gaze to the abbot, and said with deliberation: 'My lord, I have no mind to leave my lodging here in your house until I can do so free and vindicated. I give you my word on that.'

'Go, then, until I ask your attendance again. And now,' said Radulfus, rising, 'this session is adjourned. Go to your duties, every one, and bear in mind we are still in a day dedicated to the remembrance of Saint Winifred, and the saints also bear witness to all that we do, and will testify accordingly.'

'I understand you very well,' said Canon Gerbert, when he was alone with Radulfus in the abbot's parlour. Closeted thus in private with his peer, he sat relaxed, even weary, all his censorious zeal shed, a fallible man and anxious for his faith. 'Here retired from the world, or at the worst concerned largely with the region and the people close about you, you have not seen the danger of false belief. And I grant you it has not yet cast a shadow in this land, and I pray our people may be sturdy enough to resist all such devious temptations. But it comes, Father Abbot, it comes! From the east the serpents of undoing are working their way westward, and of all travellers from the east I go in dread that they may bring back with them bad seed, perhaps even unwittingly, to take root and grow even here. There are malignant wandering preachers active even now in Flanders, in France, on the Rhine, in Lombardy, who cry out against Holy Church and her priesthood, that we are corrupt and greedy, that the Apostles lived simply, in holy poverty. In Antwerp a certain Tachelm has drawn deluded thousands after him to raid churches and tear down their ornaments. In France, in Rouen itself, yet another such goes about preaching poverty and humility and demanding reform. I have travelled in the south on my archbishop's errands, and seen how error grows and spreads like a heath fire. These are not a few sick in mind and harmless. In Provence, in Languedoc, there are regions where a fashion of Manichean heresy has grown so strong it is become almost a rival church. Do you wonder that I dread even the first weak spark that may start such a blaze?'

'No,' said Radulfus, 'I do not wonder. We should never relax our guard. But also we must see every man clearly, with his words and his deeds upon him, and not hasten to cover him from sight with this universal cloak of heresy. Once the word is spoken, the man himself may become invisible. And therefore expendable! Here is certainly no wandering preacher, no inflamer of crowds, no ambitious madman whipping up a following for his own gain. The boy spoke of a master he had valued and served, and therefore tended to speak in praise of him, in defence of his bold doubts, the more loyally and fiercely if his companions raised their voices against him. He had probably drunk enough to loosen his tongue, besides. He may well have said, and repeated to us, more than he truly means, to the aggravation of his cause. Shall we do the same?'

'No,' said Gerbert heavily, 'I would not wish that. And I do see him clearly. You say rightly, here is no wild man bent on mischief, but a sound, hardworking fellow, profitable to his master and I doubt not honest and well-meaning with his neighbours. Do you not see how much more dangerous that makes him? To hear false doctrine from one himself plainly false and vile is no temptation at all, to hear it from one fair of countenance and reputation, speaking it with his heart's conviction, that can be deadly seduction. It is why I fear him.'

'It is why one century's saint is the next century's heretic,' the abbot replied drily, 'and one century's heretic the next century's saint. It is as well to think long and calmly before affixing either name to any man.'

'That is to neglect a duty we cannot evade,' said Gerbert, again bristling. 'The peril which is here and now must be dealt with here and now, or the battle is lost, for the seed will have fallen and rooted.'

'Then at least we may know the wheat from the tares. And bear in mind,' said Radulfus gravely, 'that where error is sincere and bred out of misguided goodness, the blemish may be healed by reason and persuasion.'

'Or failing that,' said Gerbert with inflexible resolution, 'by lopping off the diseased member.'

Chapter Six

LAVE passed through the gates unchallenged, and turned towards the town. Evidently the porter had not yet got word of the alarm raised against this one ordinary mortal among the abbey guests, or else he had already received the abbot's fiat that the accused's parole was given and accepted, and he was free to go and come as he pleased, provided he did not collect his belongings and take to his heels altogether, for no attempt was made to bar his way. The brother on the gate even gave him a cheerful good-day as he passed.

Out in the Foregate he paused to look both ways along the highroad, but all the witnesses against him had vanished from sight. He set off in haste towards the bridge and the town, certain that Fortunata in her distress would make straight for home. She had left the chapter-house before he had given his word he had no intention of departing unvindicated, she might well think him already a prisoner, might even blame herself for his plight. He had seen how reluctantly she had borne true witness against him, and at this moment it grieved him more that she should grieve than that his own liberty and life should be in danger. In that danger he found it hard to believe, therefore it was easy to bear. Her evident agitation he believed in utterly, and it caused him deep

87

and compelling pain. He had to speak to her, to reassure her she had done him no wrong in the world, that this commotion would pass, that the abbot was a reasonable man, and the other one, the one who wanted blood, would soon be gone and leave the judgement to saner judges. And more beyond that, that he had understood how valiantly she had striven to defend him, that he was grateful for it, perhaps even hoping in his heart to find in it a deeper meaning than sympathy, and more intimate than concern for justice. Though he must guard his tongue from saying too much, as long as even the shadow of reprobation hung over him.

He had reached the end of the enclave wall, where the ground on his left opened out over the silvery oval of the mill pool, and on the right of the road the houses of the Foregate gave way to a grove of trees that stretched as far as the approaches to the bridge over the Severn. And there she was before him, unmistakeable in her bearing and gait, hastening along the dusty highway with an impetuosity that suggested angry resolution rather than consternation and dismay. He broke into a run, and overtook her in the shadow of the trees. At the sound of his racing feet she had swung round to face him, and at sight of him, without a word said beyond his breathless 'Mistress . . .!' she caught him hastily by the hand and drew him well aside into the grove, out of sight from the road.

'What is this? Have they freed you? Is it over?' She raised to him a face glowing and intent with unmistakeable joy, but still holding it in check for fear of a fall as sudden as her elation.

'No, not yet. No, there'll be more debate yet before I'm quit of all this. But I had to speak to you, to thank you for what you did for me –'

'*Thank* me!' she said in a soft, incredulous cry. 'For digging the pit a little deeper under you? I burn with shame that I had not even the courage to lie!'

'No, no, you mustn't think so! You did me no wrong

at all, you did everything you could to help me. Why should you be forced to lie? In any case, you could not do it, it is not in you. Nor will I lie,' said Elave fiercely, 'nor give back from what I believe. What I came to say is that you must not fret for me, nor ever for a moment think that I have anything but gratitude and reverence for you. You stood my friend the only way I would have you stand my friend.'

· He had not even realised that he was holding both her hands, clasped close against his breast, so that they stood heart to heart, the rhythm of matched heartbeats and quickened breathing shaking them both. Her face, raised to his, was intent and fierce, her hazel eyes dazzlingly wide and bright.

'If they have not freed you, how are you here? Do they know you are gone? Will they not be hunting for you if you're missed?'

'Why should they? I'm free to go and come, as long as I remain a guest in the abbey until there's a judgement. The abbot took my word I would not run.'

'But you must,' she said urgently. 'I thank God that you ran after me like this, while there's time. You must go, get away from here as far as you can. Into Wales would be best. Come with me now, quickly, I'll get you to Jevan's workshop beyond Frankwell, and hide you there until I can get you a horse.'

Elave was shaking his head vigorously before she had ended her plea. 'No, I will not run! I gave the abbot my word, but even if he had never asked it or I given it, I would not run. I will not bow to such superstitious foolishness, it would be to encourage the madmen, and put other souls in worse danger than mine. This I don't believe can come to anything perilous, if I stand my ground. We have not yet come to that extreme of folly, that a man can be hounded for thinking about holy things. You'll see, the storm will all pass over.'

'No,' she insisted, 'not so easily. Things are changing, did you not smell the smoke of it even there in the chapter-house? I foresee it, if you do not. I was hurrying back now to talk to Jevan, to see what more can be brought to bear, to deliver you away out of danger. You brought me something of my own, it must have value. I want to use it to have you away and safe. What better use could I make of it?'

'No!' he said in sharp protest. 'I will not have it! I am not going to run, I refuse to run. And that, whatever it may be, is for you, for your marriage.'

'My marriage!' she said in a wondering voice, very low, and opened wide at him the greenish fire of her eyes, as though the thought was new to her and very strange.

'Never trouble for me, in the end it will all be well. I am going back now,' said Elave firmly, too dazzled to be observant. 'Never fear, I'll take good care how I speak, how I carry myself, but I will not deny what I believe, or say ay to what I do not believe. And I will not run. From what? I have no guilt from which to run.'

He loosed her hand with a gesture almost rough, because at the end it seemed such a hard thing to do. He was turning away through the trees when he looked back, and she had not moved. Her eyes were on him, fixed thoughtfully, almost severely, and her lower lip was caught between even teeth.

'There is another reason,' he said, 'why I will not go. Alone it would be enough to hold me. To run now would be to leave you.'

'And do you think,' said Fortunata, 'that I would not follow and find you?'

She heard the several voices before she entered the hall, voices raised not so much in anger or argument as in bewilderment and consternation. Either Conan or Aldwin had thought it wise to acquaint the household with the morning's sensational turn of events at once on arrival home, no doubt to put the best aspect on what they had done. She had no doubt that they were in collusion in the matter, but whatever their motives, they would not want to appear simply as squalid informers. A gloss of genuine religious revulsion and sense of duty would have to gloze over the malice entailed.

They were all there, Margaret, Jevan, Conan and Aldwin, gathered in an agitated group, baffled question and oblique answer flying at the same time, Conan standing back to be the innocent bystander caught up in someone else's quarrel, Aldwin bleating aloud as Fortunata entered: 'How could I know? I was worried that such things should be said, I feared for my own soul if I hid them. All I did was tell Brother Jerome what was troubling me –'

'And he told Prior Robert,' cried Fortunata from the doorway, 'and Prior Robert told everyone, especially that great man from Canterbury, as you knew very well he would. How can you pretend you never meant Elave harm? Once you launched it, you knew where it would end.'

They had all swung about to face her, startled by her anger rather than by the suddenness of her entry.

'No!' protested Aldwin, recovering his breath. 'No, I swear I only thought the prior might speak to him, warn him, turn him to better counsel . . .'

'And therefore,' she said sharply, 'you told him who had been present to hear. Why do that unless you meant it to go further? Why force me into your plans? That I shall never forgive you!'

'Wait, wait, wait!' cried Jevan, throwing up his hands. 'Are you telling me, chick, that *you* were called to witness? In God's name, man, what possessed you? How dared you bring our girl into such a business?'

'It was not I who wanted that,' protested Aldwin. 'Brother Jerome got it out of me who was there, I never meant to bring her into the tangle. But I am a son of the Church, I needed to slough the load from my conscience, but then it got out of hand.'

'I never knew you all that constant in observance,'

said Jevan ruefully. 'You could as well have refused to name any names but your own. Well, what's done is done. Is it over even now? Need we expect her to be called to more enquiries, more interrogations? Is it to drag on to exhaustion, now it's begun?'

'It isn't over,' said Fortunata. 'They have not pronounced any judgement, but they won't let go so easily. Elave is pledged not to go away until he's freed of the charge. I know it because I have just left him, among the trees close by the bridge, and he's on his way back now to the abbey to stand his ground. I wanted him to run, I begged him to run, but he refuses. See what you've done, Aldwin, to a poor young man who never did you any harm, who has no family or patron now, no safe home and secure living, as you have. Here are you provided for life, without a care for your old age, and he has to find work again wherever he can, and now you have put a shadow upon him that will cling round him whatever the judgement, and turn men away from employing him for fear of being thought suspect by contagion. Why did you do it? Why?'

Aldwin had been gradually recovering his composure since the shock of her entrance had upset it, but now it seemed he had lost it altogether, and his wits with it. He stood gaping at her mutely, and from her to Jevan. Twice he swallowed hard before he could find a word to say, and even then he brought out the words with infinite caution, disbelieving.

'Provided for life?'

'You know you are,' she said impatiently, and herself was struck mute the next moment, suddenly sensible that for Aldwin nothing had ever been known beyond possibility of doubt. Every evil was to be expected, every good suspect and to be watched jealously, lest it evaporate as he breathed on it. 'Oh, no!' she said on a despairing breath. 'Was *that* it? Did you think he was come to turn you out and take your place? Was that why you wanted rid of him?'

'What?' cried Jevan. 'Is the girl right, man? Did you suppose you were to be thrown out on the roads to make way for him to get his old place back again? After all the years you've lived here and worked for us? Did this house ever treat any of its people so? You know better than that!'

But that was Aldwin's trouble, that he valued himself so low he expected as low a regard from everyone else, even after years, and the respect and consideration the house of Lythwood showed towards its other dependants could not, in his eyes, be relied on as applying equally to him. He stood dumbstruck, his mouth working silently.

'My dear soul!' said Margaret, grieving. 'The thought never entered our heads to part with you. Certainly he was a good lad when we had him, but we wouldn't have displaced you for the world. Why, the boy didn't want it, either. I told him how it was, the first time he came back here, and he said surely, the place was yours, he never had the least wish to take it from you. Have you been fretting all this time over that? I thought you knew us better.'

'I've damaged him for no reason,' said Aldwin, as though to himself. 'No reason at all!' And suddenly, with a convulsive moment that shook his aging body as a gale shakes a bush, he turned and blundered towards the doorway. Conan caught him by the arm and held him fast.

'Where are you going? What can you do? It's done. You told no lies, what was said was said.'

'I'll overtake him,' said Aldwin with unaccustomed resolution. 'I'll tell him I'm sorry for it. I'll go with him to the monks, and see if I can undo what I've done – any part of what I've done. I'll own why I did it. I'll withdraw the charge I made.'

'Don't be a fool!' urged Conan roughly. 'What difference will that make? The charge is laid now, the priests won't let it be dropped, not they. It's no small matter to accuse a man of heresy and then go back on it, you'll only end in as bad case as he. And they have my witness, and Fortunata's, what use is it taking back yours? Let be, and show some sense!'

But Aldwin's courage was up, and his conscience stricken too deeply for sense. He dragged himself free from the detaining hand. 'I can but try! I will! That at least.' And he was out at the door, and halfway across the yard towards the street. Conan would have gone after him, but Jevan called him back sharply.

'Let him alone! At the very least, if he owns to his own fear and malice, he must surely shake the case against the lad. Words, words, I don't doubt they were spoken, but words can be interpreted many ways, and even a small doubt cast can alter the image. You get back to work, and let the poor devil go and ease his mind the best way he can. If he falls foul of the priests, we'll put in a word for him and get him out of it.'

Conan gave up reluctantly, shrugging off his misgivings about the whole affair. 'Then I'd best get out to the folds until nightfall. God knows how he'll fare, but by then, one way or another, I suppose we shall find out.' And he went out still shaking his head disapprovingly over Aldwin's foolishness, and they heard his solid footsteps cross the yard to the passage into the street.

'What a coil!' said Jevan with a gusty sigh. 'And I must be off, too, and fetch some more skins from the workshop. There's a canon of Haughmond coming tomorrow, and I've no notion yet what size of book he has in mind. Don't take things too much to heart, girl,' he said, and embraced Fortunata warmly in a long arm. 'If it comes to the worst we'll get the prior of Haughmond to say a word to Gerbert for any man of ours – one Augustinian must surely listen to another, and the prior owes me a favour or two.'

He released her and was off towards the door in his turn, when she demanded abruptly: 'Uncle – does Elave count as a man of ours?'

Jevan swung about to stare at her, his thin black brows

raised, and the dark, observant eyes beneath them flashed into the smile that came seldom but brilliantly, a little teasing, a little intimidating, but for her always reassuring.

'If you want him,' he said, 'he shall.'

Elave had gone but a few yards back towards the abbey gatehouse when he saw half a dozen men come boiling out of the open gate, and split two ways along the Foregate. The suddenness of the eruption and the distant clamour of their raised voices as they emerged and separated made him draw back hastily into the cover of the trees, to consider what this hubbub might have to do with him. They were certainly sent forth in a body, and carrying staves, which boded no good if they were indeed hunting for him. He worked his way cautiously along the grove to get a closer view, for they were sweeping the open road first before enlarging their field, and two were away on the run along the further length of the enclave wall, to reach the corner and get a view along the next stretch of the road. Someone or something was certainly being hunted. Not by any of the brothers. Here were no black habits, but sober workaday homespun and hard-wearing leather, on sturdy laymen. Three of them he knew for the grooms attendant on Canon Gerbert, a fourth was his body servant, for Elave had seen the man about the guest-hall, busy and pompous, jack in office by virtue of his master's status. The others must surely have been recruited from among those pilgrims ablest in body and readiest for zealous mischief. It was not the abbot who had set the dogs on him, but Gerbert.

He drew back deeper into cover, and stood scowling at the intent hunters quartering the Foregate. He had no mind to show himself, however boldly, and risk being set upon and dragged back like a felon, when he had not, in his reading of his commitment, ever broken his parole. Maybe Canon Gerbert read the terms differently, and considered his going outside the gate, even without his gear, as proof of a guilty mind and instant flight. Well, he should not have the satisfaction of being able to sustain that view. Elave was going back through that gate on his own two feet, of his own obstinate will, true to his bond and staking his liberty and perhaps his life. The peril in which he could not bring himself to believe looked more real and sinister now.

They had left a single groom, the brawniest of Gerbert's three, sentinel before the gatehouse, prowling up and down as though neither time nor force could shift him. Small hope of slipping past that great sinewy hulk! And a couple of the hounds, having beaten the road, the gardens and the cottages along the Foregate for a hundred paces either way, were crossing the road purposefully towards the trees. Better remove himself from here to a safe distance until they either abandoned the hunt, or pursued it into more remote coverts, and allowed him safe passage back into the fold. Elave drew off hastily through the trees, and followed their dwindling course north-eastward until he came round into the orchards beyond the Gaye, and the belt of bushes that clothed the riverside. They were more likely to search for him westward. Along the border, English fugitives made for Wales, Welsh fugitives for England. The two laws baulked and held off at the dyke, though trade crossed back and forth merrily enough.

There was still a matter of three hours or so before Vespers, when he could hope that everyone would be in church again, and he might be able to slip in either through the gatehouse, if the burly guard had departed, or into the church by the west door among the local parishioners. No point in going back, meantime, to risk running his head into a snare. He found himself a comfortable nest among the tall grass above the river, screened by bushes and islanded in a silence that would give him due warning of any foot rustling the grass or shoulders brushing through the branches of alder and willow for a hundred yards around, and sat thinking of

Fortunata. He could not credit that he was in the kind of danger she envisaged, and yet he could not quite put the shadow away from him.

Across the swift and sinuous currents of the Severn, sparkling in sunlight, the hill of the town rose sharply, its long, enfolding wall terminating here opposite his hiding-place in the thick sandstone towers of the castle, and giving place to the highroad launching away to the north from the Castle Foregate towards Whitchurch and Wem. And even now he could have forded the river only a little way downstream and made off at speed by that road, but he was damned if he would! He had committed no crime, he had said only what he held to be right, and there was nothing in it of blasphemy or disrespect to the Church, and he would not take back a word of it, or run away from his own utterances and afford his accusers a cheap triumph.

He had no way of knowing the time, but when he thought it must be drawing near to Vespers he left his nest, and made his way cautiously back by the same route, keeping in cover, until he could see between the trees the dusty whiteness of the road, the people passing along it, and the lively bustle about the gatehouse. He had a while to wait before the Vesper bell rang, and he spent it moving warily from one cover to another, to see whether any of his pursuers were to be noted among the people gathering outside the west door of the church. He recognised none, but in the constant movement it was difficult to be sure. The big man who had been left to guard the gate was nowhere within view. Elave's best moment would come when the little bell was heard, and the gossips passing the time of day there in the early evening sunshine would gather and move into the church.

The moment was on him as fast as the thought. The bell chimed, and the worshippers gathered their families, saluted their friends, and began to move in by the west door. Elave darted out in time to mingle with them and hide himself in the middle of the procession, and there was no outcry, no rough hand grasping him by the shoulder. Now he had a choice between continuing left with the good people of the Foregate into the church, or slipping through the open gate of the enclave into the great court, and walking calmly across to the guest-hall. If he had chosen the church all might have been well, but the temptation to walk openly into the court as from a respectable stroll was too much for him. He left the shelter of the worshippers, and turned in through the gate.

From the doorway of the porter's lodge on his right a great howl of triumph soared, and was echoed from the road he had left behind. The canon's giant groom had been talking with the porter, vengeance in ambush, and two of his colleagues were just coming back from a foray into the town. All three of them fell upon the returning prodigal at once. A heavy cudgel struck him on the back of the head, sending him staggering, and before he could regain his balance or his wits he was grappled in the big man's muscular arms, while one of the others caught him by the hair, dragging his head back. He let out a yell of rage, and laid about him with fist and foot, heaving off his assailant from behind, wrenching one arm free from the big man's embrace and lashing out heartily at his nose. A second blow on the head drove him to his knees, half stunned. Distantly he heard dismayed voices crying out at such violence on sacred ground, and sandalled feet running hastily over the cobbles. Lucky for him that the brothers were just gathering from their various occupations to the sound of the bell.

Brother Edmund from the infirmary, Brother Cadfael from the turn of the path into the garden, bore down on the unseemly struggle with habits flying.

'Stop that! Stop at once!' cried Edmund, scandalised at the profanation, and waving agitated arms impartially at all the offenders.

Cadfael, with a sharper turn of speed, wasted no

breath on remonstrance, but made straight for the cudgel that was uplifted for a third blow at the victim's already bloodied head, halted it in midair, and twisted it without difficulty out of the hand that wielded it, fetching a howl from the over-enthusiastic groom in the process. The three huntsmen ceased battering their captive, but kept fast hold of him, hauling him to his feet and pinning him between them as though he might yet slip through their fingers and make off like a hare through the gate.

'We've got him!' they proclaimed almost in unison. 'It's him, it's the heretic! He was for making off out of trouble, but we've got him for you, safe and sound –'

'Sound?' Cadfael echoed ruefully. 'You've half killed the lad between you. Did it need three of you to deal with one man? Here he was, within the pale, did you have to break his head for him?'

'We've been hunting him all the afternoon,' protested the big man, swelling with his own prowess, 'as Canon Gerbert ordered us. Were we to take any chances with such a fellow when we did lay hand on him? Find and bring him back, we were told, and here he is.'

'Bring him?' said Cadfael, shoving one of Elave's captors unceremoniously aside to take his place, with an arm about the young man's body to support him. 'I saw from the turn of the hedge there who brought him back. He walked in here of his own will. You can take no credit for it, even if you count what you're about as credit. What possessed your master to set the dogs on him in the first place? He gave his word he wouldn't run, and Father Abbot accepted it, and said he was free to go and come as he pleased for the time being. A pledge good enough for our abbot was not good enough for Canon Gerbert, I suppose?'

By that time three or four others had gathered excitedly about them, and here came Prior Robert, sailing towards them from the corner of the cloister in acute displeasure at seeing what appeared to be an agitated and disorderly gathering disturbing the procession to Vespers.

'What is this? What is happening here? Have you not heard the bell?' His eyes fell upon Elave, propped up unsteadily between Cadfael and Edmund, his clothes dusty and in disarray, his brow and cheek smeared with blood. 'Oh,' he said, satisfaction tempered with some dismay at the violence done, 'so they have brought you back. It seems the attempt at flight cost you dear. I am sorry you are hurt, but you should not have run from justice.'

'I did not run from justice,' said Elave, panting. 'The lord abbot gave me leave to go and come freely, on my word not to run, and I did not run.'

'That is truth,' said Cadfael, 'for he walked in here of his own accord. He was heading for the guest-hall, where he's lodged like any other traveller, when these fellows fell upon him, and now they claim to have recaptured him for Canon Gerbert. Did he ever give such orders?'

'Canon Gerbert understood the liberty granted him as holding good only within the enclave,' said the prior sharply. 'So, I must say, did I. When this man was found to have gone from the court we supposed him to have attempted escape. But I am sorry it was necessary to be so rough with him. Now what is to be done? He needs attention . . . Cadfael, see to his hurts, if you will, and after Vespers I will see the abbot and tell him what has happened. It may be he should be housed in isolation . . .'

Which meant, thought Cadfael, in a cell, under lock and key. Well, at worst that would keep these great oafs away from him. But we shall see what Abbot Radulfus will say.

'If I may miss Vespers,' he said, 'I'll have him away into the infirmary for now, and take care of his injuries there. He'll need no armed guards, the state he's in, but I'll stay with him until we get the lord abbot's orders concerning him.'

'Well, at least,' said Cadfael, bathing away blood from Elave's head in the small anteroom in the infirmary, where the medicine cupboard was kept, 'you left your mark on a couple of them. And though you'll have a devil of a headache for a while, you've a good hard skull, and there'll be no lasting harm. I don't know but you'd be just as well in a penitential cell till all blows over. The bed's the same as all the other beds, the cell's fine and cool in this weather, there's a little desk for reading – our delinquents are meant to spend their time during imprisonment in improving their minds and repenting their errors. Can you read?'

'Yes,' said Elave, passive under the ministering hands.

'Then we could ask books from the library for you. The right course with a young fellow who's gone astray after unblessed beliefs is to ply him with the works of the Church fathers, and visit him with good counsel and godly argument. With me to minister to your bruises, and Anselm to discuss this world and the next with you, you'd have some of the best company to be had in this enclave, and with official sanction, mind. And a solitary cell keeps out the bleatings of fools and zealous idiots who hunt three to a lone man. Keep still now! Does that hurt?'

'No,' said Elave, curiously soothed by this flow of talk which he did not quite know how to take. 'You think they will shut me up in a cell?'

'I think Canon Gerbert will insist. And it's not so easy to refuse the archbishop's envoy over details. For they've come to the conclusion, I hear, that your case cannot be simply dismissed. That's Gerbert's verdict. The abbot's is that if there is to be further probing, it must be by your own bishop, and nothing shall be done until he declares what he wishes in the matter. And little Serlo is off to Coventry tomorrow morning, to report to him all that has happened. So no harm can come to you and no one can question or fret you until Roger de Clinton has had his say. You may as well pass your time as pleasantly as possible. Anselm has built up a very passable library.'

'I think,' said Elave with quickening interest, in spite

of his aching head, 'I should like to read Saint Augustine, and see if he really did write what he's said to have written.'

'About the number of the elect? He did, in a treatise called "De Correptione et Gratia", if my memory serves me right. Which,' said Cadfael honestly, 'I have never read, though I have had it read to me in the frater. Could you manage him in the Latin? I'd be small help to you there, but Anselm would.'

'It's a strange thing,' said Elave, pondering with deep solemnity over the course of events which had brought him to this curious pass, 'all the years I worked for William, and travelled with him, and listened to him, I never truly gave any thought to these things until now. They never bothered me. They do now, they matter to me now. If no one had meddled with William's memory and tried to deny him a grave, I never should have given thought to them.'

'If it's any help to have company along the way,' admitted Cadfael, 'I begin to find my case much the same as yours. Where the seed lights, the herb grows. And there's nothing like hard usage and drought to drive its roots in deep.'

Jevan came back to the house near Saint Alkmund's when it was already dark, with a bundle of new white skins of vellum, of a silken, creamy texture, and very thin and supple. He was proud of the work he did. The prior of Haughmond would not be disappointed in the wares on offer. Jevan bestowed them carefully in the shop, and locked up there before crossing the yard to the hall, where supper was laid, and Margaret and Fortunata were waiting for him.

'Is Aldwin not back yet?' he asked, looking round with raised brows as they sat down only three to table.

Margaret looked up from serving with a somewhat anxious face. 'No, no sign of him since. I was getting worried about him. What can possibly have kept him this long?'

'He'll have fallen foul of the theologians,' said Jevan, shrugging, 'and serve him right for throwing the other lad to them, like a bone to a pack of dogs. He'll be still at the abbey, and his turn to answer awkward questions. But they'll turn him loose when they've wrung him dry. Whether they'll do as much for Elave there's no knowing. Well, I shall lock up the house as usual before I go to my bed. If he creeps back later than that he'll have to lie in the stable-loft for the night.'

'Conan's not back, either,' said Margaret, shaking her head over the distressful day that should have been all celebration. 'And I thought Girard would have been home before this. I hope nothing has happened to him.'

'Nothing will have happened,' Jevan assured her firmly, 'but some matter of business to his profit. You know he can take very good care of himself, and he has excellent relations all along the border. If he meant to be back for the festival, and has missed his day, it will be because he's added a couple of new customers to his tally. It takes time to strike a bargain with a Welsh sheep-man. He'll be back home safe and sound in a day or so.'

'And what will he find when he does get home?' She sighed ruefully. 'Elave in this trouble as soon as he shows his face here again, Uncle William dead and buried, and now Aldwin getting himself still deeper into so bad a business. Truly I hope you're right, and he has done well with the wool clip, it will be some comfort at least if one thing has gone right.'

She rose to clear away the supper dishes, still shaking her head over undefined misgivings, and Fortunata was left alone with Jevan.

'Uncle,' she said hesitantly, after some minutes of silence, 'I wanted to talk to you. Whether I like it or not, I have been drawn into this terrible charge against Elave. He will not believe he is in grave danger, but I know he is. I want to help him. I must help him.'

The solemnity of her voice had caused him to turn and regard her long and attentively, with those black, penetrating eyes that saw deep into her now as in her childhood, and always with detached affection.

'I think this matters to you,' he said, 'more than might appear, when you have barely seen him again, and after years.'

It was not a question, but she answered it. 'I think I love him. What else can this be? It is not so strange. There were years before the years of his absence. I liked him then, better than he knew.'

'And you talked with him today, as I remember,' he said keenly, 'after this hearing at the abbey.'

'Yes,' she said.

'And thereafter, I fancy, he knows better how well you like him! And has he given you cause to be as certain of his liking for you?'

'Cause enough. He said that if there were no other reason I should be reason enough to hold him fast, in despite of whatever danger there may be to him here. Uncle, you know I have a dowry now from William. When my father comes home, and that box is opened, I want to use whatever he has given me to help Elave. To offer for his fine, if a fine is allowed to pay off his debt, to bargain for his liberty if they hold him, yes, even to corrupt his guards if the worst comes, and get him away over the border.'

'And you'd feel no guilt,' said Jevan with his sharp, dark smile, 'at defying the law and flouting the Church?'

'None, because he has done no wrong. If they condemn him, it's they who are guilty. But I mean to ask Father to speak up for him. As one who knows him, and is respected by everyone, law, Church and all. If Girard of Lythwood stood guarantor for his future behaviour, I believe they might listen.'

'So they might,' agreed Jevan heartily. 'At least that and every other means can be tried. I told you – if you want him, then Elave can and shall count as a man of ours. There, you be off to your bed and sleep easy. Who knows what magic may be discovered when William's box is opened?'

* * *

Late but not too late, Conan came home just before the door was locked, only a little tipsy after celebrating the end of the day, as he freely admitted, with half a dozen boon companions at the alehouse in Mardol.

Aldwin did not come home at all.

Chapter Seven

ROTHER CADFAEL arose well before Prime, took his scrip, and went out to collect certain waterside plants, now in their full summer leaf. The morning was veiled with a light covering of cloud, through which the sun shimmered in pearly tints of faint rose and misty blue. Later it would clear and be hot again. As he went out from the gatehouse a groom was just bringing up Serlo's mule from the stable-yard, and the bishop's deacon came out from the guest-hall ready for his journey, and paused at the top of the steps to draw deep breath, as though the solitary ride to Coventry held out to him all the delights of a holiday, by comparison with riding in Canon Gerbert's overbearing company. His errand, perhaps, was less pleasurable. So gentle a soul would not enjoy reporting to his bishop an accusation that might threaten a young man's liberty and life, but by his very nature he would probably make as fair a case as he could for the accused. And Roger de Clinton was a man of good repute, devout and charitable if austere, a founder of religious houses and patron of poor priests. All might yet go well for Elave, if he did not let his newly discovered predilection for undisciplined thought run away with him.

I must talk to Anselm about some books for him,

Cadfael reminded himself as he left the dusty highroad and began to descend the green path to the riverside, threading the bushes now at the most exuberant of their summer growth, rich cover for fugitives or the beasts of the woodland. The vegetable gardens of the Gaye unfolded green and neat along the riverside, the uncut grass of the bank making a thick emerald barrier between water and tillage. Beyond were the orchards, and then two fields of grain and the disused mill, and after that trees and bushes leaning over the swift, silent currents, crowding an overhanging bank, indented here and there by little coves, where the water lay deceptively innocent and still, lipping sandy shallows. Cadfael wanted comfrey and marsh mallow, both the leaves and the roots, and knew exactly where they grew profusely. Freshly prepared root and leaf of comfrey to heal Elave's broken head, marsh mallow to soothe the surface soreness, were better than the ready-made ointments or the poultices from dried material in his workshop. Nature was a rich provider in summer. Stored medicines were for the winter.

He had filled his scrip and was on the point of turning back, in no hurry since he had plenty of time before Prime, when his eye caught the pallor of some strange water-flower that floated out on the idle current from under the overhanging bushes, and again drifted back, trailing soiled white petals. The tremor of the water overlaid them with shifting points of light as the early sun came through the veil. In a moment they floated out again into full view, and this time they were seen to be joined to a thick pale stem that ended abruptly in something dark.

There were places along this stretch of the river where the Severn sometimes brought in and discarded whatever it had captured higher upstream. In low water, as now, things cast adrift above the bridge were usually picked up at that point. Once past the bridge, they might well drift in anywhere along this stretch. Only in the swollen and turgid floods of winter storms or February thaws did the Severn hurl them on beyond, to fetch up, perhaps, as far downstream as Attingham, or to be trapped deep down in the debris of storms, and never recovered at all. Cadfael knew most of the currents, and knew now from what manner of root this pallid, languid flower grew. The brightness of the morning, opening like a rose as the gossamer cloud parted, seemed instead to darken the promising day.

He put down his scrip in the grass, kilted his habit, and clambered down through the bushes to the shallow water. The river had brought in its drowned man with just enough impetus and at the right angle to lodge him securely under the bank. He lay sprawled on his face, only the left arm in deep enough water to be moved and cradled by the stream, a lean, stoop-shouldered man in dun-coloured coat and hose, indeed with something dun-coloured about him altogether, as though he had begun life in brighter colours and been faded by the discouragement of time. Grizzled, straggling hair, more grey than brown, draped a balding skull. But the river had not taken him, he had been committed to it with intent. In the back of his coat, just where its ample folds broke the surface of the water, there was a long slit, from the upper end of which a meagre ooze of blood had darkened and corroded the coarse homespun. Where his bowed back rose just clear of the surface, the stain was even drying into a crust along the folds of cloth.

Cadfael stood calf-deep between the body and the river, in case the dead man should be drawn back into the current when disturbed, and turned the corpse face upward, exposing to view the long, despondent, grudging countenance of Girard of Lythwood's clerk, Aldwin.

There was nothing to be done for him. He was sodden and bleached with water, surely dead for many hours. Nor could he be left lying here while help was sought to move him, or the river might snatch him back again. Cadfael took him under the arms and drew him along

108

through the shallows to a spot where the bank sloped gently down, and there pulled him up into the grassy shelf above. Then he set off at speed, back along the riverside path to the bridge. There he hesitated for a moment which way to take, up into the town to carry the news to Hugh Beringar, or back to the abbey to inform abbot and prior, but it was towards the town he turned. Canon Gerbert could wait for the news that the accuser would never again testify against Elave, in the matter of heresy or any other offence. Not that his death would end the case! On the contrary, it was at the back of Cadfael's mind that an even more sinister shadow was closing over that troublesome young man in a penitent's cell at the abbey. He had no time to contemplate the implications then, but they were there in his consciousness as he hurried across the bridge and in at the town gate, and he liked them not at all. Better, far better, to go first to Hugh, and let him consider the meaning of this death, before other and less reasonable beings got their teeth into it.

'How long,' asked Hugh, looking down at the dead man with bleak attention, 'do you suppose he's been in the water?'

He was asking, not Cadfael, but Madog of the Dead-Boat, summoned hastily from his hut and his coracles by the western bridge. There was very little about the ways of the Severn that Madog did not know, it was his life, as it had been the death of many of his generation in its treacherous flood-times. Given a hint as to where an unfortunate had gone into the stream, Madog would know where to expect the river to give him back, and it was to him everyone turned to find what was lost. He scratched thoughtfully at his bushy beard, and viewed the corpse without haste from head to foot. Already a little bloated, grey of flesh and oozing water and weed into the grass, Aldwin peered back into the bright sky from imperfectly closed eyes.

'All last night, certainly. Ten hours it might be, but more likely less, it would still have been daylight then. Somewhere, I fancy,' said Madog, 'he was laid up dead until dark, and then cast into the river. And not far from here. Most of the night he's lain here where Cadfael found him. How else would there still be blood to be seen on him? If he had not washed up within a short distance, face down as you say he was, the river would have bleached him clean.'

'Between here and the bridge?' Hugh suggested, eyeing the little dark, hairy Welshman with respectful attention. Sheriff and waterman, they had worked together before this, and knew each other well.

'With the level as it is, if he'd gone in above the bridge I doubt if he'd ever have passed it.'

Hugh looked back along the open green plain of the Gaye, lush and sunny, through the fringe of bushes and trees. 'Between here and the bridge nothing could happen in open day. This is the first cover to be found beside the water. And though this fellow may be a lightweight, no one would want to carry or drag him very far to reach the river. And if he'd been cast in here, whoever wanted to be quit of him would have made sure he went far enough out for the current to take him down the next reach and beyond. What do you say, Madog?'

Madog confirmed it with a jerk of his shaggy head.

'There's been no rain and no dew,' said Cadfael thoughtfully. 'Grass and ground are dry. If he was hidden until nightfall, it would be close where he was killed. A man needs privacy and cover both to kill and to hide his dead. Somewhere there may be traces of blood in the grass, or wherever the murderer bestowed him.'

'We can but look,' agreed Hugh, with no great expectation of finding anything. 'There's the old mill offers one place where murder could be done without a witness. I'll have them search there. We'll comb this belt of trees, too, though I doubt there'll be anything here to find. And what should this fellow be doing at the mill, or here,

110

for that matter? You've told me how he spent the morning. What he did afterwards we may find out from the household up there in the town. They know nothing of this yet. They may well be wondering and enquiring about him by this time, if it's dawned on them yet that he's been out all night. Or perhaps he often was, and no one wondered. I know little enough about him, but I know he lived there with his master's family. But beyond the mill, upstream – no, the whole stretch of the Gaye lies open. There's nothing from here on could give shelter to a killing. Nothing until the bridge. But surely, if the man was killed by daylight, and left in the bushes there even a couple of hours until dark, he might be found before he could be put into the river.'

'Would that matter?' wondered Cadfael. 'A little more risky, perhaps, but still there'd be nothing to show who slipped the dagger into his back. Sending him down-river does but confuse place and time. And perhaps that was important to whoever did it.'

'Well, I'll take the news up to the wool-merchants myself, and see what they can tell me.' Hugh looked round to where his sergeant and four men of the castle garrison stood a little apart, waiting for his orders in attentive silence. 'Will can see the body brought up after us. The fellow has no other home, to my knowledge, they'll need to take care of his burying. Come back with me, Cadfael, we'll at least take a look among the trees by the bridge, and under the arch.'

They set off side by side, out of the fringe of trees into the abbey wheatfields and past the abandoned mill. They had reached the waterside path that hemmed the kitchen gardens when Hugh asked, slanting a brief, oblique and burdened smile along his shoulder: 'How long did you say that heretical pilgrim of yours was out at liberty yesterday? While Canon Gerbert's grooms went puffing busily up and down looking for him to no purpose?'

It was asked quite lightly and currently, but Cadfael understood its significance, and knew that Hugh had already grasped it equally well. 'From about an hour before Nones until Vespers,' he said, and clearly heard the unacknowledged but unmistakeable reserve and concern in his own voice.

'And then he walked into the enclave in all conscious innocence. And has not accounted for where he spent those hours?'

'No one has yet asked him,' said Cadfael simply.

'Good! Then do my work for me there, will you? Tell no one in the abbey yet about this death, and let no one question Elave until I do it myself. I'll be with you before the morning's out, and we'll talk privately with the abbot before anyone else shall know what's happened. I want to see this lad for myself, and hear what he has to say for himself before any other gets at him. For you know, don't you,' said Hugh with detached sympathy, 'what his inquisitors are going to say?'

Cadfael left them to their search of the grove of trees and the bushes that cloaked the path down to the riverside, and made his way back to the abbey, though with some reluctance at abandoning the hunt even for a few hours. He was well aware of the immediate implications of Aldwin's death, and uneasily conscious that he did not know Elave well enough to discount them out of hand. Instinctive liking is not enough to guarantee any man's integrity, let alone his innocence of murder, where he had been basely wronged, and was by chance presented with the opportunity to avenge his injury. A high and hasty temper, which undoubtedly he had, might do the rest almost before he could think at all, let alone think better of it.

But *in the back*?

No, that Cadfael could not imagine. Had there been such an encounter it would have been face to face. And what of the dagger? Did Elave even possess such a weapon? A knife for all general purposes he must possess, no sensible traveller would go far without one.

But he would not be carrying it on him in the abbey, and he certainly had not taken the time to go and collect it from his belongings in the guest-hall, before hurrying out at the gate after Fortunata. The porter could testify to that. He had come rushing straight up from the chapter-house without so much as a glance aside. And if by unlikely chance he had had it on him at that hearing, then it must be with him now in his locked cell. Or if he had discarded it, Hugh's sergeants would do their best to find it. Of one thing Cadfael was certain, he did not want Elave to be a murderer.

Just as Cadfael was approaching the gatehouse, someone emerged from it and turned towards the town. A tall, lean, dark man, frowning down abstractedly at the dust of the Foregate as he strode, and shaking his head at some puzzling frustration of his own, probably of no great moment but still puzzling. He jerked momentarily out of his preoccupation when Cadfael gave him good-day, and returned the greeting with a vague glance and an absent smile before withdrawing again into whatever matter was chafing at his peace of mind.

It was altogether too apt a reminder, that Jevan of Lythwood should be calling in at the abbey gatehouse at this hour of the morning, after his brother's clerk had failed to come home the previous night. Cadfael turned to look after him. A tall man with a long, ardent stride, making for home with his hands clasped behind his back, and his brows knotted in so far unenlightened conjecture. Cadfael hoped he would cross the bridge without pausing to look down over the parapet towards the level, sunlit length of the Gaye, where at this moment Will Warden's men might be carrying the litter with Aldwin's body. Better that Hugh should reach the house first, both to warn the household, and to harvest whatever he could from their bearing and their answers, before the inevitable burden arrived to set the busy and demanding rites of death in motion.

'What was Jevan of Lythwood wanting here?' Cadfael

asked of the porter, who was making himself useful holding a very handsome and lively young mare while her master buckled on his saddle-roll behind. A good number of the guests would be moving on today, having paid their annual tribute to Saint Winifred.

'He wanted to know if his clerk had been here,' said the porter.

'Why did he suppose his clerk should have been here?'

'He says he changed his mind, yesterday, about laying charges against that lad we've got under lock and key, as soon as he found out the young fellow had no intention of elbowing him out of his employment. Said he was all for rushing off down here on the spot to take back what he'd laid against him. Much good that would do! Small use running after the arrow once it's loosed. But that's what he wanted to do, so his master says.'

'What did you tell him?' asked Cadfael.

'What should I tell him? I told him we've seen nor hide nor hair of his clerk since he went out of the gate here early yesterday afternoon. It seems he's been missing overnight. But wherever he's been, he hasn't been here.'

Cadfael pondered this new turn of events with misgiving. 'When was it he took this change of heart, and started back here? What time of the day?'

'Very near as soon as he got home, so Jevan says. No more than an hour after he'd left here. But he never came,' said the porter placidly. 'Changed his mind again, I daresay, when he got near, and began to reason how it might fall back on him, without delivering the other fellow.'

Cadfael went on down the court very thoughtfully. He had already missed Prime, but there was ample time before the Mass; he might as well take himself off to his workshop and unload his scrip, and try to get all these confused and confusing events clear in his mind. If Aldwin had come running back with the idea of undoing what he had done, then even if he had encountered an angry and resentful Elave, it would have needed only the first hasty words of penitence and restitution to disarm the avenger. Why kill a man who is willing at least to try to make amends? Still, some might argue, an angry man might not wait for any words, but strike on sight. *In the back*? No, it would not do. That Elave had killed his accuser might be the first thought to spring into other minds, but it could find no lodging in Cadfael's. And not for mere obstinate liking, either, but because it made no sense.

Hugh arrived towards the end of chapter, alone and, somewhat to Cadfael's surprise, as well as to his profound relief, ahead of any other and untoward report. Rumour was usually so blithe and busy about the town and the Foregate that he had expected word of Aldwin's death to worm its way in with inconvenient speed and a good deal of regrettable embroidery to the plain tale, but it had not happened. Hugh could tell the story his own way, and in the privacy of Abbot Radulfus's parlour, with Cadfael to confirm and supplement. And the abbot did not say what, inevitably, someone else very soon would. Instead he said directly:

'Who last saw the man alive?'

'From what we know so far,' said Hugh, 'those who saw him go out of the house early yesterday afternoon. Jevan of Lythwood, who came enquiring for him here this morning, as Cadfael says, before ever I got the word to him of his man's death. The fosterchild Fortunata, she who was made a witness to the charge yesterday. The woman of the house. And the shepherd Conan. But that was broad daylight, he must have been seen by others, at the town gate, on the bridge, here in the Foregate, or wherever he turned aside. We shall trace his every step, to fill in the time before he died.'

'But we cannot know when that was,' said Radulfus.

'No, true, no better than a guess. But Madog judges

he was put into the river as soon as it grew dark, and that he'd lain hidden somewhere after his death, waiting for dark. Perhaps two or three hours, but there's no knowing. I have men out looking for any trace of where he may have lain hidden. If we find that, we find where he was murdered, for he could not have been moved far.'

'And all Lythwood's household are in one tale together – that the clerk, when he heard the young man made no claim to his place, started to come here, to confess his malice and withdraw the charge he had made?'

'Further, the girl says that she had parted from Elave in the trees, there not far from the bridge, and told Aldwin so. She believes he went off in such haste in the hope of overtaking him. She says also,' said Hugh with emphasis, 'that she urged Elave to take to his heels, and he refused.'

'Then what he did accords with what he said,' Radulfus allowed. 'And his accuser set out to confess and beg pardon. Yes – it argues against,' he said, holding Hugh eye to eye.

'There are those who will argue for. And it must be said,' Hugh owned fairly, 'that circumstances give body to what they'll say. He was at liberty, he had good reason to bear a grudge. We know of no one else who had cause to strike at Aldwin. He set off to meet Elave, there in the trees. In cover. It hangs together, on the face of it, all too well, for the body must surely have gone into the water below the bridge, and cover is scant there along the Gaye.'

'All true,' said Radulfus. 'But equally true, I think, that if the young man had killed he would hardly have walked back into our precinct of his own will, as admittedly he did. Moreover, if the dead man was cast into the river after dark, that was not done by Elave. At least we know at what hour he returned here, it was just when the Vesper bell sounded. That does not prove past doubt that he did not kill, but it casts it into question. Well, we have him safe.' He smiled, a little grimly. It was an ambiguous reassurance. A stone cell, securely locked, ensured Elave's personal safety not less than his close custody. 'And now you wish to question him.'

'In your presence,' said Hugh, 'if you will.' And catching the sharp, intelligent eye he said simply: 'Better with a witness who cannot be suspect. You are as good a judge of a man as I am, and better.'

'Very well,' said Radulfus. 'He shall not come to us. We will go to him, while they are all in the frater. Robert is in attendance on Canon Gerbert.' So he would be, thought Cadfael uncharitably. Robert was not the man to let slip the chance to ingratiate himself with a man of influence with the archbishop. For once his predilection for the powerful would be useful. 'Anselm has been asking me to send the boy books to read,' said the abbot. 'He points out, rightly, that we have a duty to provide good counsel and exhortation, if we are to combat erroneous beliefs. Do you feel fitted, Cadfael, to undertake an advocacy on God's behalf?'

'I am not sure,' said Cadfael bluntly, thus brought up against the measure of his own concern and partisanship, 'that the instructed would not be ahead of the instructor. I see my measure more in tending his broken head then in meddling with the sound mind inside it.'

Elave sat on his narrow pallet in one of the two stone penitential cells which were seldom occupied, and told what he had to tell, while Cadfael renewed the dressings on his gashes, and bandaged him afresh. He still looked somewhat the worse for wear, bruised and stiff from the attentions of Gerbert's over-zealous grooms, but by no means subdued. At first, indeed, he was inclined to be belligerent, on the assumption that all these officials, religious and secular alike, must be hostile, and predisposed to find fault in every word he said. It was an attitude which did not consort well with his customary openness and amiability, and Cadfael was sorry to see

117

him thus maimed, even for a brief time. But it seemed that he did not find in his visitors quite the animosity and menace he had expected, for in a little while his closed and wary face eased and warmed, and the chill edge melted from his voice.

'I gave my word I would not quit this place,' he said firmly, 'until I was fairly dismissed as free and fit to go, and I never meant to do otherwise than as I said. You told me, my lord, that I was free to come and go on my own business meantime, and so I did, and never thought wrong. I went after the lady because she was in distress for me, and that I could not abide. You saw it yourself, Father Abbot. I overtook her before the bridge. I wanted to tell her not to fret, for she did me no wrong, what she said of me I had indeed said, and I would not for the world have had her grieve at speaking truth, whatever might fall on me. And also,' said Elave, taking heart in remembering, 'I wanted to show her my thankfulness, that she felt gently towards me. For it showed plain, you also saw it, and I was glad of it.'

'And when you parted from her?' said Hugh.

'I would have come back straightway, but I saw them come boiling out of the gate here and quartering the Foregate, and it was plain they were hot on my heels already. So I drew off into the trees to wait my chance. I had no mind to be dragged back by force,' said Elave indignantly, 'when I had nothing in mind but to walk in of my own will, and sit and wait for my judgement. But they left the big fellow standing guard, and I never got my chance to get past him. I thought if I waited for Vespers I might take cover and slip in among the folk coming to church.'

'But you did not spend all that time close here in hiding,' said Hugh, 'for I hear they drew every covert for half a mile from the road. Where did you go?'

'Made my way back through the trees, round behind the Gaye and a fair way down the river, and lay up in cover there till I thought it must be almost time for

'And you saw nobody in all that time? Nobody saw or spoke to you?'

'It was my whole intent that nobody should see me,' said Elave reasonably. 'I was hiding from a hue and cry. No, there's no one can speak for me all that time. But why should I come back as I did, if I meant to run? I could have been halfway to the border in that time. Acquit me at least of going back on my word.'

'That you certainly have not done,' said Abbot Radulfus. 'And you may believe that I knew nothing of this pursuit of you, and would not have countenanced it. No doubt it was done out of pure zeal, but it was misdirected and blameworthy, and I am sorry you should have fallen victim to violence. No one now supposes that you had any intent of running away. I accepted your word, I would do so again.'

Elave peered from beneath Brother Cadfael's bandages with brows drawn together in puzzlement, looking from face to face without understanding. 'Then why these questions? Does it matter where I went, since I came back again? How is it to the purpose?' He looked longest and most intently at Hugh, whose authority was secular, and should have had nothing to do or say in a charge of heresy. 'What is it? Something has happened. What can there be new since yesterday? What is it that I do not know?'

They were all studying him hard and silently, wondering indeed whether he did or did not know, and whether a relatively simple young man could dissemble so well, and one whose word the abbot had taken without question only one day past. Whatever conclusion they came to could not then be declared. Hugh said with careful mildness: 'First, perhaps you should know what Fortunata and her family have told us. You parted from her between here and the bridge, that she confirms, and she then went home. There she encountered and reproached your accuser Aldwin for bringing such a charge against you, and it came out that he had been afraid of losing his place to you, a matter of great gravity to him, as you'll allow.'

'But it was no such matter,' said Elave, astonished. 'That was settled the first time I set foot in the house. I never wanted to elbow him out, and Dame Margaret told me fairly enough they would not oust him. He had nothing to fear from me.'

'But he thought he had. No one had put it in plain terms to him until then. And when he heard it, as they all four agree – the shepherd, too – he declared his intent of running after you to confess and ask pardon, and if he failed to overtake you – the girl having told him where she had left you – of following you here to the abbey to do his best to undo what he had done against you.'

Elave shook his head blankly. 'I never saw him. I was among the trees ten minutes or more, watching the road, before I gave up and went off towards the river. I should have seen him if he'd passed. Maybe he took fright when he saw them beating all the converts and baying after me along the Foregate, and thought better of repenting.' It was said without bitterness, even with a resigned grin. 'It's easier and safer to set the hounds on than to call them off.'

'A true word!' said Hugh. 'They have been known to bite the huntsman, if he came between them and the quarry once their blood was up. So you never saw and had speech with him, and have no notion where he went or what happened to him?'

'None in the world. Why?' asked Elave simply. 'Have you lost him?'

'No,' said Hugh, 'we have found him. Brother Cadfael found him early this morning lodged under the bank of Severn beyond the Gaye. Dead, stabbed in the back.'

'Did he know or did he not?' wondered Hugh, when they were out in the great court, and the cell door closed and locked on the prisoner. 'You saw him, do you know what to make of him? Fix him as watchfully as you will, any

120

man can lie if he must. I would rather rely on things solid and provable. He did come back. Would a man who had killed do so? He has a good, serviceable knife, well able to kill, but it's in his bundle in the guest-hall still, not on him, and we know he no sooner showed his face in the gateway than he was set on, and attended every moment after, until that door closed on him. If he had another knife, and had it on him, he must have discarded it. Father Abbot, do you believe this lad? Is he telling truth? When he offered his word, you accepted it. Do you still do so?'

'I neither believe nor disbelieve,' said Radulfus heavily. 'How dare I? But I hope!'

Chapter Eight

ILLIAM WARDEN, who was the longest serving and most experienced of Hugh's sergeants, came looking for the sheriff just as Hugh and Cadfael were crossing to the gatehouse; a big, bearded, burly man of middle age, grizzled and weatherbeaten, and with a solid conceit of himself that sometimes tended to undervalue others. He had taken Hugh for a lightweight when first the young man succeeded to the sheriff's office, but time had considerably tempered that opinion, and brought them into a relationship of healthy mutual respect. The sergeant's beard was bristling with satisfaction now. Clearly he had made progress, and was pleased with himself accordingly.

'My lord, we've found it – the place where he was laid up till dark. Or at least, where he or some other bled long enough to leave his traces clear enough. While we were beating the bushes Madog thought to search through the grass under the arch of the bridge. Some fisherman had drawn up his light boat there, and turned it up to do some caulking on the boards. He wouldn't be working on it yesterday, a feast day. When we hoisted it, there was the grass flattened the length of it, and a small patch of it blackened with blood. What with the dry weather, that ground has been uncovered a month or

122

more, it's bleached pale as straw. There's no missing that stain, meagre though it is. A dead man could lie snug enough under there, with a boat upturned over him and nothing to show.'

'So that was the place!' said Hugh on a long, thoughtful breath. 'And no great risk, slipping a body into the water there in the dark, from under the arch. No sound, no splash, nothing to see. With an oar, or a pole, you could thrust him well out into the current.'

'We were right, it seems,' said Cadfael. 'You have to deal only with that length of the water, from the bridge to where he fetched up. You did not find the knife?'

The sergeant shook his head. 'If he killed his man there, under the arch or in the bushes, he'd clean the knife in the edge of the water and take it away with him. Why waste a good knife? And why leave it lying about for some neighbour to find, and say: I know that, it belongs to John Weaver, or whoever it might be, and how comes it to have blood on it? No, we shan't find the knife.'

'True,' said Hugh, 'a man would have to be scared out of his wits to throw it away to be found, and I fancy this man was in sharp command of his. Never mind, you've done well, we know now where the thing was done, there or close by.'

'There's more yet to tell you, my lord,' said Will, gratified, 'and stranger, if he was in such a hurry as they told us, when he ran off to recant his charges. We asked the porter on the town gate if he'd seen him pass out and cross the bridge, and he said yes, he had, and spoke to him, but barely got an answer. But he hadn't come straight from Lythwood's house, that's certain. It was more than an hour later, maybe as much as an hour and a half.'

'He's sure of that?' demanded Hugh. 'There's no real check there, not in quiet times. He could be hazy about time passing.'

'He's sure. He saw them all come back after the hubbub they had here at chapter, Aldwin and the shep-

123

herd first and the girl after, and it seemed to him they were all of them in an upset. He'd heard nothing then of what had happened, but he did notice the fuss they were in, and long before Aldwin came down to the gate again the whole tale was out. The porter was all agog when he laid eyes on the very man coming down the Wyle, he was hoping to stop him and gossip, but Aldwin went past without a word. Oh, he's sure enough! He knows how long had passed.'

'So all that time he was still in the town,' said Hugh, and gnawed a thoughtful lip. 'Yet in the end he did cross the bridge, going where he'd said he was going. But why the delay? What can have kept him?'

'Or who?' suggested Cadfael.

'Or who! Do you think someone ran after him to dissuade him? None of his own people, or they would have said so. Who else would try to turn him back? No one else knew what he was about. Well,' said Hugh, 'nothing else for it, we'll walk every yard of the way from Lythwood's house to the bridge, and hammer on every door, until we find out how far he got before turning aside. Someone must have seen him, somewhere along the way.'

'I fancy,' said Cadfael, pondering all he had seen and known of Aldwin, which was meagre enough and sad enough, 'he was not a man who had many friends, nor one of any great resolution of mind. He must have had to pluck up all his courage to accuse Elave in the first place, it would cost him more to withdraw his accusation, and put himself in the way of being suspect of perjury or malice or both. He may well have taken fright on the way, and changed his mind yet again, and decided to let well or ill alone. Where would a solitary dim soul like that go to think things out? And try to get his courage back? They sell courage of a sort in the taverns. And another sort, though not for sale, a man can find in the confessional. Try the alehouses and the churches, Hugh. In either a man can be quiet and think.'

* * *

It was one of the young men-at-arms of the castle garrison, not at all displeased at being given the task of enquiring at the alehouses of the town, who came up with the next link in Aldwin's uncertain traverse of Shrewsbury. There was a small tavern in a narrow, secluded close off the upper end of the steep, descending Wyle. It was sited about midway between the house near Saint Alkmund's church and the town gate, and the lanes leading to it were shut between high walls, and on a feast day might well be largely deserted. A man overtaken by someone bent on changing his mind for him, or suddenly possessed by misgivings calculated to change it for him without other persuasion, might well swerve from the direct way and debate the issue over a pot of ale in this quiet and secluded place. In any case, the young enquirer had no intention of missing any of the places of refreshment that lay within his commission.

'Aldwin?' said the potman, willing enough to talk about so sensational a tragedy. 'I only heard the word an hour past. Of course I knew him. A silent sort, mostly. If he did come in he'd sit in a corner and say hardly a word. He always expected the worst, you might say, but who'd have thought anyone would want to do him harm? He never did anyone else any that I knew of, not till this to-do yesterday. The talk is that the one he informed on has got his own back with a vengeance. And him with trouble enough,' said the potman, lowering his voice confidentially, 'if the Church has got its claws into him, small need to go crying out for worse.'

'Did you see the man yesterday at all?' asked the man-at-arms.

'Aldwin? Yes, he was here for a while, up in the corner of the bench there, as glum as ever. I hadn't heard anything then about this business at the abbey, or I'd have taken more notice. We'd none of us any notion the poor soul would be dead by this morning. It falls on a man without giving him time to put his affairs in order.'

'He was here?' echoed the enquirer, elated. 'What time was that?'

'Well past noon. Nearly three, I suppose, when they came in.'

'They? He wasn't alone?'

'No, the other fellow brought him in, very confidential, with an arm round his shoulders and talking fast into his ear. They must have sat there for above half an hour, and then the other one went off and left him to himself another half-hour, brooding, it seemed. He was never a drinker, though, Aldwin. Sober as a stone when he got up and went out at the door, and without a word, mind you. Too late for words now, poor soul.'

'Who was it with him?' demanded the questioner eagerly. 'What's his name?'

'I don't know that I ever heard his name, but I know who he is. He works for the same master – that shepherd of theirs who keeps the flock they have out on the Welsh side of town.'

'Conan?' echoed Jevan, turning from the shelves of his shop with a creamy skin of vellum in his hands. 'He's off with the sheep, and he may very well sleep up there, these summer nights he often does. Why, is there anything new? He told you what he knew, what we all knew, this morning. Should we have kept him here? I knew of no reason you might need him again.'

'Neither did I, then,' agreed Hugh grimly. 'But it seems Master Conan told no more than half a tale, the half you and all the household could bear witness to. Not a word about running after Aldwin and haling him away into the tavern in the Three-Tree Shut, and keeping him in there more than half an hour.'

Jevan's level dark brows had soared to his hair, and his jaw dropped for a moment. 'He did that? He said he'd be off to the flock and get on with his work for the rest of the day. I took it that's what he'd done.' He came slowly to the solid table where he folded his skins, and spread the one he was carrying carefully over it, smoothing it out abstractedly with a sweep of one long hand. He was a very meticulous man. Everything in his shop was in immaculate order, the uncut skins draped over racks, the trimmed leaves ranged on shelves in their varied sizes, and the knives with which he cut and trimmed them laid out in neat alignment in their tray, ready to his hand. The shop was small, and open on to the street in this fine weather, its shutters laid by until nightfall.

'He went into the alehouse with Aldwin in his arm, so the potman says, about three o'clock. They were there a good half-hour, with Conan talking fast and confidentially into Aldwin's ear. Then Conan left him there, and I daresay did go to his work, and Aldwin still sat there another half-hour alone. That's the story my man unearthed, and that's the story I want out of Conan's hide, along with whatever more there may be to tell,'

Jevan stroked his long, well-shaven jaw and considered, with a speculative eye upon Hugh's face. 'Now that you tell me this, my lord, I must say I see more in what was said yesterday than I saw at the time. For when Aldwin said he must go and try to overtake that boy he'd done his best to ruin, and go with him to the monks to withdraw everything he'd said against him, Conan did tell him not to be a fool, that he'd only get himself into trouble, and do no good for the lad. He tried his best to dissuade him. But I thought nothing of it but that it was good sense enough, and all he meant was to haul Aldwin back out of danger. When I said let him go, if he's bent on it, Conan shrugged it off, and went off about his own business. Or so I thought. Now I wonder. Does not this sound to you as though he spent another half-hour trying to persuade the poor fool to give up his penitent notion? You say it was he was doing the talking, and Aldwin the listening. And another half-hour still before Aldwin could make up his mind to jump one way or the other.'

'It sounds like that indeed,' said Hugh. 'Moreover, if Conan went off content, and left him to himself, surely he thought he had convinced him. If it meant so much to him he would not have let go until he was satisfied he'd got his way. But what I do not understand is why it should matter so gravely to him. Is Conan the man to venture so much for a friend, or care so much into what mire another man blundered?'

'I confess,' said Jevan, 'I've never thought so. He has a very sharp eye on his own advantage, though he's a good worker in his own line, and gives value for what he's paid.'

'Then why? What other reason could he have for going to such pains to persuade the poor wretch to let things lie? What could he possibly have against Elave, that he should want him dead, or buried alive in a Church prison? The lad's barely home. If they've exchanged a dozen words that must be the measure of it. If it's not concern for Aldwin or a grudge against Elave this fellow of yours has in mind, what is it?'

'You should ask him that,' said Jevan with a slow and baffled shake of his head, but with a certain wondering note in his voice that made Hugh prick up his ears.

'So I will. But now I am asking you.'

'Well,' said Jevan cautiously, 'you must bear in mind I may be wrong. But there is a matter which Conan may be holding against Elave. Quite without provocation, and no doubt Elave would be astonished if he knew of it. You have not noticed our Fortunata? She is grown into a very fresh and winning young woman, since Elave went off with my uncle on this pilgrimage to Jerusalem, and before that, you must remember, they were here familiar in the house some years, and liked each other well enough, he condescending to a child, and she childishly fond of a pleasant young man, even if he did no better than humour her liking. A very different matter he found her when he came back. And here's Conan . . .'

'Who has known her as long, and seen her grow,' said Hugh sceptically, 'and could have offered for her long ago if he was so minded, with no Elave to stand in his way. And did he?'

'He did not,' Jevan granted, hollowly smiling. 'But times have changed. In spite of the name my uncle gave to her, Fortunata until now has had nothing of her own, to make her a good match. Young Elave has brought back from the east not only himself, but the legacy my Uncle William, bless his kindly soul, thought to send to his fosterchild when he knew he might not see her again. Oh, no, Conan has no knowledge, as yet, of what may be in the box Elave brought for her. It will not be opened until my brother gets home from his wool-buying. But Conan knows it exists, it is here, it came from a generous man, virtually on his deathbed, when such a man would open his heart. From the looks I've seen Conan giving Fortunata these last few days, he's beginning to look on her as earmarked for him, dowry and all, and on Elave as a threat to be removed.'

'By death, if need be?' hazarded Hugh doubtfully. It seemed too bold and bitter an extreme for so ordinary a man to contemplate. 'It was not he who brought the charge.'

'I have wondered if they did not hatch that rotten egg between them. It suited them both to get rid of the youngster if they could, since it turns out Aldwin feared he might be elbowed out of office. It was like him to think the worst of my brother and me, as of all others. Oh, I doubt if either of them thought of anything so final as a death sentence. It would do if the lad was whisked off into the bishop's prison, or even so harried and ill-used here that he'd make off for healthier places when he was released. And doubtless Conan misread women,' said the cynic who had never married, 'and thought even the threat against Elave would put the girl off him. He should have known better. It has put her on! She'll fight for him tooth and nail now. The priests have not heard the last of our Fortunata.'

'So that's the way of it,' said Hugh, and whistled softly. 'You make a case for more than you know. If that's how it is with him, he might well be alarmed when

Aldwin changed his tune, and wanted to get the boy out of the mire he'd thrust him into. It could well be enough to make him go after Aldwin, hang upon him, pour words into his ear, do everything possible to dissuade him. Would it be enough to make him go still further?'

Jevan stood gazing at him enquiringly, and laid down, slowly and almost absently, the edge of vellum he had taken up to fold across to its matching edge. 'Further? How further? What have you in mind? It would seem he had won his argument, and went away satisfied. Nothing further was needed.'

'Ah, but suppose he was not quite satisfied. Suppose he could not rely on it that he'd won? Knowing Aldwin for the whiffle-minded poor soul he was, with a bad conscience, his own fear removed and his grudge with it, and his resolution blown this way and that as the wind changed, suppose Conan stayed lurking somewhere to see what he would do. And saw him get up and walk out of the tavern without a word, and off down the Wyle to the town gate and the bridge. All his words gone to waste, and more than words needed, quickly, before the damage was done. Did it matter to him all that much? Aldwin would think no ill even when he was pursued a second time – by a man he'd known for years. He might even let himself be drawn aside into some quiet place to argue the cause all over again. And Aldwin,' said Hugh, 'died somewhere in cover by the bridge, and lay hidden under an upturned boat until dark, and was slipped into the water under cover of the arch.'

Jevan stood contemplating that in silence for some minutes. Then he shook his head vigorously, but without complete conviction. 'I think it's out of his scope. But agreed, it would certainly account for why he should conceal half the tale, and pretend the last he saw of Aldwin was in our yard, like the rest of us. But no, surely little men with little grievances don't kill for them. Unless,' he ended, 'it was done in a silly rage, almost by accident, instantly regretted. That they might!'

'Send and fetch him back here,' said Hugh. 'Tell him nothing. If you send, he'll come unsuspecting. And if he's wise, he'll tell the truth.'

Girard of Lythwood came home in the middle of the evening, two days later than he had intended, but highly content with his week's work, for the delay was due to his collecting two new clients on his travels, with good clips to sell, and thankful to make contact with an honest middleman and broker, after some less happy dealings in previous years. All the stores of wool he had weighed and bought were safely stowed in his warehouse outside the Castle Foregate before he came home to his own house. His hired pack-ponies, needed only once a year after the annual clip, were restored to the stable, and the two grooms hired with them were paid off and sent to their homes. Girard was a practical man, who dealt with first things first. He paid his bills on time, and expected others to pay what they owed him with as little reluctance or delay. By the end of June or the beginning of July the contract woolman who dealt with the Flemish export trade would come to collect the summer's load. Girard knew his limitations. He was content to spread his net over a quarter of the shire and its Welsh neighbours, and leave the wholesale trade to more ambitious men.

Girard was half a head shorter than his younger brother, but a good deal broader in the shoulders and thicker in the bone, a portly man in the best of health and spirits, round-faced and cheerful, with a thick thornbush of reddish brown hair and a close trimmed beard. His good humour was seldom shaken even by the unexpected, but even he was taken aback at arriving home after a week's absence to find his pilgrim Uncle William dead and buried, William's young companion back safely from all the perils of his travels only to fall headlong into mortal trouble at home, his clerk dead and laid out for burial in one of the outhouses in his yard, the parish priest of Saint Alkmund's probing anxiously into the dead man's spiritual health before he would bury him, and his shepherd sweating and dumbstruck in Jevan's shop with one of the sheriff's men standing over him. It was no help to have three people all attempting to explain at the same time how these chaotic events had come about in his absence.

But Girard was a man who saw to first things first. If Uncle William was dead, and buried with all propriety, then there was nothing to be done about that, no haste even about coming to terms with the truth of it. If Aldwin, of all improbable people had come by a violent death, then that, too, though requiring a just resolution, was hardly within his competence to set right. Father Elias's doubts about the poor fellow's spiritual condition was another matter, and would need consideration. If Elave was in a locked cell at the abbey, then at least nothing worse could happen to him at this moment. As for Conan, he was solid enough, it would do him no harm to sweat a little. There would be time to salvage him, if it proved necessary. Meantime, Girard's horse had done a good few miles that day, and needed stabling, and Girard himself was hungry.

'Come within, lass,' he said briskly, flinging a bracing arm about his wife's waist and sweeping her towards the hall, 'and, Jevan, see to my beast for me, will you, till I get this tale straight. It's too late for lamentation and too soon for panic. Whatever's gone wrong, there'll be a time for putting it right. The more haste, the less speed! Fortunata, my chick, go and draw me some ale, I'm dry as a lime-pit. And set the supper forward, for if I'm to be any use I need my food.'

They did as he bade, every one of them. The pivot of the house, hearty and heartening, was home. Jevan, who had left most of the exclaiming to the women, allowed his brother his position as prop and stay of household, business and all, as from a relaxed and acknowledged distance, having his own separate kingdom among the membranes of vellum. He stabled, groomed and fed the tired horse at leisure, before he went into the house to join the rest at table. By that time Conan had been whisked away to the castle, to answer to Hugh Beringar. Jevan smiled, somewhat wryly, as he shuttered the frontage, and went into the hall.

'Well, it's a strange thing,' said Girard, sitting back with a satisfied sigh, 'that a man can't be off about his business one week in the year but everything must happen in that week. Just as well Conan never caught up with me, or I should have missed two new customers, for I should have set off back with him if he had reached me. The wool of four hundred sheep I got from those two villages, and some of it the lowland breed, too. But I'm sorry, love, that you've had the worry of all this, and me not here to lift it from you. We'll see now what's to be done. The first thing, as I reckon, is this of Aldwin. Whatever he may have done and said against another man in his fret – was there ever such a one as Aldwin for fearing the worst and being afraid to ask in case it came true? Well, whatever he may have done, he was our man, and we'll see him properly buried. But Father Elias here is troubled about the funeral.'

Father Elias, parish priest of Saint Alkmund's, was there with them at the end of the table, swept in to supper in Girard's hospitable arm from his conscientious brooding over the dead. Small, elderly, grey and fierce in his piety, Father Elias ate like a little bird, whenever he remembered to eat at all, and ran about among his flock busy and bothered, like a flustered hen trying to round up alien ducklings under her wings. Souls tended to elude him, every one seeming at the time the only one to matter, and he spent much of his time on his knees apologising to God for the soul that slipped through his fingers. But he would not let even that fugitive in upon false recommendation.

'The man was my parishioner,' said the little priest, in a wisp of a voice that yet had an irascible resolution in it, 'and I grieve for him and will pray for him. But he died

133

by violence, and as it were in the act of bringing mortal charges against another in malice, and what can the health of his soul be? He has not been to Mass in my church these many weeks, nor to confession. He was never regular in his worship, as all men should be. I would not ban him for his slackness. But when did he last confess, and gain absolution? How can I accept him unless I know he died penitent?'

'One little act of contrition will do?' ventured Girard mildly. 'He may have gone to another priest. Who knows? The thought could have come upon him somewhere else, and seemed to him a mortal matter there and then.'

'There are four parishes within the walls,' said Elias with grudging tolerance. 'I will ask. Though one who misses Mass so often . . . Well, I will ask, here within the town and beyond. It may even be that he feared to come to me. Men are feeble, and go aside to hide their feebleness.'

'So they are, Father, so they do! Wouldn't he be ashamed to come to you, if he'd never shown his face at Mass for so long? And mightn't he go rather to another, one who didn't know him so well, and might be easier on his sins? You ask, Father, and you'll find excuse for him somewhere. Then there's this matter of Conan. He's our man, too, whatever he may have been up to. You say he gave evidence, about this lad of William's talking some foolishness about the Church? What do you say, Jevan, did they put their heads together to do him harm?'

'It's likely enough,' said Jevan, shrugging. 'Though I wouldn't say they understood rightly what they were doing. It turns out Aldwin, the silly soul, feared he'd be thrown out to let Elave back in.'

'That would be like him, surely!' agreed Girard, sighing. 'Always one to look on the black side. Though he should have had more sense, all the years he's known us. I daresay he thought the youngster would take to his heels, and be off to find his fortune elsewhere, as soon as he felt the threat. But why should Conan want to be rid of him?'

There was a brief, blank silence and some head-shaking, then Jevan said with his small, rueful smile: 'I think our shepherd has also taken to thinking of Elave as a perilous rival, though not for employment. He has an eye on Fortunata . . .'

'On me?' Fortunata sat bolt upright with astonishment, and gaped at her uncle across the table. 'I've never seen signs of it! And I'm sure I never gave him any cause.'

'. . .and fancies and fears,' continued Jevan, his smile deepening, 'that Elave, if he stays, will make a more personable suitor. Not to say a more welcome one! And who's to say he's wrong?' And he added, his black eye bent on the girl in teasing affection:'On both counts!'

'Conan has never paid me any attention,' said Fortunata, past sheer amazement now, and quick to examine what might very well be true, even if it had eluded her notice. 'Never! I can't believe he has ever given me a thought.'

'He would certainly never make a winning lover,' said Jevan, 'but there's been a change in these last few days. You've been too busy looking in another direction to notice it.'

'You mean he's been casting sheep's eyes at my girl?' demanded Girard, and laughed aloud at the notion.

'Hardly that! I would call it a very calculating eye. Has not Margaret told you, Fortunata has an endowment now from William, to be her dowry.'

'There was a box mentioned that has yet to be opened. Why, does any man think I would let my girl want for a dowry, when she has a mind to marry? Though it's good that the old man remembered her, and thought to send her his blessing, too. If she did have a mind to Conan, well, I suppose he's not a bad fellow, a girl could do worse. He should have known I'd never let her go empty-handed, whoever she chose.' And he added, with an appreciative glance at Fortunata: 'Though our girl might do a great deal better, too!'

'Coin in the hand,' said Jevan sardonically, 'is more worth than all the promises.'

'Ah, you surely do the man an injustice! What's to prevent him waking up to the fact that our little lass has grown into a beauty, and as good as she is pretty, too. And even if he did bear witness against Elave to elbow him out of the running, and urge Aldwin not to recant for the same none too creditable reason, men have done worse, and not been made to pay too highly for it. But this business of Aldwin is murder. No, that's out of Conan's scope, surely!' He looked down the length of the table to Father Elias, sitting small, attentive and sharp-eyed under his wispy grey tonsure. 'Surely, Father?'

'I have learned,' said the little priest, 'not to put any villainy out of any man's reach. Nor any goodness, either. A life is a very fragile thing, created in desperate labour and snuffed out by a breath of wind – anger, or drunkenness, or mere horseplay, it takes no more than an instant.'

'Conan has merely a few hours of time to account for,' Jevan pointed out mildly. 'He must surely have met with someone who knew him on his way out to the sheep, he has only to name them, they have only to say where and when they saw him. This time, if he tells all the truth instead of half, he cannot miscarry.'

And that would leave only Elave. The grossly offended, the most aggrieved, suddenly approached by his accuser, among trees, without witnesses, too enraged to wait to hear what his enemy wanted to say to him. It was what almost every soul in Shrewsbury must be saying, taking the ending for granted. One charge of heresy, one of murder. All that afternoon until Vespers he was at liberty, and who had seen Aldwin alive since he passed the porter on the town gate? Two and a half hours between then and Vespers, when Elave was again in custody, two and a half hours in which he could have done murder. Even the objection that Aldwin's wound was in the back could easily be set aside. He came running to plead his penitence, Elave turned on him so furious a face and so menacing a front that he took fright and turned to flee, and got the knife in his back as he fled. Yes, they would all say so. And if it was argued that Elave had no knife on him, that it was left in his bundle in the guest-hall? He had another, doubtless at the bottom of the river by now. There was an answer to everything.

'Father,' said Fortunata abruptly, rising from her place, 'will you open my box for me now? Let us see what I am worth. And then I must talk to you. About Elave!'

Margaret brought the box from the corner press, and cleared an end of the table to make room for it before her husband. Girard's bushy brows rose appreciatively at the sight of it, and he handled it admiringly.

'Why, this is a beautiful thing in itself. This could bring you in an extra penny or two if you ever need it.' He took up the gilded key and fitted it into the lock. It turned smoothly and silently, and Girard opened the lid to reveal a neat, thick swathing of felt, folded in such a way that it could be opened to disclose what the box contained without removing it. Six little bags of similar felt were packed within. All of a size, snugly fitted together to fill the space.

'Well, they're yours,' said Girard, smiling at Fortunata, who was leaning over to stare at them with her face in shadow. 'Open one!'

She drew out one of the bags, and the soft chink of silver sounded under her fingers. There was no drawstring, the top of the bag was simply folded over. She tipped the contents streaming out upon the table, a flood of silver pennies, more than she had ever seen at one time, and yet somehow curiously disappointing. The casket was so beautiful and unusual, a work of art, the contents, however valuable, mere everyday money, the traffic of trade. But yes, they might have their uses, urgent uses if it came to the worst.

'There you are, girl!' said Girard, delighted. 'Good coin of the realm, and all yours. Nigh on a hundred pence there, I should guess. And five more like it. Uncle William did well by you. Shall we count them for you?'

She hesitated for a moment, and then she said:'Yes!' and herself curved a hand round the little pile of thin, small silver pieces, and began to tell them over one by one back into the bag. There were ninety-three of them. By the time she had folded the bag closed again and restored it to its corner in the box, Girard was half-way through the next.

Father Elias had drawn back a little from the table, averting his eyes from this sudden dazzling display of comparative wealth with a curious mixture of desire and detestation. A poor parish priest seldom saw even ten silver pennies together, let alone a hundred. He said hollowly: 'I will go and enquire about Aldwin at Saint Julian's,' and walked quietly out of the room and out of the house, and only Margaret noticed his going, and ran after him to see him courteously out to the street.

There were five hundred and seventy pennies in the six bags. Fortunata fitted them all snugly back into their places in the box, and closed the lid upon them.

'Lock it again, and put it away safely for me,' she said. 'It is mine, isn't it? To use as I like?' They were all looking at her with steady, benevolent interest, and the indulgent respect they had always shown towards her, even from her intense and serious childhood.

'I wanted you to know. Since Elave came back, even more since this shadow fell, I have come close to him afresh, closer than ever I was. I think I love him. So I did long ago, but this is love in a different kind. He brought me this money to help me to a good marriage, but now I know that the marriage I want is with him, and even if I cannot have it, I want to use this gift to help him out of the shadow, even if it means he must go away from here, where they can't lay hands on him again. Money can buy a lot of things, even ways out of prison, even men to open the doors. At least I can try.'

'Girl dear,' said Girard, gently but firmly, 'it was you told me, just a while since, how you urged him to run for his life when he had the chance. And he was the one who refused. A man who won't run can't be made to run. And to my way of thinking he's right. And not only because he gave his word, but because of why he gave his word. He said he'd done no wrong, and wouldn't afford any man proof that he went in fear of justice.'

'I know it,' said Fortunata. 'But *he* has absolute faith in the justice of Church and state. And I am not sure that I have. I would rather buy him his life against his will than see him throw it away.'

'You would not get him to take it,' warned Jevan. 'He has refused you once.'

'That was before Aldwin was murdered,' she said starkly. 'Then he was accused only of heresy. Now, if he is not yet charged, it's a matter of murder. He never did it, I won't believe it, murder is not in his nature. But there he is helpless under lock and key, already in their hands. It *is* his life now.'

'He still has his life,' said Girard robustly, and flung an arm about her to draw her to his solid side. 'Hugh Beringar is not the man to take the easy answer and never look beyond. If the lad is blameless he'll come out of it whole and free. Wait! Wait a little and see what the law can discover. I won't meddle with murder. Do I know for sure that any man is innocent, whether it's Elave or Conan? But if it comes down to the simple matter of heresy, then I'll throw all the weight I have into the balance to bring him off safely. You shall have him, he shall have the place poor Aldwin grudged to him, and I'll be guarantor for his good behaviour. But murder – no! Am I God, to see guilt or innocence in a man's face?'

Chapter Nine

ATHER ELIAS, having visited all his fellow-priests within the town, came down to the abbey next morning, and appealed at chapter as to whether any of the brothers who were also priests had by any chance taken confession from the clerk Aldwin before the services of Saint Winifred's translation. The eve of a festival day must have found plenty of work for the confessors, since it was natural for any worshippers who had neglected their spiritual condition for some time to find their consciences pricking them into the confessional, to come purged and refreshed to the celebrations of the day, and rest content in their renewed virtue and peace of mind. If any cleric here had been approached by Aldwin, he would be able to declare it. But no one had. It ended with Father Elias scurrying out of the chapter-house disappointed and distrait, shaking his shaggy grey head and trailing the wide, frayed sleeves of his gown like a small, dishevelled bird.

Brother Cadfael went out from chapter to his work in the garden with the rear view of that shabby little figure still before his mind's eye. A stickler, was Father Elias, he would not easily give up. Somewhere, somehow, he must find a reason to convince himself that Aldwin had died in a state of grace, and see to it that his soul had all the consolation and assistance the rites of the Church could provide. But it seemed he had already tried every cleric in the town and the Foregate, and so far fruitlessly. And he was not a man who could simply shut his eyes and pretend that all was well, his conscience had a flinty streak, and would pay him out with a vengeance if he lowered his standards without due grounds for clemency. Cadfael felt a dual sympathy for the perfectionist priest and back-sliding parishioner. At this moment their case seemed to him to take precedence even over Elave's plight. Elave was safe enough now until Bishop Roger de Clinton declared his will towards him. If he could not get out, neither could any zealot get in, to break his head again. His wounds were healing and his bruises fading, and Brother Anselm, precentor and librarian, had given him the first volume of Saint Augustine's 'Confessions' to pass the time away. So that he might discover, said Anselm, that Augustine did write on other themes besides predestination, reprobation and sin.

Anselm was ten years younger than Cadfael, a lean, active, gifted soul with a grain of irrepressible mischief still alive if usually dormant within him. Cadfael had suggested that he should rather give Elave Augustine's 'Against Fortunatus' to read. There he might find, written some years before the saint's more orthodox outpourings, in one of his periods of sharply changing belief: 'There is no sin unless through a man's own will, and hence the reward when we do right things also of our own will.' Let Elave commit that to memory, and he could quote it in his own defence. More than likely Anselm would take him at his word, and feed the suspect all manner of quotations supportive to his cause. It was a game any well-read student of the early fathers could play, and Anselm better than most.

So for some days at least, until Serlo could reach his bishop in Coventry and return with his response, Elave was safe enough, and could do with the time to get over his rough handling. But Aldwin, dead and in need of burial, could not wait.

Cadfael could not but wonder how things were going with Hugh's enquiries within the town. He had seen nothing of him since the morning of the previous day, and the revelation of murder had removed the centre of action from the abbey into the wide and populated field of the secular world. Even if the original root of the case was within these walls, in the cloudy issue of heresy, and the obvious suspect here in close keeping, there outside the walls the last hours of Aldwin's life remained to be filled in, and there were hundreds of men in town and Foregate who had known him, who might have old grudges or new complaints against him, nothing whatever to do with the charges against Elave. And there were frailties in the case against Elave which Hugh had seen for himself, and would not lightly discard in favour of the easy answer. No, Aldwin was the more urgent priority.

After dinner, in the half-hour or so allowed for rest, Cadfael went into the church, into the grateful stony coolness, and stood for some minutes silent before Saint Winifred's altar. Of late, if he felt the need to speak to her in actual words at all, he found himself addressing her in Welsh, but usually he relied on her to know all the preoccupations of his mind without words. Doubtful, in any case, if the young and beautiful Welsh girl of her first brief life had known any English or Latin, or even been able to read and write her own language, though the stately prioress of her second life, pilgrim to Rome and head of a community of holy women, must have had time to learn and study to her heart's content. But it was as the girl that Cadfael always imagined her. A girl whose beauty was legendary, and caused her to be coveted by princes.

Before he left her, though he was not conscious of having expressed any need or request, he felt the quietude and certainty the thought of her always gave him. He circled the parish altar into the nave, and there was Father Boniface just filling the little altar lamp and

142

straightening the candles in their holders. Cadfael stopped to pass the time of day.

'You'll have had Father Elias from Saint Alkmund's after you this morning, I daresay? He came to us at chapter on the same errand. A sad business, this of Aldwin's death.'

Father Boniface nodded his solemn dark head, and wiped oily fingers, boylike, in the skirt of his gown. He was thin but wiry, and almost as taciturn as his verger, but that deferent shyness was gradually easing as he worked his way into the confidence of his flock.

'Yes, he came to me after Prime. I never knew this Aldwin, living. I wish I could have helped him, dead, but to my knowledge I never saw him until the wool-merchant's funeral, the day before the festival. Certainly he never came to me for confession.'

'Nor to any of those within here,' said Cadfael. 'Nor in the town, for Elias asked there first. And your parish is a wide one. Poor Father Elias would have to walk a few miles to find the next priest. And if Aldwin never knocked on the door of any of his own neighbours, I doubt if he made a long journey to seek his penance elsewhere.'

'True, I have occasion to walk a few miles myself in the way of duty,' agreed Boniface, with pride rather than regret in the breadth of his cure. 'Not that I grudge it, God knows! Night or day, it's a joy to know that from the furthest hamlet they can call me when they need me, and know that I'll come. Sometimes I question my fortune, knowing it so little deserved. Only two days ago I was called away to Betton, and missed all but the morning Mass. I was sorry it should be that day, but no choice, there was a man dying, or he and all his kin thought he was dying. It was worth the journey, for he took the turn for life and I stayed until we were sure. It was getting dusk when I got back – ' He broke off suddenly, open mouthed and round-eyed. 'So it was!' he said slowly. 'And I never thought to say!'

'What is it?' asked Cadfael curiously. It had been a long and confiding speech for this quiet, reticent young man, and this sudden halt was almost startling. 'What have you thought of now?'

'Why, that there was one more priest here then who is not here now. Father Elias will not know. I had a visitor came for the day of Saint Winifred's translation, one who was my fellow-student, and ordained only a month ago. He came on the eve of the festival, early in the afternoon, and stayed through the next day, and when I was called away that morning after Mass I left him here to take part in all the offices in my place. I knew that would please him. He stayed until I came back, but that was when it was growing dark, and he was in haste then to be on his way home. It's only a short while, from past noon one day to nightfall the next, but how if he did have a penitent come asking?'

'He said no word of any such before he went?' asked Cadfael.

'He was in haste to be off, he had a walk of four miles. I never asked him. He was very proud to take my place, he said Compline for me. It could be!' said Boniface. 'Thin it may be, but it is a chance. Should we not make sure?'

'So we can,' said Cadfael heartily, 'if he's still within reach. But where should we look for him now? Four miles, you said? That's no great way.'

'He's nephew to Father Eadmer at Attingham, and named for his uncle. Whether he's still there, with him, is more than I know. But he has no cure yet. I would go,' said Boniface, hesitating, 'but I could hardly get back for Vespers. If I'd thought of it earlier . . .'

'Never trouble yourself,' said Cadfael. 'I'll ask leave of Father Abbot and go myself. For such a cause he'll give permission. It's the welfare of a soul at stake. And in this warm weather,' he added practically, 'there's need of haste.'

* * *

It was, as it chanced, the first day for over a week to grow lightly overcast, though before night the cloud cover cleared again. To set out along the Foregate with the abbot's blessing behind him and a four-mile walk ahead was pure pleasure, and the lingering *vagus* left in Cadfael breathed a little deeper when he reached the fork of the road at Saint Giles, and took the left-hand branch towards Attingham. There were times when the old wandering desire quickened again within him, and the very fact that he had been sent on an errand even beyond the limits of the shire, only three months back, in March, had rather roused than quenched the appetite. The vow of stability, however gravely undertaken, sometimes proved as hard to keep as the vow of obedience, which Cadfael had always found his chief stumbling-block. He greeted this afternoon's freedom – and justified freedom, at that, since it had sanction and purpose – as a refreshment and a holiday.

The highroad had a broad margin of turf on either side, soft green walking, the veil of cloud had tempered the sun's heat, the meadows were green on either hand, full of flowers and vibrant with insects, and in the bushes and headlands of the fields the birds were loud and full of themselves, shrilling off rivals, their first brood already fledged and trying their wings. Cadfael rolled contentedly along the green verge, the grass stroking silken cool about his ankles. Now if the end came up to the journey, every step of the way would be repaid with double pleasure.

Before him, beyond the level of the fields, rose the wooded hogback of the Wrekin, and soon the river reappeared at some distance on his left, to wind nearer as he proceeded, until it was close beside the highway, a gentle, innocent stream between flat grassy banks, incapable of menace to all appearances, though the local people knew better than to trust it. There were cattle in the pastures here, and waterfowl among the fringes of reeds. And soon he could see the square, squat tower of the parish church of Saint Eata beyond the curve of the Severn, and the low roofs of the village clustered close to it. There was a wooden bridge somewhat to the left, but Cadfael made straight for the church and the priest's house beside it. Here the river spread out into a maze of green and golden shallows, and at this summer level could easily be forded. Cadfael tucked up his habit and splashed through, shaking the little rafts of water crowfoot until the whole languid surface quivered.

Over the years, summer by summer, so many people had waded the river here instead of turning aside to the bridge that they had worn a narrow, sandy path up the opposite bank and across the grassy level between river and church, straight to the priest's house. Behind the mellow red stone of the church and the weathered timber of the modest dwelling in its shadow a circle of old trees gave shelter from the wind, and shaded half of the small garden. Father Eadmer had been many years in office here, and worked lovingly upon his garden. Half of it was producing vegetables for his table, and by the look of it a surplus to eke out the diet of his poorer neighbours. The other half was given over to a pretty little herber full of flowers, and the undulation of the ground had made it possible for him to shape a short bench of earth, turfed over with wild thyme, for a seat. And there sat Father Eadmer in his midsummer glory, a man lavish but solid of flesh, his breviary unopened on his knees, his considerable weight distilling around him, at every movement, a great aureole of fragrance. Before him, hatless in the sun, a younger man was busy hoeing between rows of young cabbages, and the gleam of his shaven scalp above the ebullient ring of curly hair reassured Cadfael, as he approached, that he had not had his journey for nothing. At least enquiry was possible, even if it produced disappointing answers.

'Well, well!' said the elder Eadmer, sitting up straight and almost sliding the breviary from his lap. 'Is it you, off on your travels again?'

'No further than here,' said Cadfael, 'this time.'

'And how's that unfortunate young brother you had with you in the spring?' And Eadmer called across the vegetable beds to the young man with the hoe:'Leave that, Eddi, and fetch Brother Cadfael here a beaker of ale. Bring pitcher and all!'

Young Eadmer laid aside the hoe cheerfully, and was off into the house on fine long legs. Cadfael sat down beside the priest on the green bench, and waves of spicy fragrance rose around him.

'He's back with his pens and brushes, doing good work, and none the worse for his journey, indeed all the better in spirit. His walking improves, slowly but it improves. And how have you been? I hear this is your nephew, the young one, and newly made priest.'

'A month since. He's waiting to see what the bishop has in mind for him. The lad was lucky enough to catch his eye, it may work out well for him.'

It was clear to Cadfael, when the young Eadmer came striding out with a wooden tray of beakers and the pitcher, and served them with easy and willing grace, that the new priest was likely to catch any observant eye, for he was tall, well made and goodlooking, and blessedly unselfconscious about his assets. He dropped to the grass at their feet as soon as he had waited on them, and acknowledged his presentation to this Benedictine elder with pleasant deference, but quite without awe. One of those happy people for whose confidence and fearlessness circumstances will always rearrange themselves, and rough roads subside into level pastures. Cadfael wondered if his touch could do as much for other less fortunate souls.

'Time spent sitting here with you and drinking your ale,' admitted Cadfael with mild regret, 'is stolen time, I fear, however delightful. I'm on an errand that won't wait, and once it's done I must be off back. And my business is with your nephew here.'

'With me?' said the young man, looking up in surprise.

'You came visiting Father Boniface, did you not, for Saint Winifred's translation? And stayed with him from past noon on the eve until after Compline on the feast day?'

'I did. We were deacons together,' said young Eadmer, stretching up to refill their beakers without stirring from his grassy seat. 'Why? Did I mislay something for him when I disrobed? I'll walk back and see him again before I leave here.'

'And he had to leave you in his place most of that day, from after the morning Mass until past Compline. Did any man come to you, during all that time, asking advice or wanting you to hear his confession?'

The straight-gazing brown eyes looked up at him thoughtfully, very grave now. Cadfael could read the answer and marvel at it even before Eadmer said:'Yes. One man did.'

It was too early yet to be sure of achievement. Cadfael asked cautiously:'What manner of man? Of what age?'

'Oh, fifty years old, I should guess, going grey, and balding. A little stooped, and lined in the face, but he was uneasy and troubled when I saw him. Not a craftsman, by his hands, perhaps a small tradesman or someone's house servant.'

More and more hopeful, Cadfael thought, and went on, encouraged:'You did see him clearly?'

'It was not in the church. He came to the little room over the porch, where Cynric sleeps. Looking for Father Boniface, but found me instead. So we were face to face.'

'You did not know him, though?'

'No, I know very few in Shrewsbury. I never was there before.'

No need to ask if he had been at chapter, or at the session that followed, to know Aldwin again from that encounter. Cadfael knew he had not. He had too sure a sense of the limitations of his fledgling rights to overstep them.

148

'And you confessed this man? And gave him penance and absolution?'

'I did. And helped him through the penance. You will understand that I can tell you nothing about his confession.'

'I would not ask you. If this was the man I believe it was, what matters is that you did absolve him, that his soul's peace was made. For, you see,' said Cadfael, considerately mirroring the young man's severe gravity, 'if I am right, the man is now dead. And since his parish priest had reason to wonder about the state of his strayed sheep, he is enquiring as to his spiritual standing before he will bury him with all the rites of the Church. It's why every priest in the town has been questioned, and I come at last to you.'

'Dead?' echoed Eadmer, dismayed. 'He was in sound health for a man of his years. How is that possible? And he was happier when he left me, he would not. . . No! So how comes it he is dead so soon?'

'You will surely have heard by now,' said Cadfael, 'that the morning after the feast day a man was taken out of the river? Not drowned, but stabbed. The sheriff is hunting for his murderer.'

'And this is the man?' asked the young priest, aghast.

'This is the man who so sorely needs a guarantor. Whether he is the man you confessed I cannot yet be certain.'

'I never knew his name,' said the boy, hesitant.

'You would know his face,' said his uncle, and spared to comment or prompt him further. There was no need. Young Eadmer set a hand to the ground and bounded to his feet, brushing down the skirt of his cassock briskly. 'I will come back with you,' he said, 'and I hope with all my heart that I can speak for your murdered man.'

There were four of them about the trestle table on which Aldwin's body had been laid out decently for burial: Girard, Father Elias, Cadfael and young Eadmer. In this narrow storeshed in the yard, swept out and sweetened with green branches, there was no room for more. And these witnesses were enough.

There had been very little said on the walk back to Shrewsbury. Eadmer, bent on preserving the sacredness of what had passed between them, had banished even the mention of their meeting until he should know that this dead man was indeed his penitent. Possibly his first penitent, and approached with awe, humility and reverence in consequence.

They had gone first to Father Elias, to ask him to accompany them to Girard's house, for if this promise came to fruit it would be both ease for his mind, and due licence to hasten the arrangements for burial. The little priest came with them eagerly. He stood at the head of the bier, the place granted to him as of right, and his aging hands, thin and curled like a small bird's claws, trembled for a moment as he turned back the covering from the dead man's face. At the foot Eadmer stood, the fledgling priest fronting the old man worn but durable, after years of gain and loss in his strivings to medicine the human condition.

Eadmer did not move or utter a sound as the sheet was drawn down to uncover a face now somewhat eased, Cadfael thought, of its living discouragement and suspicion. The sinews of the cheeks and jaw had relaxed their sour tightness, and with it some years had slipped from him, leaving him almost serene. Eadmer gazed at him with prolonged wonder and compassion, and said simply: 'Yes, that is my penitent.'

'You are quite sure?' said Cadfael.

'Quite sure.'

'And he made confession and received absolution? Praise be to God!' said Father Elias, drawing up the sheet again. 'I need not hesitate further. On the very day of his death he cleansed his soul. He did perform his penance?'

'We said what was due together,' said Eadmer. 'He

150

was distressed, I wanted to see him depart in better comfort, and so he did. I saw no cause to be hard on him. It seemed to me he might have done enough penance in his lifetime to be somewhat in credit. There are those who make their own way stony. There's no merit in it, but I doubt if they can help it, and I felt it should count in extenuation of some small sins.'

For that Father Elias gave him a sharp and somewhat disapproving glance, but forebore from reproving what an austere old man might well consider the presumption, even levity, of youth. Eadmer was certainly innocent of having set out to arouse any such reservations. He opened his honest brown eyes wide on Father Elias, and said simply: 'I'm glad out of measure, Father, that Brother Cadfael thought to come looking for me in time. And even more glad that I was there when this man was in need. God knows I have failings of my own to confess, for I was vexed at first when he came stumbling up the stairs. I came near to telling him to go away and come back at a better time, until I saw his face clearly. And all because he was making me late for Vespers.'

It was said so naturally and simply that it passed Brother Cadfael by for a long moment. He had turned towards the open doorway, where Girard was already leading the way out, and the early evening hung textured like a pearl, the westering sun veiled. He had heard the words without regarding them, and enlightenment fell on him so dazzlingly that he stumbled on the threshold. He swung about to stare at the young man following him.

'What was that you said? For Vespers? He made you late for *Vespers*?'

'So he did,' said Eadmer blankly. 'I was just opening the door to go down and into the church when he came. The office was half over by the time I sent him away consoled.'

'Dear God!' said Cadfael reverently. 'And I never even thought to ask about the time! And this was on the festival day? Not the Vespers of the day you arrived? Not the eve?'

'It was the festival day, when Boniface was away. Why, what's in that to shake you? What is it I've said?'

'The moment I clapped eyes on you, lad,' said Cadfael joyfully, 'I knew you had a happy touch about you. You've delivered not one man, but two, God bless you for it. Now come, come with me round the corner to Saint Mary's close, and tell the sheriff what you've just told me.'

Hugh had come back to his house and family after a long and exasperating day of pursuing fruitless enquiries among an apparently unobservant populace, and trying to extract truth from a scared and perspiring Conan, who was willing to admit that he had spent an hour or so trying to persuade Aldwin to let sleeping dogs lie, since it was known already, but insisted that after that he had wasted no more time, but gone straight to his work in the pastures west of the town. And that might well be true, even if he could cite no acquaintance who had met and spoken to him on the way. But there remained the possibility that he was still lying, and had followed and made one more disastrous attempt to sway a mind normally only too easily deflected from any purpose.

Enough and more than enough for one day. Hugh had taken himself off home to his own house, to his wife and his son and his supper, and he was sitting in the clean rushes of the hall floor, stripped down to shirt and hose in the mild evening, helping three-year-old Giles to build a castle, when Cadfael came rapping briskly at the open door, and marched in upon him shining with portentous news, and towing by the sleeve an unknown and plainly nonplussed young man.

Hugh abandoned his tower of wooden blocks unfinished, and came alertly to his feet. 'Truant again, are you? I looked for you in the herbarium an hour ago. Where have you been off to this time? And who is this you've brought me?'

'I've been no further than Attingham,' said Cadfael,

152

'to visit Father Eadmer. And here I've brought you his nephew, who is also Father Eadmer, ordained last month. This young man came to join his friend Father Boniface at Holy Cross for Saint Winifred's celebrations. You know Father Elias has been fretting as to whether Aldwin died in a fit state to deserve all the rites of the Church, seeing he seldom showed his face at Mass in his own parish church. Elias had tried every priest he knew of, in and out of the town, to see if any could stand sponsor for the poor fellow. Boniface told me of one more who was here for a day and half a day, however unlikely it might be that a local man should find his way to him in so short a time. Howbeit, here he is, and he has a tale to tell you.'

Young Eadmer told it accommodatingly, though hardly comprehending what significance it could have here, beyond what he already knew. 'And I walked back here with Brother Cadfael to see the man himself, whether he was indeed the one who came to me. And he is,' he ended simply. 'But what Brother Cadfael sees in it more, of such moment that it must come at once to you, my lord, that he must tell you himself, for I can't guess at it.'

'But you have not mentioned,' said Cadfael, 'at what time this man came to you with his confession.'

'It was just when the bell had rung for Vespers,' Eadmer repeated obligingly, still mystified. 'Because of him I came very late to the office.'

'Vespers?' Hugh had stiffened, turning upon them a face ablaze with enlightenment. 'You are sure? That very day?'

'That very day!' Cadfael confirmed triumphantly. 'And just at the ringing of the Vesper bell, as I have good reason to know, Elave walked into the great court and was set upon by Gerbert's henchmen and battered to the ground, and has been prisoner in the abbey ever since. Aldwin was alive and well and seeking confession at that very moment. Whoever killed him, it was not Elave!'

Chapter Ten

HAPTER WAS nearly over, next morning, when Girard of Lythwood presented himself at the gatehouse, requesting a hearing before the lord abbot. As a man of consequence in the town, and like his late uncle a good patron of the abbey, he came confidently, aware of his own merit and status. He had brought his fosterdaughter Fortunata with him, and they both came roused and girded, if not for battle, at least for possible contention, to be encountered courteously but with determination.

'Certainly admit them,' said Radulfus. 'I am glad Master Girard is home again, his household has been greatly troubled and needs its head.'

Cadfael watched their entry into the chapter-house with fixed attention. They were both in their best, adorned to cut the most impressive figure possible, the ideal respected citizen and his modest daughter. The girl took her stance a pace behind her father, and kept her eyes devoutly lowered in this monastic assembly, but when they opened wide for an instant, to flash a glance round the room and take a rapid estimate of possible friends and enemies, they were very shrewd, fierce and bright. The first calculating glance had noted the continuing presence of Canon Gerbert, and recorded it with regret. In his presence she would contain her grief, anger and anxiety on Elave's behalf, and let Girard speak for her. Gerbert would deplore a froward woman, and Fortunata had certainly primed her father by this time in every detail. They must have spent the remainder of the past evening, after Cadfael's departure, preparing what they were now about to propound.

The significance of one detail was not yet apparent, though it did suggest interesting possibilities. Girard carried under his arm, polished to that lovely dark patina by age and handling, and with the light caressing the gilded curves of its carving, the box that contained Fortunata's dowry.

'My lord,' said Girard, 'I thank you for this courtesy. I come in the matter of the young man you have detained here as a prisoner. Everyone here knows that his accuser was done to death, and though no charge has been made against Elave on that count, your lordship must know that it has been the common talk everywhere that he must be a murderer. I trust you have now heard from the lord sheriff that it is not so. Aldwin was still alive and well when Elave was taken and made prisoner here. In the matter of the murder he is proven innocent. There is the word of a priest to vouch for him.'

'Yes, this has been made known to us,' said the abbot. 'On that head Elave is cleared of all blame. I am glad to publish his innocence.'

'And I welcome your good word,' said Girard with emphasis, 'as one who has a right to speak in all this, and to be heard, seeing that both Aldwin and Elave were of my uncle's household, and now of mine, and the weight of both falls upon me. One man of mine has been killed unlawfully, and I want justice for him. I do not approve all that he did, but I understand his thinking and his actions, knowing his nature as I do. For him I can at least do this much, bury him decently, and if I can, help to run to earth his murderer. I have a duty also to Elave, who is living, and against whom the mortal charge now falls to the ground. Will you hear me on his behalf, my lord?'

'Willingly,' said Radulfus. 'Proceed!'

'Is this the time or place for such a plea?' objected Canon Gerbert, shifting impatiently in his stall and frowning at the solid burgess who stood straddling the flags of the floor so immovably. 'We are not now hearing this man's case. The withdrawal of one charge – '

'The charge of murder was never made,' said Radulfus, cutting him off short, 'and as now appears, never can be made.'

'The withdrawal of one suspicion,' snapped Gerbert, 'does not affect the charge which has been made, and which awaits judgement. It is not the purpose of chapter to hear pleas out of place, which may prejudice the case when the bishop declares his wishes. It would be a breach of form to allow it.'

'My lords,' said Girard with admirable smoothness and calm, 'I have a proposition to make, which I feel to be reasonable and permissible, if you find yourselves so minded. To put it before you I needs must speak as to my knowledge of Elave, of his character, and the service he has done my household. It is relevant.'

'I find that reasonable,' said the abbot imperturbably. 'You shall have your hearing, Master Girard. Speak freely!'

'My lord, I thank you! You must know, then, that this young man was in the employ of my uncle for some years, and proved always honest, reliable and trustworthy in all matters, so that my uncle took him with him as servant, guard and friend on his pilgrimage to Jerusalem, Rome and Compostela, and throughout those years of travelling the lad continued always dutiful, tended his master in illness, and when the old man died in France, brought back his body for burial here. A long and devoted service, my lords. Among other charges faithfully carried out, at his master's wish he brought back this treasury, here in this casket, as a dowry for William's fosterdaughter here, now mine.'

'This is not disputed,' said Gerbert, shifting restlessly

156

in his seat, 'but it is hardly to the purpose. The charge of heresy remains, and cannot be put aside. In my view, having seen elsewhere to what horrors it can lead, it is graver than that of murder. We know, do we not, how this poison can exist in vessels otherwise seen by the world as pure and virtuous, and yet contaminate souls by the thousand. A man cannot prevail by good works, only by divine grace, and who strays from the true doctrine of the Church has repudiated divine grace.'

'Yet we are told a tree shall be known by its fruit,' remarked the abbot drily. 'Divine grace, I think, will know where to look for a responsive human grace, without instruction from us. Go on, Master Girard. I believe you have a proposal to make.'

'I have, Father. At the least it is now known that my clerk's death happened through no fault of Elave, who never coveted his place or tried to oust him, nor did him any harm. Yet there is the place vacant now, nonetheless. And I, who have known Elave and trusted him, say that I am prepared to take him back in Aldwin's place, and advance him in my business. If you will release him into my charge, I make myself his guarantor that he shall not leave Shrewsbury. I engage that he shall remain in my house, and be available whenever your lordships require him to attend, until his case is heard and justly judged.'

'And regardless,' asked Radulfus mildly, 'of what the verdict may be?'

'My lord, if the judging is just, so will the verdict be. And after that day he will need no guarantor.'

'It is presumptuous,' said Gerbert coldly, 'to be so certain of your own rightness.'

'I speak as I have found. And I know as well as any man that in the heat of argument or ale words can be spoken beyond what was ever meant, but I do not think God would condemn a man for folly, not beyond the consequences of folly, which can be punishment enough.'

Radulfus was smiling behind his austere mask, though only those who had grown close and familiar with him would have known it. 'Well, I appreciate the kindliness of your intentions,' he said. 'Have you anything more to add?'

'Only this voice to add to mine, Father. Here in this casket are five hundred and seventy silver pence, the dowry sent by my uncle for the girl-child he took as his daughter. As Elave took great pains to deliver it to her safely, so Fortunata desires, in reverence to William who sent it, to use it now for Elave's deliverance from prison. Here she offers it in bail for him, and I will guarantee that when the time comes he shall answer to it.'

'Is this indeed your own wish, child?' asked the abbot, studying Fortunata's demure and wary calm with interest. 'No one has persuaded you to this offer?'

'No one, Father,' she said firmly. 'The thought was mine.'

'And do you know,' he insisted gently, 'that all those who go bail for another do take the risk of loss?'

She raised her ivory eyelids, lofty and smooth, for one brief and brilliant flash of hazel eyes. 'Not all, Father,' she said, uttering defiance in the soft, discreet voice of daughterly submission. And to Cadfael, watching, it was plain that Radulfus, even if he kept his formidable countenance, was not displeased.

'You may not know, Father,' explained Girard considerately, and even somewhat complacently, 'that women stake only on certainties. Well, that is what I propose, and I promise you I will fulfill my part of it, if you agree to release him into my custody. At any time you may be assured you will find him at my house. I am told he would not run from you when he was loose before; he certainly will not this time, when Fortunata stands to lose by him. As *you* suppose,' he added generously, 'for *I* am in no doubt.'

Radulfus had Canon Gerbert on his right hand, and Prior Robert on his left, and knew himself between two monuments of orthodoxy in more than doctrine. The precise letter of canon law was sacred to Robert, and the influence of an archbishop, distilled through his confidential envoy, hung close and convincing at his elbow, stiffening a mind already disposed to rigidity. As between his abbot and Theobald's vicarious presence Robert might be torn, and would certainly endeavour to remain compatible with both, but in extremes he would go with Gerbert. Cadfael, watching him manipulating inward argument, with devoutly folded hands, arched silver brows and tightly pursed mouth, could almost find the words in which he would endorse whatever Gerbert said, whilst subtly refraining from actually echoing it. And if he knew his man, so did the abbot. As for Gerbert himself, Cadfael had a sudden startling insight into a mind utterly alien to his own. For the man really had, somewhere in Europe, glimpsed yawning chaos and been afraid, seen the subtleties of the devil working through the mouths of men, and the fragmentation of Christendom in the eruption of loud-voiced prophets bursting out of limbo like bubbles in the scum of a boiling pot, and the dispersion into the wilderness in the malignant excesses of their deluded followers. There was nothing false in the horror with which Gerbert looked upon the threat of heresy, though how he could find it in an open soul like Elave remained incomprehensible.

Nor could the abbot afford to oppose the archbishop's representative, however true it might be that Theobald probably held a more balanced and temperate opinion of those who felt compelled to reason about faith than did Gerbert. A threat that troubled pope, cardinals and bishops abroad, however nebulous it might feel here, must be taken seriously. There is much to be said for being an island off the main. Invasions, curses and plagues are slower to reach you, and arrive so weakened as to be almost exhausted beforehand. Yet even distance may not always be a perfect defence.

'You have heard,' said Radulfus, 'an offer which is

generous, and comes from one whose good faith may be taken for granted. We need only debate what is right for us to do in response. I have only one reservation. If this concerned only my own monastic household, I should have none. Let me hear your view, Canon Gerbert.'

There was no help for it, he would certainly be expressing it very forcibly; as well compel him to speak first, so that his rigours could at least be moderated afterwards.

'In a matter of such gravity,' said Gerbert, 'I am absolutely against any relaxation. It is true, and I acknowledge it, that the accused has been at liberty once, and returned as he was pledged to do. But that experience may itself cause him to do otherwise if the chance is repeated. I say we have no right to take any risk with a prisoner accused of such a perilous crime. I tell you, the threat to Christendom is not understood here, or there would be no dispute, none! He must remain under lock and key until the cause is fully heard.'

'Robert?'

'I cannot but agree,' said the prior, looking studiously down his long nose. 'It is too serious a charge to take even the least risk of flight. Moreover, the time is not wasted while he remains in our custody. Brother Anselm has been providing him with books, for the better instruction of his mind. If we keep him, the good seed may yet fall on ground not utterly barren.'

'True,' said Brother Anselm without detectable irony, 'he reads, and he thinks about what he reads. He brought back more than silver pence from the Holy Land. An intelligent man's baggage on such a journey must be light, but in his mind he can accumulate a world.' Wisely and ambiguously he halted there, before Canon Gerbert should wind his slower way through this speech to understanding, and spy an infinitesimal note of heresy in it. It is not wise to tease a man with no humour in him.

'It seems I should be outvoted if I came down on the side of release,' said the abbot drily, 'but it so chances that I, too, am for continuing to hold the young man here

160

in the enclave. This house is my domain, but jurisdiction has already passed out of my hands. We have sent word to the bishop, and expect to hear his will very soon. Therefore the judgement is now with him, and our part is simply to ensure that we hand over the accused to him, or to his representatives, as soon as he makes his will known. I am now no more in this matter than the bishop's agent. I am sorry, Master Girard, but that must be my answer. I cannot take you as bail, I cannot give you custody of Elave. I can promise you that he shall come to no harm here in my house. Nor suffer any further violence,' he added with intent, if without emphasis.

'Then at least,' said Girard quickly, accepting what he saw to be unalterable, but alert to make the most of what ground was left to him, 'can I be assured that the bishop will give me as fair a hearing, when it comes to a trial, as you have given me now?'

'I shall see to it that he is informed of your wish and right to be heard,' said the abbot.

'And may we see and speak with Elave, now that we are here? It may help to settle his mind to know that there is a roof and employment ready for him, when he is free to accept them.'

'I see no objection,' said Radulfus.

'In company,' added Gerbert quickly and loudly. 'There must be some brother present to witness all that may be said.'

'That can quite well be provided,' said the abbot. 'Brother Cadfael will be paying his daily visit to the young man after chapter, to see how his injuries are healing. He can conduct Master Girard, and remain throughout the visit.' And with that he rose authoritatively to cut off further objections that might be forming in Canon Gerbert's undoubtedly less agile mind. He had not so much as glanced in Cadfael's direction. 'This chapter is concluded,' he said, and followed his secular visitors out of the chapter-house.

* * *

Elave was sitting on his pallet under the narrow window of the cell. There was a book open on the reading desk beside him, but he was no longer reading, only frowning over some deep inward consideration drawn from what he had read, and by the set of his face he had not found much that was comprehensible in whichever of the early fathers Anselm had brought him. It seemed to him that most of them spent far more time in denouncing one another than in extolling God, and more venom on the one occupation than fervour on the other. Perhaps there were others who were less ready to declare war at the drop of a word, and actually thought and spoke well of their fellow theologians, even when they differed, but if so, all their books must have been burned, and possibly they themselves into the bargain.

'The longer I study here,' he had said to Brother Anselm bluntly, 'the more I begin to think well of heretics. Perhaps I am one, after all. When they all professed to believe in God, and tried to live in a way pleasing to him, how could they hate one another so much?'

In a few curiously companionable days they had arrived at terms on which such questions could be asked and answered freely. And Anselm had turned a page of Origen and replied tranquilly: 'It all comes of trying to formulate what is too vast and mysterious to be formulated. Once the bit was between their teeth there was nothing for it but to take exception to anything that differed from their own conception. And every rival conception lured its conceiver deeper and deeper into a quagmire. The simple souls who found no difficulty and knew nothing about formulae walked dryshod across the same marsh, not knowing it was there.'

'I fancy that was what I was doing,' said Elave ruefully, 'until I came here. Now I'm bogged to the knees, and doubt if I shall ever get out.'

'Oh, you may have lost your saving innocence,' said Anselm comfortably, 'but if you are sinking, it's in a

162

morass of other men's words, not your own. They never hold so fast. You have only to close the book.'

'Too late! There are things I want to know, now. How did Father and Son first become three? Who first wrote of them as three, to confuse us all? How can there be three, all equal, who are yet not three but one?'

'As the three lobes of the clover leaf are three and equal but united in one leaf,' suggested Anselm.

'And the four-leaved clover, that brings luck? What is the fourth, humankind? Or are we the stem of the three-some, that binds all together?'

Anselm shook his head over him, but with unperturbed serenity and a tolerant grin. 'Never write a book, son! You would certainly be made to burn it!'

Now Elave sat in his solitude, which did not seem to him particularly lonely, and thought about this and other conversations which had passed between precentor and prisoner during the past few days, and seriously considered whether a man was really better for reading anything at all, let alone these labyrinthine works of theology that served only to make the clear and bright seem muddied and dim, by clothing everything they touched in words obscure and shapeless as mist, far out of the comprehension of ordinary men, of whom the greater part of the human creation is composed. When he looked out from the cell window, at a narrow lancet of pale blue sky fretted with the tremor of leaves and feathered with a few wisps of bright white cloud, everything appeared to him radiant and simple again, within the grasp of even the meanest, and conferring benevolence impartially and joyously upon all.

He started when he heard the key grate in the lock, not having associated the murmur of voices outside with his own person. The sounds of the outer world came in to him throughout the day by the window, and the chime of the office bell marked off the hours for him. He was even becoming used to the horarium, and celebrated the regular observances with small inward genuflections of

163

his own. For God was no part of the morass or the labyrinth and could not be blamed for what men had made of a shining simplicity and certainty.

But the turning of the key in the lock belonged to his own practical workaday world, from which this banishment could only be temporary, possibly for a purpose, a halting place for thought after the journey half across the world. He sat watching the door open upon the summer day outside, and it was not opened inch by cautious inch but wide and generously, back to touch the wall, as Brother Cadfael came in.

'Son, you have visitors!' He waved them past him into the small, stony room, watching the sudden brightness flood over Elave's dazzled face and set him blinking. 'How is your head this morning?'

The head in question had shed its bandages the previous day, only a dry scar was left in the thick hair. Elave said in a daze: 'Well, very well!'

'No aches and pains? Then that's my business done. And now,' said Cadfael, withdrawing to perch on the foot of the bed with his back to the room, 'I am one of the stones of the wall. I am ordered to stay with you, but you may regard me as deaf and mute.'

It seemed that he had made mutes of two of the three thus unceremoniously brought together, for Elave had come to his feet in a great start, and stood staring at Fortunata as she was staring at him, flushed and great-eyed, and stricken silent. Only their eyes were still eloquent, and Cadfael had not turned his back so completely that he could not observe them from the corner of his own eye, and read what was not being said. It had not taken those two long to make up their minds. Yet he must remember that this was not so sudden, except in its discovery. They had known each other and lived in the same household from her infancy until her eleventh year, and in another fashion there had surely been a strong fondness, indulgent and condescending, no doubt, on his part, probably worshipping and wistful on hers, for girls tend to achieve grown-up and painful affections far earlier than boys. She had had to wait for her fulfilment until he came home, to find the bud had blossomed, and to stand astonished at its beauty.

'Well, lad!' Girard said heartily, eyeing the young man from head to foot and shaking him warmly by both hands. 'You're home at last after all your ventures, and I not here to greet you! But greet you I do now, and gladly. I never looked to see you in this trouble, but God helping, it will all pass off safely in the end. From all accounts you did well by Uncle William. So far as is in us, we'll do well by you.'

Elave drew himself out of his daze with an effort, gulped, and sat down abruptly on his bed. 'I never thought,' he said, 'they would have let you in to see me. It was good of you to trouble for me, but take no chances on my behalf. Touch no pitch, and it can't stick to you! You know what they're holding against me? You should not come near me,' he said vehemently, 'not yet, not until I'm freed. I'm contagious!'

'But you do know,' said Fortunata, 'that you're not suspect of ever harming Aldwin? That's over, proven false.'

'Yes, I know. Brother Anselm brought me word, after Prime. But that's but the half of it.'

'The greater half,' said Girard, plumping himself down on the small, high stool, which his amplitude overflowed on every side.

'Not everyone within here thinks so. Fortunata has already put herself in disfavour with some because she was not hot enough against me when they questioned her. I would not for the world,' said Elave earnestly, 'bring harm upon her or upon you. Stay from me, I shall be easier in my mind.'

'We have the abbot's leave to come,' said Girard, 'and for all I could see his goodwill, too. We came here to chapter, Fortunata and I, to make an offer on your behalf. And if you think we shall either of us draw off and leave you unfriended for fear of a few over-zealous sniffers-out of evil, with tongues that wag at both ends, you're mistaken in us. My name stands sturdy enough in this town to survive a deal of buffeting by gossips. And so shall yours, before this is over. What we hoped was to have you released to come home with us, on my guarantee of your good behaviour. I pledged you to answer to your bail when you were called, and told them there's now a place for you in my employ. Why not? You had no hand in Aldwin's death and neither did I, nor would either of us ever have turned him off to make way for you. But for all that, it's done! The poor soul's gone, I need a clerk, and you need somewhere to lay your head when you get out of here. Where better than in the house you know, dealing with a business you used to know well, and can soon master again? So if you're willing, there's my hand on it, and we're both bound. What do you say?'

'I say there's nothing in the world I'd like better!' Elave's face, carefully composed these last days into a wary calm, had slipped its mask and flushed into a warmth of pleasure and gratitude that made him look very young and vulnerable. It would cost him something to reassemble his breached defences when these two were gone, Cadfael reflected. 'But we should not be talking of it now. We must not!' Elave protested, quivering. 'God knows I'm grateful to you for such generosity, but I dare hardly think of the future until I'm out of here. Out of here, and vindicated! You have not told me what they answered, but I can guess at it. They would not turn me loose, not even into your charge.'

Girard owned it regretfully. 'But the abbot gave us leave to come and see you, and tell you what I propose for you, so that you may at least know you have friends who are stirring for you. Every voice raised in your support must be of some help. I've told you of what I am keeping for you. Now Fortunata has somewhat to say to you on her own account.'

Girard on entering had sensibly laid down the burden he was carrying upon the pallet beside Elave. Fortunata stirred out of her tranced stillness, and leaned to take it up and sit down beside him, nursing the box on her knees.

'You remember how you brought this to our house? Father and I brought it here today to pledge as bail for your release, but they would not let you go. But if we could not buy your liberty with it one way,' she said in a low deliberate voice, 'there are other ways. Remember what I said to you when last we were together.'

'I do remember,' he said.

'Such matters need money,' said Fortunata, choosing her words with aching care. 'Uncle William sent me a lot of money. I want it to be used for you. In whatever way may be needful. You've given no parole now. The one you did give *they* violated, not you.'

Girard laid a restraining hand upon her arm, and said in a warning whisper, which nevertheless found a betraying echo from the stone walls: 'Gently, my girl! Walls have ears!'

'But no tongues,' said Cadfael as softly. 'No, speak freely, child, it's not me you need fear. Say all you have to say to him, and let him answer you. Expect no interference from me, one way or the other.'

For answer Fortunata took up the box she was nursing, and thrust it into Elave's hands. Cadfael heard the infinitesimal chink of small coins shifting, and turned his head in time to see the slight start Elave made as he received the weight, the stiffening of the young man's shoulders and the sharp contraction of his brows. He saw him tilt the box between his hands to elicit a fainter echo of the small sound, and weigh it thoughtfully on his palms.

'It was money Master William sent you?' said Elave consideringly. 'I never knew what was in it. But it's yours. He sent it for you, I brought it here for you.'

'If it profits you, it profits me,' said Fortunata. 'Yes, I will say what I came to say, even though I know Father does not approve. I don't trust them to do you justice. I am afraid for you. I want you far away from here, and safe. This money is mine, I may do what I choose with it. It can buy a horse, shelter, food, perhaps even a man to turn a key and open the door. I want you to accept it – to accept the use of it, and whatever I can buy with it for you. I'm not afraid, except for you. I'm not ashamed. And wherever you may go, however far, I'll follow you.'

She had begun in a bleak, defiant calm, but she ended with contained and muted passion, her voice still level and low, her hands clenched together in her lap, her face very pale and fierce. Elave's hand shook as he closed it tightly over hers, pushing the box aside on his bed. After a long pause, not of hesitation, rather of an unbending resolution that had difficulty in finding the clearest but least hurtful words in which to express himself, he said quietly: 'No! I cannot take it, or let you make such use of it for my sake. You know why. I have not changed, I shall not change. If I ran away from this charge I should be opening the door to devils, ready to bay after other honest men. If this fight is not fought out to the end now, heresy can be cried against anyone who offends his neighbour, so easy is it to accuse when there are those willing to condemn for a doubt, for a question, for a word out of place. And I will not give way. I will not budge until they come to me and tell me they find no blame in me, and ask me civilly to come forth and go my way.'

She had known all along, in spite of her persistence, that he would say no. She withdrew her hand from his very slowly, and rose to her feet, but could not for a moment bring herself to turn away from him, even when Girard took her gently by the arm.

'But then,' said Elave deliberately, his eyes holding hers, 'then I will take your gift – if I can also have the bride who comes with it.'

Chapter Eleven

 HAVE A request to make of you, Fortunata,' said Cadfael, as he crossed the great court between the silent vistors, the girl disconsolate, her fosterfather almost certainly relieved at Elave's dogged insistence on remaining where he was and relying on justice. Girard undoubtedly believed in justice. 'Will you allow me to show this box to Brother Anselm? He's well versed in all the crafts, and may be able to say where it came from, and how old it is. I should be interested to see for what purpose he thinks it was made. You certainly can't lose by it, Anselm carries weight as an obedientiary, and he's well disposed to Elave already. Have you time now to come to the scriptorium with me? You may like to know more about your box. It surely has a value in itself.'

She gave her assent almost absently, her thoughts still left behind with Elave.

'The lad needs all the friends he can get,' said Girard ruefully. 'I had hoped that now the worse charge has fallen to the ground those who blamed him for all might feel some shame, and soften even on the other charge. But here's this great prelate from Canterbury claiming that over-bold thinking about belief is worse than murder. What sort of values are those? I don't know but

I'd help the boy to a horse myself if he'd agreed, but I'd rather my girl had no part in it.'

'He will not let me have any part,' said Fortunata bitterly.

'And I think the more of him for it! And what I can do within the law to haul him safely out of this coil, that I'll do, at whatever cost. If he's the man you want, as it seems he wants you, then neither of you shall want in vain,' said Girard roundly.

Brother Anselm had his workshop in a corner carrel of the north walk of the cloister, where he kept the manuscripts of his music in neat and loving store. He was busy mending the bellows of his little portative organ when they walked in upon him, but he set it aside willingly enough when he saw the box Girard laid before him. He took it up and turned it about in the best light, to admire the delicacy of the carving, and the depth of colour time had given to the wood.

'This is a beautiful thing! He was a true craftsman who made it. See the handling of the ivory, the great round brow, as if the carver had first drawn a circle to guide him, and then drawn in the lines of age and thought. I wonder what saint is pictured here? An elder, certainly. It could be Saint John Chrysostom.' He followed the whorls and tendrils of the vine leaves with a thin, appreciative fingertip. 'Where did he pick up such a thing, I wonder?'

'Elave told me,' said Cadfael, 'that William bought it in a market in Tripoli, from some fugitive monks driven out of their monasteries, somewhere beyond Edessa, by raiders from Mosul. You think it was made there, in the east?'

'The ivory may well have been,' said Anselm judicially. 'Somewhere in the eastern empire, certainly. The full-faced gaze, the great, fixed eyes . . . Of the carving of the box I am not so sure. I fancy it came from nearer home. Not an English house – perhaps French or German. Have we your leave, daughter, to examine it inside?'

Fortunata's curiosity was already caught and held, she was leaning forward eagerly to follow whatever Anselm might have to demonstrate. 'Yes, open it!' she said, and herself proffered the key.

Girard turned the key in the lock and raised the lid, to lift out the little felt bags that uttered their brief insect sound as he handled them. The interior of the box was lined with pale brown vellum. Anselm raised it to the light and peered within. One corner of the lining was curled up slightly from the wood, and a thin edge of some darker colour showed there, pressed between vellum and wood. He drew it out carefully with a finger-nail, and unrolled a wisp of dark purple membrane, frayed from some larger shape, for one edge of it was fretted away into a worn fringe, where it had parted, the rest presented a clear, cut edge, the segment of a circle or half-circle. So small a wisp, and so inexplicable. He smoothed it out flat upon the desk. Hardly bigger than a thumbnail, but the cut side was a segment of a larger curve. The colour, though rubbed, and perhaps paler than it had once been, was nevertheless a rich, soft purple.

The pale lining in the base of the box seemed also to have the faintest of darker blooms upon its surface here and there, Cadfael drew a nail gently from end to end of it, and examined the fine dust of vellum he had collected, bluish rose, leaving a thin, clean line where he had scratched the membrane. Anselm stroked along the mark and smoothed down the ruffled pile, but the streak was still clear to be seen. He looked closely at his fingertip, and the faintest trace of colour was there, the translucent blue of mist. And something more, that made him look even more closely, and then take up the box again and hold it in full sunlight, tilting and turning it to catch the rays. And Cadfael saw what Anselm had seen, trapped in the velvety surface of the leather, invisible except by favour of the light, the scattered sparkle of gold dust.

Fortunata stood gazing curiously at the wisp of purple

smoothed out upon the desk. A breath would have blown it away. 'What can this have been? What was it part of?'

'It is a fragment from a tongue of leather, the kind that would be stitched to the top and base of the spines of books, if they were to be stored in chests. Stored side by side, spine upwards. The tongues were an aid to drawing out a single book.'

'Do you think, then,' she pursued, 'that there was once a book kept in this box?'

'It's possible. The box may be a hundred, two hundred years old. It may have been in many places, and used for many things before it found its way into the market in Tripoli.'

'But a book kept in this would have no use for these tongues,' she objected alertly, her interest quickening. 'It would lie flat. And it would lie alone. There is no room for more than one.'

'True. But books, like boxes, may travel many miles and be carried in many ways before they match and are put together. By this fragment, surely it did once carry a book, if only for a time. Perhaps the monks who sold the box had kept their breviary in it. The book they would not part with, even when they were destitute. In their monastery it may have been one of many in a chest, and they could not carry all, when the raiders from Mosul drove them out.'

'This leather tongue was well worn,' Fortunata continued her pursuit, fingering the frayed edge worn thin as gauze. 'The book must have fitted very close within here, to leave this wisp behind.'

'Leather perishes in the end,' said Girard. 'Much handling can wear it away into dry dust, and the books of the office are constantly in use. If there's such a threat from these mamluks of Mosul, the poor souls round Edessa would have little chance to copy new service books.'

Cadfael had begun thoughtfully restoring the felt bags of coins to the casket, packing them solidly. Before the base was covered he drew a finger along the vellum again, and studied the tip in the sunlight, and the invisible grains of gold caught the light, became visible for a fleeting instant, and vanished again as he flexed his hand. Girard closed the lid and turned the key, and picked up the box to tuck it under his arm. Cadfael had rolled up the bags tightly to muffle all movement, but even so, when the box was tilted, he caught the very faint and brief clink as silver pennies shifted.

'I'm grateful to you for letting me see so fine a piece of craftmanship,' said Anselm, relaxing with a sigh. 'It's the work of a master, and you are a fortunate lady to possess it. Master William had an eye for quality.'

'So I've told her,' Girard agreed heartily. 'If she should wish to part with it, it would fetch her in a fair sum to add to what is inside.'

'It might well fetch more than the sum it holds,' Anselm said seriously. 'I am wondering if it was made to hold relics. The ivory suggests it, but of course it may not be so. The maker took pleasure in embellishing his work, whatever its purpose.'

'I'll go with you to the gatehouse,' said Cadfael, stirring out of his private ponderings as Girard and Fortunata turned to walk along the north range on their way out. He fell in beside Girard, the girl going a pace or two ahead of them, her eyes on the flags of the walk, her lips set and brows drawn, somewhere far from them in a closed world of her own thoughts. Only when they were out in the great court and approaching the gate, and Cadfael halted to take leave of them, did she turn and look at him directly. Her eyes lit on what he was still carrying in his hand, and suddenly she smiled.

'You've forgotten to put away the key to Elave's cell. Or,' she wondered, her smile deepening and warming from lips to eyes, 'are *you* thinking of letting him out?'

'No,' said Cadfael. 'I am thinking of letting myself in. There are things Elave and I have to talk about.'

* * *

Elave had quite lost by this time the sharp, defensive, even aggressive front he had first presented to anyone who entered his cell. No one visited him regularly except Anselm, Cadfael, and the novice who brought his food, and with all these he was now on strangely familiar terms. The sound of the key turning caused him to turn his head, but at sight of Cadfael re-entering, and so soon, his glance of rapid enquiry changed to a welcoming smile. He had been reclining on his bed with his face uplifted to the light from the narrow lancet window, but he swung his feet to the floor and moved hospitably to make way for Cadfael on the pallet beside him.

'I hardly thought to see you again so soon,' he said. 'Are they gone? God forbid I should ever hurt her, but what else could I do? She will not admit what in her heart she knows! If I ran away I should be ashamed, and so would she, and that I won't bear. I am not ashamed now, I have nothing to be ashamed of. Do *you* think I'm a fool for refusing to take to my heels?'

'A rare kind of fool, if you are,' said Cadfael. 'And every practical way, no fool at all. And who should know everything there is to be known about that box you brought for her, so well as you? So tell me this – when she plumped it in your arms a while ago, what did you note about it that surprised you? Oh, I saw you handle it. The moment the weight was in your hands it jarred you, for all you never said a word. What was there new to discover about it? Will you tell me, or shall I first tell you? And we shall see if we both agree.'

Elave was gazing at him along his shoulder, with wonder, doubt and speculation in his eyes. 'Yes, I remember you handled it once before, the day I took it up into the town. Should that be enough for you to notice so small a difference when you had it in your hands again?'

'It was not that,' said Cadfael. 'It was you who made it clear to me. You knew the weight of it from carrying it, from living with it and handling it all the way from

France. When she laid it in your hands you knew what to expect. Yet as you took it your hands rose. I saw it, and saw that you had recorded all that it meant. For then you tilted it, this way and then that. And you know what you heard. That the box should be lighter by some small measure than when you last held it, that startled you as it startled me. That it should give forth the clinking of coin was no surprise to me, for we had just been told at chapter that it held five hundred and seventy silver pence. But I saw that it was a surprise to you, for you repeated the test. Why did you say nothing then?'

'There was no certainty,' said Elave, shaking his head. 'How could I be sure? I knew what I heard, but since last I had the box in my hands it has been opened, perhaps something not replaced when they put back what was in it, more wrappings, no longer needed ... Enough to change the weight, and let the coins within move, that were tight-packed before, and could not shift. I needed time to think. And if you had not come ...'

'I know,' said Cadfael, 'You would have put it out of your mind as of no importance, a mistaken memory. After all, you delivered your charge where it was sent, Fortunata had her money, what possible profit to waste time and thought over a morsel of weight and a few coins jingling? Especially for a man with graver matters on his mind. And you have just accounted for all, very sensibly. But now here am I, stirring the depths that were just beginning to settle. Son, I have just been handling that box again myself. I won't say I noted the difference in weight, except when it jarred you as it did. But what I do most clearly remember is how solid, how stable was that weight. Nothing moved in it when first I held it. It might have been a solid mass of wood in my hands. It is not so now. I doubt if any discarded wrappings of felt could quite have silenced the coins that are in it now, for I have just packed it again myself – six small felt bags, rolled up tightly and pressed in, and still I heard them chink when the box was taken up and carried. No, you were not

175

'mistaken. It is lighter than it was, and it has lost that solidity that formerly it had.'

Elave sat silent for a long moment, accepting what was set before him, but dubious of its sense or relevance. 'But I do not see,' he said slowly, 'of what use it is to know these things, even to think them, even to wonder. What bearing has it on anything? Even if it is all true, *why* should it be so? It's not worth solving so small a mystery, since no one is the better or the worse whether we fathom it or not.'

'Everything that is not what it seems, and not what it reasonably should be,' said Cadfael firmly, 'must have significance. And until I know what that significance is, in particular if it manifests itself in the middle of murder and malice, I cannot be content. Thank God, no one now supposes that you had any part in Aldwin's death, but *someone* killed him, and whatever his own faults and misdoings, worse was done to him, and he has a right to justice. I grant it was but natural that most people should take it as certain his sudden death had to do with you and the accusation he made against you. But now, with you out of the reckoning, is not that out of the reckoning, too? Who else in that quarrel had any cause to kill him? So is it not logic to look for another cause? Nothing to do with you and your troubles? But something, nevertheless, to do with your return here. Death came within days of your coming. And whatever is strange, whatever cannot be explained, during these few days since your return may indeed have a bearing.'

'And the box came with me,' said Elave, following this path to its logical ending. 'And here is something strange about the box, something that cannot be explained. Unless you will now tell me that you have an explanation for it?'

'A possible one, yes. For consider . . . We have just been examining the box, emptied of its bags of pence, inside and out. And in the vellum lining of the base there are traces of gold leaf, powdered into a fine dust, but the light finds them. And on the deep ivory vellum there is a fine blue bloom, as on a plum. And I think, and so I know does Brother Anselm, though we have not yet spoken of it, that it is the delicate frettings of another vellum once in constant contact with it, and dyed purple. And pressed into a corner there was a fragment of purple vellum frayed from an end-tag such as we use on the spines of books in our chests in the library.'

'You are saying,' said Elave, watching him in bright-eyed speculation, 'that what the box contained at some time was a book – or books. A book that had formerly been kept among others in a chest. That could well be true, but need it mean anything to us, now? The thing is old, it could have been used in many ways since it was made. It could be a hundred years since it held a book.'

'So it could,' agreed Cadfael, 'but for this one thing. That both you and I handled it only five days ago, and have handled it again today, and found it to be lighter in weight, changed in balance, and filled with something that rings audibly when it is tilted or shaken. What I am saying, Elave, is that what it held, not a hundred years ago, but five short days ago, on the twentieth day of this very month of June, is not what it holds now, on the twenty-fifth.'

'A standard size,' said Brother Anselm, demonstrating with his hands on the desk before him. 'The skin folded to make eight leaves – it would fit the box exactly. Most probably the box was made for it.'

'But if they had been made together,' objected Cadfael, 'the book would not have been given the tabs at the spine. They would not have been needed.'

'That could well be, though the maker may have added them simply as common practice. But the box may have been made for it later. If the book was commissioned first, scribe and binder would finish it in the usual fashion. But if it was the kind of book it may well have been, by the traces left behind, the owner may

177

very well have had a casket made for it to his own wishes, afterwards, to keep it from being rubbed by being drawn in and out from a chest among others of less value.'

Cadfael was smoothing out under his fingers the scrap of purple vellum, teasing out the fringe of gossamer fluff along the torn edge. Minute threads clung to his fingers, motes of bluish mist. 'I spoke to Haluin, who knows more about pigments and vellum than I shall ever know. I wish he had been here to see for himself. So does he! But he said what you have said. Purple is the imperial colour, gold on purple vellum should be a book made for an emperor. East or west, they both had such books made. Purple and gold were the imperial symbols.'

'They still are. And here we have the purple, and traces of the gold. In old Rome,' said Anselm, 'the Caesars used the same fashion, and were jealous of it. I doubt if any other dared so exalt himself. In Aachen or Byzantium, they've been known to follow the Caesars.'

'And from which empire, supposing we are right about this book and the box that contained it, did these works of art come? Can you read the signs?'

'You might do better than I can,' said Anselm. 'You have been in those parts of the world, as I have not. Read your own riddle.'

'The ivory was carved by a craftsman from Constantinople or near it, but it need not have been made there. There is traffic between the two courts, as there has been since Charles the Great. Strange that the box brings the two together as it does, for the carving of the wood is not eastern. The wood itself I cannot fathom, but I think it must be from somewhere round the Middle Sea. Perhaps Italy? How all these materials and talents come together from many places to create so small and rare a thing!'

'And once it contained, perhaps, a smaller and rarer. And who knows who was the scribe who wrote – in gold throughout, do you think, on purple vellum? – whatever that text might be, or for what prince of Byzantium or

Rome it was written? Or who was the painter who adorned it, and in which style, of the east or the west?'

Brother Anselm was gazing out across the sunny garth in a dream of treasure, the fashion of treasure that best pleased him, words and neums inscribed with loving care for the pleasure of kings, and ornamented with delicate elaborations of tendril and blossom.

'It may well have been a marvel,' he said fondly.

'I wonder,' said Cadfael, rather to himself than to any other, 'where it is now.'

Fortunata came into Jevan's shop in the early evening and found him putting his tools tidily away, and laying aside on his shelves the skin he had just folded, creamy white and fine-textured. Three folds had made of it a potential sheaf of eight leaves, but he had not yet trimmed the edges. Fortunata came to his shoulder and smoothed the surface with a forefinger.

'That would be the right size,' she said thoughtfully.

'The right size for many purposes,' said Jevan. 'But what made you say it? Right for what?'

'To make a book to fit my box.' She looked up at him with wide, clear hazel eyes. 'You know I went with Father to try and get them to release Elave, to live with us here until his case is heard? They wouldn't do it. But they took a great interest in the box. Brother Anselm, who keeps all the abbey books, wanted to examine it. Do you know, they think it must once have held a book. Because of the size being so right for a sheepskin folded three times. And the box being so fine, it must have been a very precious book. Do you think they could be right?'

'All things are possible,' said Jevan. 'I hadn't thought of it, but the size is certainly suggestive, now you speak of it. It would indeed make a splendid case for a book.' He looked down into her grave face with his familiar dark smile. 'A pity it had lost its contents before Uncle William happened on it in Tripoli, but I daresay it had been through a great many changes of use and fortune by then. Those are troubled regions. Easier to plant a kingdom there for Christendom than to maintain it.'

'Well, I'm glad,' said Fortunata, 'that it was good silver coin in the box when it reached me, rather than some old book. I can't read, what use would a book be to me?'

'A book would have its value, too. A high value if it was well penned and painted. But I'm glad you're content with what you have, and I hope it will bring you what you want.'

She was running a hand along a shelf, and frowning at the faint fur of dust she found on her palm. Just as the monks had smoothed at the lining of the box, and found something significant in whatever minute residue it left upon the skin. She had caught the tiny flashes of gold in the sunlight, but the rest she had not understood. She studied her own hand, and wiped away the almost imperceptible velvety dust. 'It's time I cleaned your rooms for you,' she said. 'You keep everything so neatly, but it does need dusting.'

'Whenever you wish!' Jevan took a detached look about the room, and agreed placidly: 'It does build up, even here with the finished membranes there's a special dust. I live in it, I breathe it, so it slips my notice. Yes, dust and polish if you want to.'

'It must be much worse in your workshop,' she said, 'with all the scraping of the skins, and going back and forth to the river, coming in with muddy feet, and then the skins, when you bring them first to soak, and all the hair . . . It must smell, too,' she said, wrinkling her nose at the very thought.

'Not so, my lady!' Jevan laughed at her fastidious countenance. 'Conan cleans my workshop for me as often as it needs it, and makes a good job of it, too. I could even teach him the trade, if he was not needed with the sheep. He's no fool, he knows a deal already about the making of vellum.'

'But Conan is shut up in the castle,' she reminded him

seriously. 'The sheriff is still hunting for anyone who can show just where he went and what he did before he went out to the pastures, that day that Aldwin was killed. You don't believe, do you, that he really could kill?'

'Who could not,' said Jevan indifferently, 'given the time and the place? But no, not Conan. They'll let him go in the end. He'll be back. It won't hurt him to sweat for a few days. And it won't hurt my workshop to wait a while for its next cleaning. Now, madam, are you ready for supper? I'll shut the shop, and we'll go in.'

She was paying no attention. Her eyes were roaming the length of his shelves, and the rack where the largest finished membranes were draped, cut and trimmed to order into the great bifolia intended for some massive lectern Bible. These she passed by to dwell upon the eight-leaved gatherings of the size that fitted her box.

'Uncle, you have some books this same size, haven't you?'

'It's the most usual,' he said. 'Yes, the best thing I have is of that measure. It was made in France. God knows how it ever found its way to the abbey fair here in Shrewsbury. Why did you ask?'

'Then it would fit into my box. I'd like you to have it. Why not? If it's so fine, and has a value, it should stay in the household, and I'm unlettered, and have no book to put in it, and besides,' she said, 'I'm happy with my dowry, and grateful to Uncle William for it. Let's try it, after supper. Show me your books again. I may not be able to read, but they're beautiful to look at.'

Jevan stood looking down at her from his lean height, solemn and still. Thus motionless, everything about him seemed a little more elongated than usual, like a saint carved into the vertical moulding of a church porch, from his narrow, scholarly face to the long-toed shoes on his thin, sinewy feet, and the lean, clever, adept's hands. His deep eyes searched her face. He shook his head at such rash and thoughtless generosity.

'Child, you should not so madly give away everything

you have, before you know the value of it, or what need you may have of it in the future. Do nothing on impulse, you may pay for it with regret.'

'No,' said Fortunata. 'Why should I regret giving a thing for which I have no use to someone who will make good and proper use of it? And dare you tell me that you don't want it?' Certainly his black eyes were glittering, if not with covetousness, with unmistakeable longing and pleasure. 'Come to supper, and afterwards we'll try how they match together. And I'll get Father to mind my money for me.'

The French breviary was one of seven manuscripts Jevan had acquired over the years of his dealings with churchmen and other patrons. When he lifted the lid of the chest in which he kept them Fortunata saw them ranged side by side, spines upward, leaning towards one side because he had not quite enough as yet to fill the space neatly. Two had fading titles in Latin inscribed along the spine, one was in a cover dyed red, the rest had all originally been bound in ivory leather drawn over thin wooden boards, but some were old enough to have mellowed into the pleasant pale brown of the lining of her box. She had seen them several times before, but had never paid them such close attention. And there at head and foot of every spine were the little rounded tongues of leather for lifting them in and out.

Jevan drew out his favourite, its binding still almost virgin white, and opened it at random, and the brilliant colours sprang out as if they were just freshly applied, a right-hand border the length of the page, very narrow and delicate, of twining leaves and tendrils and flowers, the rest of the page written in two columns, with one large initial letter, and five smaller ones to open later paragraphs, each one using the letter as a frame for vivid miniatures of flower and fern. The precision of the painting was matched by the limpid lucidity of the blues and reds and golds and greens, but the blues in particular filled and satisfied the eyes with a translucent coolness that was pure pleasure.

'It's in such mint condition,' said Jevan, stroking the smooth binding lovingly, 'that I fancy it was stolen, and brought well away from the place where it belonged before the merchant dared sell it. This is the beginning of the Common of the Saints, hence the large initial. See the violets, and how true their colour is!'

Fortunata opened her box on her knees. The colour of the lining blended softly with the paler colour of the breviary's binding. The book fitted comfortably within. When the lid was closed on it the soft clinging of the lining held the book secure.

'You see?' she said. 'How much better that it should have a use! And truly it does seem that this is the purpose for which it was made.'

There was room for the box within the chest. Jevan closed that lid also over his library, and kneeled for a moment with both long hands pressed upon the wood, caressing and reverent. 'Very well! At least you may be sure it will be valued.' He rose to his feet, his eyes still lingering upon the chest that held his treasure, a shadowy private smile of perfect contentment playing round his lips. 'Do you know, chick, that I've never locked this before? Now I have your gift within it I shall keep it locked for safety.'

They turned towards the door together, his hand on her shoulder. At the head of the stairs that went down into the hall she halted, and turned her face up to him suddenly. 'Uncle, you know you said Conan had learned a great deal about your business, through helping you there sometimes? Would he know what value to set on books? Would he recognise it, if by chance he lit on one of immense value?'

Chapter Twelve

O N THE twenty-sixth day of June Fortunata rose early, and with her first waking thought recalled that it was the day of Aldwin's funeral. It was taken for granted that the entire household would attend, so much was owed to him, for many reasons, years of service, undistinguished but conscientious, years of familiarity with his harmless, disconsolate figure about the place, and the pity and the vague sense of having somehow failed him, now that he had come to so unexpected an end. And the last words she had ever said to him were a reproach! Deserved, perhaps, but now, less reasonably, reproaching her.

Poor Aldwin! He had never made the most of his blessings, always feared their loss, like a miser with his gold. And he had done a terrible thing to Elave in his haunting fear of being discarded. But he had not deserved to be stabbed from behind and cast into the river, and she had him somehow on her conscience in spite of her anxiety and dread for Elave, whom he had injured. On this of all mornings he filled Fortunata's mind, and drove her on along a road she was reluctant to take. But if justice is to be denied to the inadequate, grudging and sad, to whom then is it due?

Early as she was, it seemed that someone else was earlier. The shop would remain closed all this day, shuttered and dim, so there was no occasion for Jevan to be up so early, but he had risen and gone out before Fortunata came down into the hall.

'He's off to his workshop,' said Margaret, when Fortunata asked after him. 'He has some fresh skins to put into the river to soak, but he'll be back in good time for poor Aldwin's funeral. Were you wanting him?'

'No, nothing that won't wait,' said Fortunata. 'I missed him, that's all.'

She was glad that the household was fully occupied with the preparations for one more memorial gathering, so soon after the first, the evening of Uncle William's wake when this whole cycle of misfortune had begun. Margaret and the maid were busy in the kitchen, Girard, as soon as he had broken his fast, was out in the yard arranging Aldwin's last dignified transit to the church he had neglected in life. Fortunata went into the shuttered shop, and without more light than filtered through the joints of the shutters, began swiftly and silently to search along the shelves among the array of uncut skins, tools, every corner of a neat, sparsely furnished room. Everything was open to view. She had scarcely expected to find anything alien in here, and did not spend much time on it. She closed the door again upon the shadowy interior, and went back into the empty hall, and up the staircase to Jevan's bedchamber, over the entry from the street.

Perhaps he had forgotten that she had known from infancy where everything in this house was kept, or overlooked the fact that even those details which had never interested her before might be of grave importance now. She had not yet given him any cause to reflect on such matters, and she was praying inwardly at this moment that she never need give him cause. Whatever she did now, she was going to feel guilt, but that she could bear, since she must. The haunting uncertainty she could not bear.

Never before, Jevan had said, had he troubled to lock

up his manuscripts, never until her precious dower box was laid among them. And that might well have been a light, affectionate gesture of praise and thanks to flatter her, but for the fact that he had indeed turned the key on her gift when he was alone in the room at night. She knew it, even before she laid hand to the lid to raise it, and found it locked. Now, if he had kept his keys on his person when he left the house, she could go no further along this fearful road. But he had seen no need for that, for they were there in their usual place, on a hook inside the chest where his clothes were kept, in a corner of the room. Her hand shook as she selected the smallest, and metal grated acidly against metal before she could insert it in the lock of the book-chest.

She raised the lid, and kneeled motionless beside the chest, gripping the carved edge with both hands, so hard that her fingers stiffened and ached with tension. It needed only one glance, not the long, dismayed stare she fixed upon the interior, the serried spines upturned, the vacant space at one end. There was no dark casket there, no great-eyed, round-browed ivory saint returning her wide stare. Whitest of the pale spines, cheek by jowl with its one red-dyed companion, Jevan's treasured French breviary, bought from some careful thief or trader in stolen goods at Saint Peter's Fair a couple of years ago, rested in its accustomed place among the others, deprived of its new and sumptuous casket.

The book remained, the box into which it fitted so harmoniously had been removed, and Fortunata could think of only one reason, and only one place where it could have gone.

She closed the lid in a sudden spurt of haste and panic, and turned the key, and a tress of her hair caught in the fretted edge of the lock, and she tugged it loose as she rose, in a fever to escape from this room, and take refuge elsewhere among ordinary events and innocent people, from the knowledge she wished she had let lie, but now could not unknow, and the path on to which she had stepped hoping it would fade from under her feet, and now must follow to its end.

Aldwin was carried to his burial at mid-morning, escorted by Girard of Lythwood and all his household, and guided into the next world with all solemnity by Father Elias, satisfied now of his parishioner's credentials and relieved of all his former doubts. Fortunata stood beside Jevan at the graveside, and felt the counter-currents of pity and horror tearing her mind between them as his sleeve brushed hers. She had watched him make one among those carrying the bier, scatter a handful of earth into the grave, and gaze down into the dark pit with austere and composed face as the clods fell dully and covered the dead. A life lived in discouragement and pessimism might not seem much to lose, but when it is snatched away by murder the offence and the deprivation show as monstrous.

So there went Aldwin out of this world, which had never seen fit to content him, and home went Girard and his family, having done their duty by their unfortunate dependent. They were all quiet at table, but the gap Aldwin had left was narrow at best, and would soon close up like a trivial wound, to leave no scar.

Fortunata cleared away the dishes, and went into the kitchen to help wash the pots after dinner. She could not be sure whether she was delaying what she knew she must do out of care to arouse no special interest in her movements, or out of desperate longing not to do it at all. But in the end she could not leave it unfinished. She might yet be agonising needlessly. There might be a good answer, even now, and if she did not finish what she had begun she might never find it out. Truth is a terrible compulsion.

She crossed the yard and slipped unnoticed into the shuttered shop. The key of the Frankwell workshop was dangling in its proper place, where Jevan had hung it openly and serenely when he returned from his early morning expedition. Fortunata took it down, and hid it in the bodice of her gown.

'I'm going down to the abbey,' she said, looking in at the hall door, 'to see if they'll let me see Elave again. Or at least to find out if anything has happened yet. The bishop must surely send a message any day now, Coventry is not so far.'

No one objected, no one offered to go with her. No doubt they felt that after the morning's preoccupation with death it would be the best thing in the world for her to go out into the summer afternoon, and turn her thoughts, however anxious they might be, towards life and youth.

Since only the eyes of the shop, blind and shuttered now, looked out upon the street, the house windows being all in the upright of the L and looking out upon the long strip of yard and garden, no one saw her emerge from the passageway and turn, not left towards the town gate and the abbey, but right, towards the western bridge and the suburb of Frankwell.

Brother Cadfael, not usually given to hesitation, had spent the entire morning and an hour of the early afternoon pondering the events of the previous day, and trying to determine how much of what was troubling his mind was knowledge, and how much was wild speculation. Certainly at some stage Fortunata's box had contained a book, and by the traces left it had been so used for a very considerable time, to leave that faint lavender bloom on the lining, and a frayed, wafer-thin wisp of purple leather trapped in a corner between lining and wood. Gold leaf is applied over glue, and then burnished, and though the sheets are too frail and fine to be handled safely out in the cloister, or in any trace of wind, properly finished gilding is very durable. It would take much use and frequent lifting in and out of a well fitted container, to fret away even those few infinitesimal grains of gold. The more he thought of it the more he felt sure that some-

188

where there was a book meant for this casket, and that they had kept company together for a century or more. If they had parted long ago, the book perhaps stolen, raided away into paynim hands, even destroyed, then what had been the nature of the dowry old William had sent to his fosterdaughter? For he was certain, as Elave was now certain, that it had not been those six felt bags of silver pence.

And supposing it had indeed still been the book, secure in its beautiful coffin, carried across half the world unhandled and unread, for its value to a girl when she had reached marriageable age? Value as something to be sold, and sold shrewdly, to bring in the best profit. Books have another value, to those who have fallen for ever and wholly in love with them. There are those who would cheat for them, steal for them, lie for them, even if then they could never show nor boast of their treasures to any other creature. Kill for them? It was not impossible.

But that was surely looking far beyond the present case, for where was the connection? Who threatened? Who stood in the way? Not a barely literate clerk, who certainly cared not at all about exquisite manuscripts worked long ago by consummate artists.

Abruptly, and somewhat to his own surprise, for he was unaware of the intention forming, Cadfael stopped fretting out small weeds from between his herb beds, put away his hoe, and went to look for Brother Winfrid, weeding by hand in the vegetable garden.

'Son, I have an errand to do, if Father Abbot allows. I should be back before Vespers, but if I come late, see everything in order and close up my workshop for me before you go.'

Brother Winfrid straightened up to his full brawny country height for a moment to acknowledge his orders, with one large fist full of the greenery he had uprooted. 'I will. Is there anything within needs a stir?'

'Nothing. You can take your ease when you are finished here.' Not that he was likely to take that literally.

Brother Winfrid had so much energy in him that it had to find constant outlet, or it would probably split him apart. Cadfael clapped him on the shoulder, left him to his vigorous labours, and went off in search of Abbot Radulfus.

The abbot was in his office, poring over the cellarer's accounts, but he put them aside when Cadfael asked audience, and gave his full attention to the petitioner.

'Father,' said Cadfael, 'has Brother Anselm told you what we discovered yesterday concerning the box that was brought back from the east for the girl Fortunata? And what, with reservations, we concluded from examining it?

'He has,' said the abbot. 'I would trust Anselm's judgement on such matters, but it is still speculation. It does seem likely that there was such a book. A great pity it should be lost.'

'Father, I am not sure that it is lost. There is reason to believe that what came to England in that box was not the money that is in it now. There was a difference of weight and balance. So says the young man who brought it from the east, and so say I, also, for I handled it on the same day he delivered it to Girard of Lythwood's house. I think,' said Cadfael vehemently, 'that what we have noted should also be reported to the sheriff.'

'You believe,' said Radulfus, eyeing him gravely, 'that it may have some bearing on the only case I know of that Hugh Beringar now has in hand? But that is a case of murder. What can a book, present or absent, have to say regarding that crime?'

'When the clerk was killed, Father, was it not taken as proven by most men that the young man he had injured had killed him in revenge? Yet we know now it was not so. Elave never harmed him. And who else had cause to move against the man's life in the matter of that accusation he made? No one. I have come to believe that the cause of his death had nothing to do with his denunciation of Elave. Yet it does still seem that it had something to do with Elave himself, with his coming home to

Shrewsbury. Everything that has happened has happened since that return. Is it not possible, Father, that it has to do with what he brought back to that house? A box that changes in weight, and one day handles like a solid carving of wood, and a few days later rings with silver coins. This in itself is strange. And whatever is strange within and around that household, where the dead man lived and worked for years, may have a bearing.'

'And should be taken into account,' concluded the abbot, and sat pondering what he had heard for some minutes in silence. 'Very well, so be it. Yes, Hugh Beringar should know of it. What he may make of it I cannot guess. God knows I can make nothing of it myself, not yet, but if it can shed one gleam of light to show the way a single step towards justice, yes, he must know. Go to him now, if you wish. Take whatever time may be needed, and I pray it may be used to good effect.'

Cadfael found Hugh, not at his own house by Saint Mary's, but at the castle. He was just striding across the outer ward in a preoccupied haste that curiously managed to indicate both buoyancy and irritation as Cadfael came up the ramp from the street, and in through the deep tunnel of the gate-tower. Hugh checked and turned at once to meet him.

'Cadfael! You come very timely, I've news for you.'

'And so have I for you,' said Cadfael, 'if mine can be called news. But for what it may be worth, I think you should have it.'

'And Radulfus agreed? So there must be substance in it. Come within, and let's exchange what we have,' said Hugh, and led the way forthwith towards the guardroom and anteroom in the gate-tower, where they could be private. 'I was about to go in and see our friend Conan,' he said with a somewhat wry smile, 'before I turn him loose. Yes, that's my news. It's taken a time to fill in all the comings and goings of his day, but we've dredged up at last a cottar at the edge of Frankwell who knows him, and saw him going up the pastures to his flock well before Vespers that afternoon. There's no way he could have killed Aldwin, the man was alive and well a good hour later.'

Cadfael sat down slowly, with a long, breathy sigh. 'So he's out of it, too! Well, well! I never thought him a likely murderer, I confess, but certainty, that's another matter.'

'Neither did I think him a likely murderer,' agreed Hugh ruefully, 'but I grudge him the days it's cost us to prise out his witnesses for him, and the fool so sick with fright he could barely remember the very acquaintances he'd passed on his way through Frankwell. And still lying, mark you, when his wits worked at all. But clean he is, and soon he'll be on his way back to his work, free as a bird. I wish Girard joy of him!' said Hugh disgustedly. He leaned his elbows on the small table between them, and held Cadfael eye to eye. 'Will you credit it? He swore he'd seen nothing of Aldwin after the girl's reproof sent the poor devil off in a passion of guilt to try and retrieve what he'd done – until he knew we'd found out about the hour or so they spent together in the alehouse. Then he admitted that, but swore that was the end of it. No such thing, as it turned out. It was one of the eager hounds baying along the Foregate after Elave who told us the next part of the story. He saw the pair of them cross over the bridge and come along the road towards the abbey with Conan's arm persuasively about Aldwin's shoulders, and Conan talking fast and urgently into Aldwin's ear. Until they both saw and heard the hunt in full cry! Frightened them out of their wits, he says, you'd have thought it was them the hounds were coursing. They went to ground among the trees so fast nothing showed but their scuts. I fancy that was what put an end once and for all to Aldwin's intention of going to the abbey with his bad conscience. Who knows, after the young priest confessed him he might have got his courage back, if . . . Only today has Conan admitted that he went after him a second time. They were both a shade drunk, I expect. But finally he did go out to his flock, when he was certain Aldwin was far too frightened to involve himself further.'

'So you've lost your best suspect,' said Cadfael thoughtfully.

'The only one I had. And not sorry, so far as the fool himself is concerned, that he should turn out to be blameless. Well, short of murder, at least,' Hugh corrected himself. 'But contenders were thin on the ground from the start. And what follows now?'

'What follows,' said Cadfael, 'is that I tell you what I've come to tell you, for with even Conan removed from the field it becomes more substantial even than I thought. And then, if you agree, we might drain Conan dry of everything he knows, to the last drop, before you turn him loose. I can't be sure, even, that anyone has so much as mentioned to you the box that Elave brought home for the girl, by way of a dowry? From the old man, before he died in France?'

'Yes,' said Hugh wonderingly, 'it was mentioned. Jevan told me, by way of accounting for Conan's wanting to get rid of Elave. He liked the daughter, did Conan, in a cool sort of way, but he began to like her much better when she had a dowry to bring with her. So says Jevan. But that's all I know of it. Why? How does the box have any bearing on the murder?'

'I have been baffled from the start,' said Cadfael, 'by the absence of motive. Revenge, said everyone, pointing the finger at Elave, but when that was blown clear away by young Father Eadmer, what was left? Conan may have been eager to prevent Aldwin from withdrawing his denunciation, but even that was thin enough, and now you tell me that's gone, too. Who had anything against Aldwin so grievous as to be worth even a clout in a quarrel, let alone murder? It was hard enough to see the poor devil at all, let alone resent him. He had nothing worth coveting, had done no great harm to anyone until now. No wonder suspects were thin on the ground. Yet he stood in someone's way, or menaced someone, surely, whether he knew it or not. so since his betrayal of Elave was not the cause of his death, I began to look more closely at all the affairs of the household to which both men were attached, however loosely, every detail, especially anything that was new, this outbreak being so sudden and so dire. All was quiet enough until Elave came home. The only thing but himself he brought into that house was Fortunata's box. And even at first sight it was no ordinary box. So when Fortunata brought it to the abbey, thinking to use the money in it to procure Elave's release, I asked if we could examine it more closely. And this, Hugh, this is what we found.'

He told it scrupulously, in every detail of the gold and purple, the change in its weight, the possible and disturbing change in its contents. Hugh listened without comment to the end. Then he said slowly: 'Such a thing, if indeed it did enter that house, might well be enough to tempt any man.'

'Any who understood its value,' said Cadfael. 'Either in money, or for its own rare sake.'

'And before all, it would have to be a man who had opened the box, and seen what was there. Before it was made known to them all. Do we know whether it was opened at once, when the boy delivered it? Or how soon after?'

'That,' said Cadfael, 'I do not know. But you have one in hold who may know. One who may even know where it was laid by, who went near it, what was said about it, through those few days, as Elave could not know at all, not being there. Why do we not question Conan once more, before you set him free?'

'Bearing in mind,' Hugh warned, 'that this, too, may blow away in the wind. It may all along have been coins within there, but better packed.'

'English coin, and in such quantity?' said Cadfael, catching at a thread he had not considered, but finding it frail. 'At the end of such a journey, and committed to her from France? But if he sent her money at all, it must needs be English money. He could have been holding it in reserve for such a purpose, once he began to be a sick man. No, there's nothing certain, everything slips through the fingers.'

Hugh rose decisively. 'Come, let's go and see what can be wrung out of Master Conan, before I let him slip through mine.'

Conan sat in his stone cell, and eyed them doubtfully and slyly from the moment they entered. He had a slit window on the air, a hard but tolerable bed, ample food and no work, and was just getting used to the fact, at first surprising, that no one was interested in using him roughly, but for all that he was uneasy and anxious whenever Hugh appeared. He had told so many lies in his efforts to distance himself from suspicion of the murder that he had difficulty in remembering now exactly what he had said, and was wary of trapping himself in still more tangled coils.

'Conan, my lad,' said Hugh, walking in upon him breezily, 'there's still a little matter in which you can be of help to me. You know most of what goes on in Girard of Lythwood's house. You know the box that was brought for Fortunata from France. Answer me some questions about it, and let's have no more lies this time. Tell me about the box. Who was there when it first came into the house?

Uneasy at this or any diversion he could not understand, Conan answered warily: 'There was Jevan, Dame Margaret, Aldwin and me. And Elave! Fortunata wasn't there, she came in later.'

'Was the box opened then?'

'No, the mistress said it should wait until Master Girard came home.' Chary of words until he understood the drift, Conan added nothing more.

'So she put it away, did she? And you saw where, did you not? Tell us!'

He was growing ever more uneasy. 'She put it away in the press, on a high shelf. We all saw it!'

'And the key, Conan? The key was with it? And were you not curious about it? Did you not want to see what was in it? Didn't your fingers begin to itch before nightfall?'

'I never meddled with it!' cried Conan, alarmed and defensive. 'It wasn't me who pried into it. I never went near it.'

So easy it was! Hugh and Cadfael exchanged a brief glance of astonished gratification. Ask the right question, and the road ahead opens before you. They closed in almost fondly on the sweating Conan.

'Then who was it?' Hugh demanded.

'Aldwin! He pried into everything. He never took things,' said Conan feverishly, desperate to point the bolts of suspicion away from himself at all costs, 'but he couldn't bear not knowing. He was always afraid there was something brewing against him. *I* never touched it, but *he* did.'

'And how do you know this, Conan?' asked Cadfael.

'He told me, afterwards. But I heard them, down in the hall.'

'And when was it you heard *them* – down in the hall?'

'That same night.' Conan drew breath, beginning to be somewhat reassured again, since nothing of all this seemed to be pointing in his direction, after all. 'I went to bed, and left Aldwin down in the kitchen, but I wasn't asleep. I never heard him come into the hall, but I did hear Jevan suddenly shout down at him from the top of the stairs, "What are you doing there?" and then Aldwin, down below, all in a hurry, said he'd left his penknife in the press, and he'd be needing it in the morning. And Jevan says take it, then, and get to bed, and give over disturbing other people. And Aldwin came up in haste, with his tail between his legs. And I heard Jevan go on down into the hall and cross to the press, and I think he locked it and took the key away, for it was locked next morning. I asked Aldwin later what he'd been up to, and he said he only wanted to have a look inside, and he had the box open, and then had to shut and lock it again in a hurry, and try to hide what he was about, when Jevan shouted at him.'

'And *did* he see what was in it?' asked Cadfael, already foreseeing the answer, and tasting its bitter irony.

'Not he! He pretended at first he had, but he wouldn't tell me what it was, and in the end he had to admit he never got a glimpse. He'd barely raised the lid when he had to close it again in a hurry. It got him nothing!' said Conan, almost with satisfaction, as if he had scored over his fellow in some way by that wasted curiosity.

It got him his death, thought Cadfael, with awful certainty. And all for nothing! He never had time to see what the box held. Perhaps no one had then seen it. Perhaps it was that prying inquisitiveness that set off another man's quickening curiosity, fatal to them both.

'Well, Conan,' said Hugh, 'you may take heart and think yourself lucky. There's a man from the Welsh side of the town can swear to it you were on your way to Girard's fold well before Vespers, the night Aldwin was killed. You're clear of blame. You can be off home when you choose, the door's open.'

'And he did not even see it,' said Hugh, as they recrossed the outer ward side by side.

'But there was one who believed he had. And looked for himself,' said Cadfael, 'and was lost. Fathoms deep! And in one more day, or two, three at the most, Girard would be home, the box would be opened, what was in it would be known to all, and would be Fortunata's. Girard is a shrewd merchant, he would get for her the highest sum possible – not that it would approach its worth. But if he did not himself know where best to sell it, he would know where to ask. If it was what I begin to believe, the sum left her in its place would not have bought one leaf.'

'And only one life stood in the way, to threaten

betrayal,' said Hugh. 'Or so it seemed! And all for nothing, the poor wretch never did have time to see what should have been there to be seen when the box was opened. Cadfael, my mind misgives me – yesterday, when Anselm examined that box, gold leaf, purple dye and all, Girard and the girl were present? How if one of them proved sharp enough to think as we are thinking? Having gone so far, could a man stop short now, if the same danger threatened his gains all over again?'

It was a new and disturbing thought. Cadfael checked for an instant in midstride, shaken into considering it.

'I think Girard never gave it much thought. The girl – I would not say! She is deeper than she seems, and she it is who has so much at stake. And she's young and kind, and sudden undeserved death has never before come so near her. I wonder! Truly I wonder! She did pay close attention, missing nothing, saying little. Hugh, what will you do?'

'Come!' said Hugh, making up his mind. 'You and I will go and visit the Lythwood household. We have pretext enough. They have buried their murdered man this morning, I have released one suspect from their retinue this afternoon, and I am still bent on finding a murderer. No need for one member rather than another to be wary of my probing, as yet, not until I have filled up the score of that day's movements for him as I took so long to do for Conan. At least we'll take note here and now of where the girl is, until you or I can talk with her again, and make sure she does nothing to draw danger upon herself.'

At about the same time that Hugh and Cadfael set out from the castle, Jevan of Lythwood had occasion to go up to his chamber, to discard and fold away the best cotte he had worn for Aldwin's funeral, and put on the lighter and easier coat in which he worked. He seldom entered the room without casting a pleased, possessive glance at the chest which held his books, and so he did now. The sunlight, declining from the zenith into the golden, sated hours of late afternoon, came slanting in by the south-facing window, gilded a corner of the lid and just reached the metal plate of the lock. Something gossamer-fine fluttered from the ornate edge, appearing and disappearing as it stirred in an air not quite motionless. Four or five long hairs, dark but bright, showing now and then a brief scintillation of red. But for the light, which just touched them against shadow, they would have been invisible.

Jevan saw them and stood at gaze, his face unchanging. Then he went to take the key from its place, and unlocked the chest and raised the lid. Nothing within was disturbed. Nothing was changed but those few sunlit filaments that stirred like living things, and curled about his fingers when he carefully detached them from the fretted edge in which they were caught.

In thoughtful silence he closed and locked the chest again, and went down into the shuttered shop. The key of his workshop upriver, on the right bank of Severn well clear of the town, was gone from its hook.

He crossed the yard and looked in at the hall, where Girard was busy over the accounts Aldwin had left in arrears, and Margaret was mending a shirt at the other end of the table.

'I'm going down to the skins again,' said Jevan. 'There's something I left unfinished.'

Chapter Thirteen

HE WELCOME at Girard's house was all the warmer because Conan had arrived home only a quarter of an hour earlier, ebullient wth relief and none the worse for his few days' incarceration, and Girard, a practical man, was disposed to let the dead bury their dead, once the living had seen to it that they got their dues and were seen off decently into a better world. What was left of his establishment seemed now to be clear of all aspersions, and could proceed about its business without interference.

Two members, however, were missing.

'Fortunata?' said Margaret in answer to Cadfael's enquiry. 'She went out after dinner. She said she was going to the abbey, to try to see Elave again, or at least to find out if anything had happened yet in his case. I daresay you'll be meeting her on the way down, but if not, you'll find her there.'

That was a load lifted from Cadfael's mind, at least. Where better could she be, or safer? 'Then I'd best be on my way home,' he said, pleased, 'or I shall be outstaying my leave.'

'And I came hoping to pick your brother's brains,' said Hugh. 'I've been hearing a great deal about this box of your daughter's, and I'm curious to see it. I'm told it may have been made to hold a book, at one time. I wondered what Jevan thought of that. He knows everything about the making of books, from the raw skin to the binding. I should like to consult him when he has time to spare. But perhaps I might see the box?'

They were quite happy to tell him what they could. There was no foreboding, no tremor in the house. 'He's away to his workshop just now,' said Girard. 'He was down there this morning, but he said he'd left something unfinished. He'll surely be back soon. Come in and wait a while, and he'll be here. The box? I doubt it's locked away until he comes. Fortunata gave it to him last night. If it's meant to hold a book, she says, Uncle Jevan is the man who has books, let me give him the box. And he's using it for the one he most values, as she wanted. He'll be pleased to show it to you. It is a very fine thing.'

'I won't trouble you now, if he's not here,' said Hugh. 'I'll look in later, I'm close enough.'

They took their leave together, and Hugh went with Cadfael as far as the head of the Wyle. 'She gave him the box,' said Hugh, frowning over a puzzle. 'What should that mean?'

'Bait,' said Cadfael soberly. 'Now I do believe she has been following the same road my mind goes. But not to prove – rather to disprove if she can. But at all costs needing to *know*. He is her close and valued kin, but she is not one who can shut her eyes and pretend no wrong has ever been done. Yet still we may both be wrong, she as well as I. Well, at the worst, she is safe enough if she's at the abbey. I'll go and find her there. And as for the other one . . .'

'The other one,' said Hugh, 'leave to me.'

Cadfael walked in through the arch of the gatehouse into a scene of purposeful activity. It seemed he had arrived on the heels of an important personage, to whose reception the hierarchies of the house were assembling busily. Brother Porter had come in a flurry of skirts to take one bridle, Brother Jerome was contending with a groom for another one, Prior Robert was approaching from the cloister at his longest stride, Brother Denis hovered, not yet certain whether the newcomer would be housed in the guest hall or with the abbot. A flutter of brothers and novices hung at a respectful distance, ready to run any errands that might arise, and three or four of the school-boys, sensibly withdrawn out of range of notice and censure, stood frankly staring, all eyes and ears.

And in the middle of this flurry of arrival stood Deacon Serlo, just dismounted from his mule and shaking out the skirts of his gown. A little dusty from the ride, but as rounded and pink-cheeked and wholesome as ever, and decidedly happier now that he had brought his bishop with him, and could leave all decisions to him with a quiet mind.

Bishop Roger de Clinton was just alighting from a tall roan horse, with the vigour and spring of a man half his age. For he must, Cadfael thought, be approaching sixty. He had been bishop for fourteen years, and wore his authority as easily and forthrightly as he did his plain riding clothes, and with the same patrician confidence. He was tall, and his erect bearing made him appear taller still. A man austere, competent, and of no pretensioms because he needed none, there was something about him, Cadfael thought, of the warrior bishops who were becoming a rare breed these days. His face would have done just as well for a soldier as for a priest, hawk-featured, direct and resolute, with penetrating grey eyes that summed up as rapidly and decisively as they saw. He took in the whole scene about him in one sweeping glance, and surrendered his bridle to the porter as Prior Robert bore down on him, all reverence and welcome.

They moved off together towards the abbot's lodging, and the group broke apart gradually, having lost its centre. The horses were eased of their saddle-bags and led away to the stables, the hovering brothers dispersed about their various businesses, the children drifted off in search of other amusement until they should be rounded up for their early supper. And Cadfael thought of Elave, who must have heard, distantly across the court, the sounds that heralded the coming of his judge. Cadfael had seen Roger de Clinton only twice before, and had no means of knowing in what mood and what mind he came to this vexed cause. But at least he had come in person, and looked fully capable of wresting back the responsibility for his diocese and its spiritual health from anyone who presumed to trespass on his writ.

Meantime, Cadfael's immediate business was to find Fortunata. He approached the porter with his enquiry. 'Where am I likely to find Girard of Lythwood's daughter? They told me at the house she would be here.'

'I know the girl,' said the porter, nodding. 'But I've seen nothing of her today.'

'She told them at home she was coming down here. Soon after dinner, so the mother told me.'

'I've neither seen nor spoken to her, and I've been here most of the time since noon. An errand or two to do, but I was only a matter of minutes away. Though she may have come in while my back was turned. But she'd need to speak to someone in authority. I think she'd have waited here at the gate until I came.'

Cadfael would have thought so, too. But if she'd caught sight of the prior as she waited, or Anselm, or Denis, she might very well have accosted one of them with her petition. Cadfael sought out Denis, whose duties kept him most of the time around the court, and within sight of the gate, but Denis had seen nothing of Fortunata. She was acquainted now with Anselm's little kingdom in the north walk, she might have made her way there, seeking for someone she knew. But Anselm shook his head decidedly, no, she had not been there. Not only was she not to be found within the precinct now, but it seemed she had not set foot in it all day.

The bell for Vespers found Cadfael hovering irresolute over what he ought to do, and reminded him sternly of his obligations to the vocation he had accepted of his own free will, and sometimes reproached himself for neglecting. There are more ways of approaching a problem than by belligerent action. The mind and the will have also something to say in the unending combat. Cadfael turned towards the south porch and joined the procession of his brothers into the dim, cool cavern of the choir, and prayed fervently for Aldwin, dead and buried in his piteous human imperfection, and for William of Lythwood, come home contented and shriven to rest in his own place, and for all those trammelled and tormented by suspicion and doubt and fear, the guilty as well as the innocent, for who needs succour more? Whether he was building a fantastic folly round a book which might not even exist, or confronting a serious peril for any who blundered on too much knowledge, one crime was hard and clear as black crystal, someone had taken the sad, inoffensive life of Aldwin the clerk, of whom the one man he had injured had said honestly: 'Everything he has said that I said, I *did* say.' But someone else, to whom he had done nothing, had slipped a dagger between his ribs from behind and killed him.

Cadfael emerged from Vespers consoled, but not the less aware of his own responsibilities. It was still full daylight, but with the slanting evening radiance about it, and the stillness of the air that seemed to dim all colours into a diaphanous pearly sheen. There remained one enquiry he could still make, before going further. It was just possible that Fortunata, grown dubious of venturing to ask admittance to Elave so soon after a first visit, had simply asked someone at the gate, in the porter's brief absence, to carry a message to the prisoner, nothing to which any man could raise objection, merely to remind him his friends thought of him, and beg him to keep up his courage. It might not mean anything that Cadfael had not encountered her on her way home, she might already have been back in the town, and used the time to some other purpose before returning home. At least he would

204

have a word with the boy, and satisfy himself he was anxious to no purpose.

He took the key from where it hung in the porch, and went to let himself into the cell. Elave swung round from his little desk, and turned a frowning face because he had been narrowing his eyes and knitting his brows in the dimming light over one of Augustine's more humane and ecstatic sermons. The apparent cloud cleared as soon as he left poring over the cramped minuscule of the text. Other people feared for him, but it seemed to Cadfael that Elave himself was quite free from fear, and had not shown even as restive in his close confinement.

'There's something of the monk in you,' said Cadfael, speaking his thoughts aloud. 'You may end up under a cowl yet.'

'Never!' said Elave fervently, and laughed aloud at the notion.

'Well, perhaps it would be a waste, seeing what other ideas you have for the future. But you have the mind for it. Travelling the world or penned in a stone cell, neither of them upsets your balance. So much the better for you! Has anyone thought to tell you that the bishop's come? In person! He pays you a compliment, for Coventry's nearer the turmoil than we are here, and he needs to keep a close eye on his church there, so time given to your case is a mark of your importance. And it may be a short time, for he looks a man who can make up his mind briskly.'

'I heard the to-do about someone arriving,' said Elave. 'I heard the horses on the cobbles. But I didn't know who it might be. Then he'll be wanting me soon?' At Cadfael's questioning glance he smiled, though seriously enough. 'I'm ready. I want it, too. I've made good use of my time here. I've found that even this Augustine went through many changes of mind over the years. You could take some of his early writings, and they say the very opposite of what he said in old age. That, and a dozen changes between. Cadfael, did you ever think what a waste it would be if you burned a man for what he believed at twenty, when what he might believe and write at forty would be hailed as the most blessed of holy writ?'

'That is the kind of argument to which the most of men never listen,' said Cadfael, 'Otherwise they would baulk at taking any life. You haven't been visited today, have you?'

'Only by Anselm. Why?'

'Nor had any message from Fortunata?'

'No. Why?' repeated Elave with sharper urgency, seeing Cadfael frown. 'All's well with her, I trust?'

'So I trust also,' agreed Cadfael, 'and so it should be. She told her family she was coming down to the abbey to ask if she could see you again, or get word of any progress in your case, that's why I asked. But no one has seen her. She hasn't been here.'

'And that troubles you,' said Elave sharply. 'Why should it matter? What is it you have in mind? Is there some threat to her? Are you *afraid* for her?'

'Let's say I should be glad to know that she's safe at home. As surely she must be. Afraid, no! But you must remember there is a murderer loose among us, and close to that household, and I would rather she kept to home and safe company than go anywhere alone. But as for today, I left Hugh Beringar keeping a close watch on the house and all who stir in and out of it, so set your mind at rest.'

They had neither of them been paying any attention to the passing sounds without, the brief ring of hooves distant across the court, the rapid exchange of voices, short and low, and then the light feet coming at an impetuous walk. It startled them both when the door of the cell was flung open before a gust of evening air and the abrupt entry of Hugh Beringar.

'They told me I should find you here,' he said, high and breathless with haste. 'They say the girl is *not* here, and has not been since yesterday. It that true?'

'She has not come home?' said Cadfael, aghast.

206

'Nor she nor the other. The dame's beginning to be anxious. I thought best to come down and fetch the girl home myself if she was still here, but now I find she has not been here, and I know she is not at home, for I'm fresh come from there. So long away, and not where she said she'd be!'

Elave clutched at Cadfael's arm, shaking him vehemently in his bewilderment and alarm. 'The other? What other? What is happening? Are you saying she may be in danger?'

Cadfael fended him off with a restraining arm, and demanded of Hugh: 'Have you sent to the workshop?'

'Not yet! She might have been here, and safe enough. Now I'm going there myself. Come with me! I'll see you excused to Father Abbot afterwards.'

'I will well!' said Cadfael fervently, and was starting for the door, but Elave hung upon him desperately, and could not be shaken off.

'You *shall* tell me! What other? What man? Who is it threatens her? The workshop . . whose?' And on the instant he knew, and moaned the name aloud:'Jevan! The book – you believe in it . . . You think it was *he* . . .?' He was on his feet, hurling himself at the open doorway, but Hugh stood solidly in his way, braced between the jambs.

'Let me go! I *will* go! Let me out to go to her!'

'Fool!' said Hugh brusquely, 'don't make things worse for yourself. Leave this to us, what more could you do than we can and will? Now, with the bishop already here, see to your own weal, and trust us to take care of hers.' And he shifted aside enough to order Cadfael, with a jerk of his head: 'Out, and fit the key!' and forthwith gripped Elave struggling in his arms, and bore him back to trip him neatly with a heel and tip him onto his bed. By the time he had sprung again like a wildcat, Hugh was outside the door, Cadfael had the key in the lock, and Elave thudded against the timber with a bellow of rage and despair, still a prisoner.

They heard him battering at the door and shouting wild appeals after them as they made for the gate-house. They would surely hear him right across the court and into the guest-hall, all the windows being open to the air.

'I sent to saddle up a horse for you,' said Hugh, 'as soon as I heard she was not here. I can think of nowhere else she might have gone, and seeing he went back there . . . Has she been searching? Did he find out?'

The porter had accepted the sheriff's orders as if they came from the abbot himself, and was already leading a saddled pony up from the stable yard at a brisk trot.

'We'll go straight through the town, it's quicker than riding round.'

The thunderous battering on the cell door had already ceased. Elave's voice was silent, But the silence was more daunting then the fury had been. Elave nursed his forces and bided his time.

'I pity whoever opens that door again tonight,' said Cadfael breathlessly, reaching for the rein. 'And within the hour someone will have to take him his supper.'

'You'll be back with better news by then, God willing,' said Hugh, and swung himself into the saddle and led the way out to the Foregate.

Between the bells that signalled the offices of the hor-arium, Elave's timepiece was the light, and he could judge accurately the passing of another clear day by those he had already spent in this narrow room. He knew, as soon as he drew breath and steeled himself into silence, that it could not be long now before the novice who brought his food would come with his wooden platter and pitcher, expecting nothing more disturbing than the courteous reception to which he had become accustomed, from a prisoner grimly resigned to patience, and too just to blame a young brother under orders for his predicament. A big, strapping young man they had chosen for the duty, with a guileless face and a friendly manner. Elave wished him no ill and would do him none if he could help it, but whoever stood between him and the way to Fortunata must look out for himself.

Yet the very arrangement of the cell was advantageous. The window and the desk beneath it were so situated that the opening of the door partly obscured them from anyone entering, until the door was closed again, and the natural place for the novice to set down his tray was on the end of the bed. Visit by visit he had lost all wariness, having had no occasion for it thus far, and his habit was to walk in blithely, pushing the door wide open with elbow and shoulder, and go straight to the bed to lay down his burden. Only then would he close the door and set his broad back to it, and pass the time of morning or evening companionably until the meal was done.

Elave withdrew from the indignity of shouting appeals that no one would heed or answer, and settled down grimly to wait for the footsteps to which he had grown used. His nameless novice had a giant's stride and a weighty frame, and the slap of his sandals on the cobbles was more of a hearty clout. There was no mistaking him, even if the narrow lancet of window had not afforded a glimpse of the wiry brown ring of his tonsure passing by before he turned the corner and reached the door. And there he had to balance his tray on one hand, while he turned the key. Ample time for Elave to be motionless behind the door when the young man walked in as guilelessly as ever, and made straight for the bed.

The smallness of the space caused Elave to collide sidelong with the unsuspecting boy and send him reeling to the opposite wall but even so the prisoner was round the door and out into the court, and running like a hare for the gatehouse, before anyone in sight realised what had happened. After him came the novice, with longer legs and a formidable turn of speed, and a bellow that alerted the porter, and fetched out brothers, grooms and guests like a swarm of bees, from hall and cloister and stableyard. Those quickest to comprehend and most willing to join any pursuit converged upon Elave's flying figure. Those less active drew in more closely to watch. And it seemed that the first shouted alarm had reached even the abbot's lodging, and brought out Radulfus and his guest in affronted dignity to suppress the commotion.

There had been from the first a very poor prospect of success. Yet even when four or five scandalised brothers had run to mass in Elave's path and pinion him between them, he drove the whole reeling group almost to the arch of the gate before they hung upon him so heavily that he was dragged to a standstill. Writhing and struggling, he was forced to his knees, and fell forward on his face on the cobbles, winded and sobbing for breath.

Above him a voice said, quite dispassionately: 'This is the man of whom you told me?'

'This is he,' said the abbot.

'And thus far he as given no trouble, threatened none, made no effort to escape?'

'None,' said Radulfus, 'and I expected none.'

'Then there must be a reason,' said the equable voice. 'Had we not better examine what it can be?' And to the captors, who were still distrustfully retaining their grip on Elave as he lay panting: 'Let him rise.'

Elave braced his hands against the cobbles and got to his knees, shook his bruised head dazedly, and looked up from a pair of elegant riding-boots, by way of plain dark chausses and cotte to a strong, square, masterful face, with a thin, aquiline nose, and grey eyes that were bent steadily and imperturbably upon the dishevelled hair and soiled face of his reputed heretic. They looked at each other with intent and fascinated interest, judge and accused, taking careful stock of a whole field of faith and error, justice and injustice, across which, with all its quicksands and pitfalls, they must try to meet.

'You are Elave?' said the bishop mildly. 'Elave, why run away now?'

'I was not running away, but towards!' said Elave, drawing wondering breath. 'My lord, there's a girl in danger, if things are as I fear. I learned of it only now. And I brought her into peril! Let me but go to her and fetch her off safe, and I'll come back, I swear it. My lord, I love her, I want her for my wife . . . If she is threatened I must go to her.' He had got his breath back now, he reached forward and gripped the skirt of the bishop's cotte, and clung. An incredulous hope was springing up within him, since he was neither repelled nor avoided. 'My lord, my lord, the sheriff is gone to try and find her, he will tell you afterwards, what I say is true. But she is mine, she is part of me and I of her, and I must go to her. My lord, take my word, my most sacred word, my oath that I will return to face my judgement, whatever it may be, if only you will loose me for these few hours of this night.'

Abbot Radulfus took two paces back from this encounter, very deliberately, and with so strong a suggestion of command that all those standing by also drew off silently, still watching wide-eyed. And Roger de Clinton, who could make up his mind about a man in a matter of moments, reached a hand to grip Elave strongly by the hand and raise him from the ground, and stepping with an authoritative gesture from between Elave and the gate, said to the porter: 'Let him go!'

The workshop where Jevan of Lythwood treated his sheepskins lay well beyond the last houses of the suburb of Frankwell, solitary by the right bank of the river, at the foot of a steep meadow backed by a ridge of trees and bushes higher up the slope. Here the land rose, and the water, even at its summer level, ran deep, and with a rapid and forceful current, ideal for Jevan's occupation. The making of vellum demanded an unfailing supply of water, for the first several days of the process running water, and this spot where the Severn ran rapidly provided perfect anchorage for the open wooden frames covered with netting, in which the raw skins were fastened, so that the water could flow freely down the whole length of them, day and night, until they were ready to go into the solution of lime and water in which they would spend a fortnight, before being scraped clean of all remaining hair, and another fortnight afterwards to complete the long bleaching. Fortunata was familiar with the processes which produced at last the thin, creamy-white membranes of which her uncle was so justly proud. But she wasted no time on the netted cages in the river. No one would hide anything of value there, no matter how many folds of cerecloth were wrapped round it for protection. A faint drift of a fleshy odour from the soaking skins made her nostrils quiver as she passed, but the current was fast enough to disperse any stronger stench. Within the workshop the fleshy taint mingled with the sharp smell from the lime tanks, and the more acceptable scent of finished leather.

She turned the key in the lock, and went in, taking the key in with her and closing the door. It was heavy and dark within there, having been closed since morning, but she did not dare open the shutters that would let in light directly on to Jevan's great table, where he cleaned, scraped and pumiced his skins. Everything must appear closed and deserted. There were no houses near, no path passing close by. and surely now she had time enough, and no need for haste. What was no longer in the house must be here. He had no other place so private and so his own.

She knew the layout of the place, where the tanks of lime lay, one for the first soaking when the skins came from the river, one for the second, after both sides had been scraped clean of hair and traces of flesh. The final rinsing was done in the river, before the membranes were stretched over a frame and dried in the sun, and subjected to repeated and arduous cleanings with pumice and water. Jevan had taken in the single frame in use on his morning visit; the skin stretched over it felt smooth and warm to the touch.

212

She waited some minutes to allow her eyes to grow used to the dimness. A little light filtered in where the shutters joined. The roof was of thick straw thatch, sunwarmed, sagging a little between the supporting beams, and the air was heavy to stifling.

Jevan's place of work was meticulously kept, but it was also overfilled, with all the tools of his trade, his lime tanks, nets in reserve for the river cages, piles of skins at various stages of manufacture, the drying frames, and racks of his knives, pumice, cloths for rubbing. He kept also a little oil lamp, in case he needed to finish some process in a failing light, and a box with flint and tinder, charred cloth and touchwood and sulphur-tipped spunks for kindling it. Fortunata began her search by what light came in through the shutters. The lime tanks could be disregarded, but they were so placed as to shroud one end of the workshop in darkness, and behind them lay the long shelf piled with skins still at varied stages of their finishing. Easy enough to use those to shroud a relatively small box, it could lie between them with the untrimmed edges draped to hide it. It took her a long time to go through them all, for they had to be laid aside in scrupulous order, to be restored just as she found them, all the more if she was in error, and there was still nothing to find but the box. But it was far too late to believe in that. If it had been true, why hide it, why remove it from its place in the chest, and leave his breviary stripped of its splendid covering?

The faint, furry dust danced in the thin chink of late sunlight, and tickled her throat and nostrils as she disturbed skin after skin. One pile was gradually stacked back into place, the second began to be stripped down, fold by fold, but there was nothing there but sheepskins. When that was done, the light was failing, for the sun had moved westward and vacated the chink in the shutters. She needed the lamp in order to see into the dark corners of the room, where two or three wooden chests housed a miscellany of offcuts, faulty pieces worth saving for smaller uses, and the finished gatherings of leaves ready for use, from a few great bifolia to the little, narrow, sixteen-leaf foldings used for small grammars or schooling texts. She was well aware that Jevan did not lock these. The workshop itself was locked up when vacant, and vellum was not a common temptation to theft. If one of the chests was locked now, that very fact would be significant.

It took her a little time to get the touchwood to nurse a spark, and kindle grudgingly into a tiny flame, enough to set to the wick of the lamp. She carried it to the line of chests and set it on the lid of the middle one, to shed its light within when she opened the first. If there was nothing alien here, there was nowhere else to look, the racks of tools stood open to view, the solid table was empty, but for the key of the door, which she had laid down there.

She had reached the third chest, in which the waste cuts and trimmings of vellum were tumbled, but here, too, all was as it should be. She had searched everywhere and found nothing.

She was on her knees on the beaten earth floor, lowering the lid, when she heard the door begin to open. The faint creak of the hinges froze her into stillness, her breath held. Then, very slowly, she closed the chest.

'You have found nothing,' said Jevan's voice behind her, low and mild. 'You will find nothing. There is nothing to find.'

Chapter Fourteen

ORTUNATA braced her hands upon the chest on which she leaned, and came slowly to her feet before she turned to face him. In the yellow gleam of the lamp she saw his face in white bone highlights and deep hollows of shadow, perfectly motionless, betraying nothing. And yet it was too late for dissembling, they had both betrayed themselves already, she by whatever sign she had inadvertently left at home to warn him, and this present search, he by following her here. Too late by far to pretend there was nothing to hide, nothing to answer, nothing to be accounted for. Too late to attempt to reconstruct the simple trust she had always had in him. He knew it was gone, as she knew now, beyond doubt, that there was reason for its going.

She sat down on the chest she had just closed, and set the lamp safely apart on the one beside it. And since silence seemed even more impossible than speech, she said simply: 'I wondered about the box. I saw that it was gone from its place.'

'I know,' he said. 'I saw the signs you left for me. I thought you had given me the box. Am I still to account for whatever I do with it?'

'I was curious,' she said. 'You were going to use it for the best of your books. I wondered that it had gone out

215

of favour in one day. But perhaps you have found a better,' she said deliberately, 'to take its place.'

He shook his head, advancing into the room the few steps that took him to the corner of the table where she had laid down the key. That was the moment when she was quite sure, and something withered in her memories of him, forcing her, like a wounded plant, in urgent haste towards maturity. The lamp showed his face arduously smiling, but it was more akin to a spasm of pain. 'I don't understand you,' he said. 'Why must you meddle secretly? Could you not have asked me whatever you wanted to know?'

His hand crept almost stealthily to the key. He drew back into the shadows by the door, and without taking his eyes from her, felt behind him with a grating fumble for the lock, and locked them in together.

It seemed to Fortunata then that she would do well to be a little afraid, but all she could feel was a baffled sadness that chilled her to the heart. She heard her own voice saying: 'Had Aldwin meddled secretly? Was that what ailed him?'

Jevan braced his shoulders back against the door, and stood staring at her with stubborn forbearance, as though dealing with someone unaccountably turned idiot, but his consciously patient smile remained fixed and strained, like a convulsion of agony.

'You are talking in riddles,' he said. 'What has this to do with Aldwin? I can't guess what strange fancy you've got into your head, but it is an illusion. If I choose to show the gem you gave me to a friend who would appreciate it, does that mislead you into thinking I have somehow misprised or misused it?'

'Oh, no!' said Fortunata in the flat tone of helpless despair. 'It will not do! Today you have been nowhere but here, not alone. If there had been no more than that, you would have taken book and all to show, you would have said what you were about. And you would not have followed me here! It was a mistake! You should have

216

waited. I've found nothing. But by your coming I do know now there is something here to be found. Why else should you trouble what I did?' A sudden gust of rage took her at his immovable and self-deceiving attempt at condescension, which struggled and failed to diminish her. 'Why do we keep pretending?' she cried. 'What is the use? If I had known I would have *given* you the book, or taken your price for it if that was what you wanted. But now there's murder, murder, murder in between us, and there's no turning back or putting that away out of mind. And you know it as well as I. Why do we not speak openly? We cannot stay here for ever, unable to go forward or back. Tell me, what *are* we to do now?'

But that was what neither he nor she could answer. Her hands were tied like his, they were suspended in limbo together, and neither of them could cut the cord that fettered them. He would have to kill, she would have to denounce, before either of them could ever be free again, and neither of them could do it, and neither of them, in the end, would be able to refrain. There was no answer. He drew deep breath, and uttered something like a groan.

'You meant that? You could forgive me for robbing you?'

'Without a thought! What you took from me I can do without. But what you took from Aldwin there's no replacing, and no one who is not Aldwin has the right to forgive it.'

'How do you know,' he demanded with abrupt ferocity, 'that I ever did any harm to Aldwin?'

'Because if you had not you would have denied it here and now, in defiance of what I may believe I know. Oh, why, why? But for that I could have held my tongue. For you I would have! But what had Aldwin ever done, to come by such a death?'

'He opened the box,' said Jevan starkly, 'and looked inside. No one else knew. When it was opened before us all he would have blabbed it out. Now you have it! An inquisitive fool who walked in my way, and he could have betrayed me, and I should have lost it . . . lost it for ever . . . It was the box, the box that made me marvel. And he was before me, and had seen what afterwards I saw . . . and coveted!'

Long, heavy silences had broken the low, furious thread of this speech, as if for minutes at a time he forgot where he was, and what manner of audience he was addressing. Outside, the light was gently dimming. Within, the lamp began to burn lower. It seemed to Fortunata that they had been there together for a very long time.

'I had only until Girard came home. I took it that very night, and put what I had in its place. I did not want to cheat you of all, I paid what I had . . . But then there was Aldwin. When could he ever keep to himself anything he knew? And my brother on his way home . . .'

Another haunted silence, in which he began to stir from his post by the door, moving restlessly the length of the room, past where she sat almost forgotten, silent and still.

'When he went running back after Elave, that day, I had almost grown reconciled. My word against his! A risk . . . but almost I came to terms with it. Even now – do you see it? – all this is my word against yours, if you so choose!' He said it without emphasis, almost indifferently. But he had remembered her again, a danger like the other. His unquiet prowling drove him back to the table. He ran the hand that was not clutching the key along the rack of his knives, in a kind of absent caress for a profession he had enjoyed and at which he had excelled.

'In the end it was pure chance. Can you believe that? Chance that I had the knife . . . It was no lie, I came out here to work that afternoon. I had been using a knife – this knife . . .'

Time and silence hung for a long while as he took it

from the rack and drew it slowly out of its leather sheath, running long fingers down the thin, sharp blade.

'I had the sheath strapped to my belt, I forgot and left it there when I locked up to go home. And I thought I would go on through the town and go to Vespers at Holy Cross, seeing it was the day of Saint Winifred's translation . . .'

He turned to look at her, darkly and intently, she sitting there slender and still on the chest beside the lamp, her grave eyes fixed unwaveringly on him. Just once he saw her glance down briefly at the knife in his hand. He turned the blade thoughtfully to catch the light. Now how easily he could end her, take the prize for which he had killed, and set out towards the west, as many and many a wanted man had done from here before him. Wales was not far, fugitives crossed that border both ways at need. But more is needed than mere opportunity. Time was passing, and it seemed this dead-lock must last for ever, in a kind of self-created purgatory.

'. . . I came late, they were all within, I heard the chanting. And then he came out from the little door that leads to the priest's room! If he had not, I should have gone into the church, and there would have been no death. Do you believe that?'

Once again he had remembered her fully, as the niece of whom he had been humanly fond. And this time he wanted a reply, there was hunger in the very vibration of his voice.

'Yes,' she said, 'I do believe it.'

'But he came. And seeing he turned towards the town, to go home, I changed my mind. It happens in a moment in a breath, and everything is changed. I fell in beside him and went with him. There was no one to see, they were all in the church. And I remembered the knife – this knife! It was very simple . . . nothing unseemly . . . He was just newly confessed and shriven, as near content as ever I knew him. At the head of the path down to the riverside I slid it into him, and drew him away in my arm down through the bushes, down to the boat under the bridge. It was still almost full daylight then, I hid him there until dark. So there was no one left to betray me.'

'Except yourself,' she said, 'and now me.'

'And you will not,' said Jevan. 'You cannot . . . any more than I can kill you . . .'

This time the silence was longer and even more strained, and the close, stifling air within the room dulled Fortunata's senses. It was as if they had shut themselves for ever into a closed world where no one else could come, to shatter the tension between them and set them free to move again, to act, to go forward or back. Jevan began once more to pace the floor, turning and twisting at every few steps as though intense pain convulsed him. It went on for a long time, before he suddenly halted, and lowering with a long sigh the hands that still gripped the knife and key, went on as though only a second had passed since he last spoke:

'. . . and yet in the end one of us will have to give way. There is no one else to deliver us.'

He had barely uttered it when a fist banged briskly at the door, and Hugh Beringar's voice called loudly and cheerfully: 'Are you within there, Master Jevan? I saw your light through the shutters. I brought your kin some good news a while ago, but you weren't there to hear it. Open the door and hear it now!'

For one shocked moment Jevan froze where he stood. She felt him stiffen into ice, but his rigor lasted no longer than the flicker of an eyelid, before he heaved himself out of it with a contortion of effort like a man plucking up the weight of the world, and summoned up from somewhere the most matter-of-fact of voices to call back an answer.

'One moment only! I'm just finishing here.'

He was at the door and turning the key as silently and softly as a cat moves. She had risen to her feet, but had not moved from her place, uncertain what he meant to do, but filled with a kind of passive wonder that kept her from making any move of her own. He gripped her by the arm with his left hand, sliding his arm through hers to hold her close and fondly by the wrist, close as a lover or an affectionate father. There was never a word said of threatening or pleading, no request for her silence and submission. Perhaps he was already sure of it, if she was not. But she watched him turn the naked knife he held in his right hand, so that the blade lay along his forearm, and the sleeve concealed it. His long fingers were competent and assured on the shaped haft. He drew her with him to the door, and she went unresisting. With the hand that nursed the knife he set the door wide open, and led her out with him on to the green meadow, into the gentle, cloudless evening light that from within had seemed to be ultimate darkness.

'Good news is always welcome,' he said, confronting Hugh at a few yards' distance with an open and untroubled countenance, from which he had banished the brief, icy pallor by force of will. 'I should have heard it soon – we're bound for home now. My niece has been sweeping and tidying my workshop for me. You need not have gone out of your way for me, my lord, but it was gracious in you.'

'I am not out of my way,' said Hugh. 'We were close, and your brother said you would be here. The matter is, I've set your shepherd free. A liar Conan may be, but a murderer he is not. Every part of his day is accounted for at last, and he's back home and clear of blame. As well you should hear it from me, you may well have been wondering yourself, after all the lies he told, how deep he was mired in this business.'

'Then does this mean,' asked Jevan calmly, 'that you have found the real murderer?'

'Not yet,' said Hugh, with an equally confident and deceptive face, 'though it narrows the field. You'll be glad to get your man back. And he's mortal glad to be back, I can tell you. I suppose that affects your brother's side of the business rather than yours, but according to Conan he has been known to help you with the skins sometimes.' He had advanced to the door of the workshop, and was peering curiously within, into a cavern dimly lit by the little glow-worm lamp, still burning on the lid of the chest. The yellow gleam faded in the light flooding in through the wide open door. Hugh's eyes roamed with an inquisitive layman's interest over the great table under the shuttered windows, the chests and the lime tanks, and arrived at the long rack of knives ranged along the wall, knives for dressing, for fleshing, for scraping, for trimming.

And one of the sheaths empty.

Cadfael, standing a little apart with the horses, between the belt of trees that curved round close to the river on his left hand and the open slope of meadow on his right, had a brightly lit view of the exterior of the workshop, the grassy slope, and the three figures gathered outside the open door. The sun was low, but not yet sunk behind the ridge of bushes, and the slanting westward light picked out detail with golden, glittering clarity, and found every point from which it could reflect. Cadfael was watching intently, for from this retired position he might see things hidden from Hugh, who stood close. He did not like the way Jevan was clasping Fortunata's arm, holding her hard against his side. That embrace, uncharacteristic of so cool and self-sufficient a person as Jevan of Lythwood, Hugh certainly would not have missed. But had he seen, as Cadfael had, in one ruby-red shaft from the setting sun, and for one instant only, the steel of the knife flashing from under the cuff of Jevan's right sleeve?

There was nothing strange in the girl's appearance, except perhaps the unusual stillness of her face. She had nothing to say, made no motion of fear or distrust, was not uneasy at being held so, or if she was, there was no discerning it in her bearing. But she knew, quite certainly, what Jevan had in his other hand.

'So this is where you perform your mysteries,' Hugh was saying, advancing curiously into the workshop. 'I've often wondered about your craft. I know the quality of what you produce, I've seen it in use, but how the leaves come by that whiteness, seeing what the raw hides are like, I've never understood.'

Like any inquisitive stranger, he was prowling about the room, probing into corners, but avoiding the rack of knives, since the gap would be too obvious to be missed if he went near it and made no comment. He was tempting Jevan, if he felt any anxiety or had things to hide within, to loose his hold on the girl and follow, but Jevan never relaxed his grip, only drew Fortunata with him to the doorway, and followed no further. And now indeed that strained and tethered movement began to seem sinister, and how to break the link began to seem a matter of life and death. Cadfael moved a little nearer, leading the horses.

Hugh had emerged from the hut again, still at gaze, still curious. He passed by the close-linked pair and went down towards the edge of the bank, where the netted cages were moored in the river. Jevan followed, but still retaining the girl's arm, cramped into the hollow of his side. Woman walks on the left, so that her man's right arm may be free to defend her, whether with fist or sword. Jevan held Fortunata so fast on his left in order that she might be within instant reach of his knife, if this matter ended past hope. Or was the knife for himself?

Elave had come, as the riders had, through the town, in by one bridge, out by the other, running, after the first frenzy, no longer like a demented man, but steadily, at a pace and rhythm he knew he could maintain. From past years he knew exactly the quickest path beyond the suburb, upriver to the curve where the current had carved its bed deep and fast. When he came over the

223

ridge, and was able to halt and look down towards the solitary workshop in the meadow, withdrawn far enough up the slope to evade even the thaw-water spate unless in a very bad year, he lingered in cover among the trees to take in the scene below, and get his breath back while he assessed it.

And there they were, just outside the door of the workshop, which was in the upstream end of the hut, to prolong the evening light from the west, as the wide opening in the inland, south-facing wall admitted it through the main part of the day. He could see the two netted frames in the water by the way the surface eddies span; they lay slightly downstream, where the raised bank afforded firm anchorage. Behind the linked figures of Jevan and Fortunata the door of the hut stood wide open, in a deceptive suggestion of honesty, as the linked arms of uncle and niece presented a travesty of affection. In all the years of her childhood, never had Jevan handled and petted the girl freely, as Girard would do by his nature. This was a different kind of man, private, self-sufficient, not given to touching or being touched, not effusive in his likings. He had been a kind uncle to her in his cool, teasing way, surely he had loved her, but never thus. It was not love that joined them now. What had she become? His hostage? His protection. for a short while if no more? No, if she had nothing to reveal against him, and he was sure of her, what need to clasp her so close? She could have stood apart, and helped him all the better to an appearance of normality, to fend off the sheriff at least for today. He held fast to her because he was not sure of her, he had to remind her by his grip that if she spoke the wrong word he could avenge himself.

Elave crept round in the cover of the trees, which swept in a long, thinning curve down towards the Severn, upstream of the hut, and shrank into scrub and bushes perhaps fifty paces from the bank. He was nearer now, he could hear the sound of voices but not what was said. Between him and the group at the door stood Brother

224

Cadfael with the horses, for the time being holding off from a nearer approach. And it was all a play, Elave saw that now, a play to preserve the face of normality between all these people. Nothing must shatter it; a too open word, a threatening move might precipitate disaster. The very voices were casual, light and current, like acquaintances exchanging the day's trivial news in the street.

He saw Hugh go into the workshop, and saw that Jevan did not loose his hold of Fortunata to follow him, but stood immovably without. He saw the sheriff emerge again, animated and smiling, brushing past the pair of them and waving Jevan with him towards the river, but when they followed him they moved as one. Then Cadfael stirred himself abruptly and led the horses down the slope to join them, suddenly treading close on Jevan's heels as it seemed, but Jevan never turned his head or relaxed his hold. And Fortunata all this time went silently where she was led, with a still and wary face.

What they needed, what they were trying to achieve, was a diversion, anything that would break that mated pair apart, enable Hugh to pluck the girl away from the man, unhurt. Once robbed of her, Jevan could be dealt with. But they were only two, and he was well aware of both of them, and could so contrive as to keep them both at arm's length and beyond. As long as he held Fortunata by the arm he was safe, and she in peril, and no one could afford to demolish the pretence that everything was as it always was.

But he, Elave, could! Of him Jevan was not aware, and against him he could not be on guard. And there must be something that would shatter his pretence and startle his hand from its attendant shield, and leave him defenceless. Only there would be no more than one chance.

A last long, red ray of the setting sun before it sank pierced the veil of bushes, and at once paled the small yellow glow from within the hut, which Elave had all this time seen without seeing, and glittered for one instant at the wrist of Jevan's right hand. Elave recognised at once fire and steel, and knew why Hugh held off so patiently. Knew, also, what he was about to do. For the whole group with the led horses, had moved downstream towards the netted cages where skins swayed and writhed in the current. A few yards more, and he could put the bulk of the workshop between him and them as he crossed the meadow to the open door.

Hugh Beringar was doing the talking, pretending interest in the processes involved in vellum-making, trying to occupy Jevan's attention to such an extent that he should relax his vigilance. Cadfael ranged distractingly close with the horses, but Jevan never looked round. He had surely left the door of the hut open and the lamp burning to force the sheriff to draw off in the end, mount and ride away, and leave the tolerant craftsman to close up his affairs for the night. Hugh was just as set on outstaying even this relentless patience. And while they were deadlocked there, standing over the bank of the Severn, here was one free agent who could act, and only one.

Elave broke cover and ran, using the hut as shield, headlong for the open doorway and the dim interior, and caught up the lamp. The thatch of the roof was old, dried from a fine summer, bellying loosely between its supporting beams. he set the flame of the lamp to it in two places, over the long table where the draught from the shutters would fan it, and again close to the doorway as he backed out again. Outside he plucked out the burning wick and flung it up on the slope of the roof, and the remaining oil after it. The breeze that often stirred at sunset after a still day was just waking from the west, and caught at the small spurt of flame, sending a thin, sinuous serpent of fire up the roof. Inside the hut he heard what sounded like a giant's gusty sigh, and flames exploded and licked from truss to truss along the thatch between

226

the rafters. Elave ran, not back into the cover of the bushes, but round to the shutters on the landward side of the hut, and gripped and tore at the best hold he could get on the boards until one panel gave and swung clear, and billowing smoke gushed out first, and after it tall tongues of flame as the air fanned the fire within. He sprang back, and stood off to see the fearful thing he had done, as smoke billowed and flame soared above the roof.

Cadfael was the first to see, and cry an alarm: 'Fire! Look, your hut's afire!'

Jevan turned his head, perhaps only half believing, and saw what Cadfael had seen. He uttered one awful scream of despair and loss, flung Fortunata away from him so suddenly and roughly that she almost fell, flung off the knife he held to quiver upright in the turf, and ran frenziedly straight for the hut. Hugh yelled after him: 'Stop! You can do nothing!' and ran after, but Jevan heeded nothing but the tower of fire and smoke, dimming the sunset against which he saw it, and blackening the rose and pale gold of the sky. Round to the far wall of the workshop he ran headlong, and in through the drifting smoke that filled the doorway.

Elave, rounding the corner of the building just in time to confront him face to face, beheld a horrified mask with open, screaming mouth and frantic eyes, before Jevan plunged without pause into the choking darkness within. Elave even grasped at his sleeve to halt him from such madness, and Jevan turned on him and hurled him off with a blow in the face, sending him reeling as a spurt of flame surged between them and drove them apart. Stumbling backwards and falling in the tufted grass, Elave saw the drifting smoke momentarily coiled aside in an eddy of wind. He was staring full into the open doorway, and could not choose but see what happened within.

Jevan had blundered heedless through the smoke, and clambered on to the long table, and was stretching up with both arms plunged to the elbow in the burning thatch, that dangled in swags above his head, reaching for something secreted there. He had it, he tugged wildly to bring it down into his arms, moaning and writhing at the pain of his burned hands. Then it seemed that half the disturbed thatch collapsed in a great explosion of flame on top of him, and he vanished in a dazzling rose of fire and a long howl of anguish and rage.

Elave clawed his way up from the ground and lunged forward with arms over his face to shield him. Hugh came up breathless and baulked in the doorway, as the heat drove them both back, coughing and retching for clean air. And suddenly a blackened figure burst out between them, trailing a comet's tail of smoke and sparks, his clothing and hair on fire, something muffled and shapeless hugged protectively and passionately in his arms. He was keening in a thin wail, like wind in winter in door and chimney. They sprang to intercept him and try to beat out the flames, but he was too sudden and too swift. Down the slope of the grass he went, a living torch, and leaped far out into the mid-current. The Severn hissed and spat, and Jevan was gone, swept downstream past his own nets and skins, past Fortunata, rigid and mute with shock in Cadfael's arms, down this free-flowing reach of the river, to drift ashore somewhere in the slower stretches and lower water where the Severn encircled the town.

Fortunata saw him pass, turning with the current, very soon lost to sight. He was not swimming. Both arms embraced fiercely the swathed burden for which he had killed and now was dying.

It was over. There was nothing now to be done for Jevan of Lythwood, nothing for his blackened and blazing property but to let it burn out. There was nothing near enough to catch fire from it, only the empty field. What mattered now, to Hugh as to Cadfael, was to get these two shocked and inarticulate souls safely back into a real

228

world among familiar things, even if for one of them it must be a return to a household horrified and bereaved, and for the other to a stone cell and a threatened condemnation. Here and now, all Fortunata could say, over and over again, was: 'He would not have hurt me – he would not!' and at last, after many such repetitions, almost inaudibly: *'Would he?'* And nothing as yet could be got out of Elave but the horrified protest: 'I never wanted that! How could I know? How could I know? I never wished him that!' And at last, in a kind of fury against himself, he said: 'And we do not even know he is guilty of anything, even now we do not know!'

'Yes,' said Fortunata then, quickening out of her icy numbness. 'I do know! He told me.'

But that was a story she was not yet able to tell fully, nor would Hugh allow her to waste present time on it, for she was cold with an unnatural cold from within, and he wanted her home.

'See to the lad, Cadfael, and get him back where his bishop wants him, before his truancy is added to the charges against him. I'll take the lady back to her mother.'

'The bishop knows I'm gone,' said Elave, rousing himself to respond, with a great heave of his shoulders that still could not shrug off the stunning load they carried. 'I begged him, and he gave me leave.'

'Did he so?' said Hugh, surprised. 'Then the more credit to him and to you. I have hopes of such a bishop.' He was up into the saddle with a vigorous spring, and reaching down a hand to Fortunata. His favourite rawboned grey would never notice the slight extra weight. 'Hand her up, boy . . . that's it, your foot on mine. And now be wise, leave all till tomorrow. What more needs be done, I'll do.' He had shed his coat to wrap round the girl's shoulders, and settled her securely in his arm. 'Tomorrow, Cadfael, I'll be early with the abbot. Doubtless we shall all meet before the day's out.'

They were gone, away at a canter up the slope of the field, turning their backs on the blaze that was already settling down into a blackened, smouldering heap of roofless timber, and the netted sheepskins weaving and swaying in the sharp current, while the water under the opposite bank lay smooth and almost still.

'And we'll be on our way, too,' said Cadfael, gathering the pony's rein, 'for there's nothing any man can do more here. All's done now, and by the same token, might have been much worse done. Here, you ride and I'll walk with you, and we'll just make our way quietly home.'

'*Would* he have harmed her?' Elave asked after long silence, when they were threading the highroad through the thriving houses and shops of Frankwell and approaching the western bridge.

'How can we know, when she herself cannot be certain? God's providence decreed that he should not. That must be enough for us. And you were his instrument.'

'I have been the death of his brother for Girard,' said Elave. 'How can he but blame me? What better could I expect from him now?'

'Would it have been better for Girard if his brother had lived to be hanged?' asked Cadfael. 'And his name blown about in the scandal of it? No, leave Girard to Hugh. He's a man of sense, he'll not hold it against you. You sent him back a daughter, he won't grudge her to you when the time comes.'

'I never killed a man before.' Elave's voice was weary and reflective. 'In all those miles we travelled, and with dangers and fights enough along the way, I doubt if I ever drew blood.'

'You did not kill him, and must not claim more than your due. His own actions killed him.'

'Do you think he may have dragged himself ashore somewhere? Living? *Could* he live? After that?'

'All things are possible,' said Cadfael. But he remembered the arms in their smouldering sleeves clamped fast over the thing Jevan had snatched from the fire, the long body swept past beneath the water without struggle or sound, and he had not much doubt what would be found next day, somewhere in the circuit of the town.

Over the bridge and through the streets the pony paced placidly, and at the descent of the Wyle he snuffed the evening air and his pace grew brisker, scenting his stable and the comforts of home.

When they entered the great court, the brothers had just come out from Compline. Abbot Radulfus emerged from the cloister to cross to his own lodging, with his distinguished guests one on either side. They came at the right moment to see a brother of the house leading in, on one of the abbey's ponies, the prisoner accused of heresy, and released on his parole some three hours earlier. The rider was soiled and blackened by smoke, his hands and his hair at the temples somewhat scorched by fire, a circumstance he had not so far noticed, but which rendered the whole small procession a degree more outrageous in Canon Gerbert's eyes. Brother Cadfael's calm acceptance of this unseemly spectacle only redoubled the offence. He helped Elave to dismount, patted him encouragingly on the back, and ambled off to the stables with the pony, leaving the prisoner to return to his cell of his own volition, even gladly, as if he were indeed coming home. This was no way to hold an alleged heretic. Everything about the procedures here in the abbey of Saint Peter and Saint Paul scandalised Canon Gerbert.

'Well, well!' said the bishop, unshaken, even appreciative. 'Whatever else the young man may be, he's a man of his word.'

'I marvel,' said Gerbert coldly, 'that your lordship should ever have taken such a risk. If you had lost him it would have been a grave dereliction, and a great injury to the Church.'

'If I had lost him,' said the bishop, unmoved, 'he would have lost more and worse. But he comes back as he went, intact!'

Chapter Fifteen

ROTHER CADFAEL asked audience with the abbot early next morning, to recount all that had happened, and was glad to meet Hugh arriving just as he himself was leaving. Hugh's session with Abbot Radulfus lasted longer. There was much to tell, and still much to do, for nothing had yet been seen of Jevan of Lythwood, dead or alive, since he had leaped into the Severn a lighted torch, his hair erected and ablaze. For Radulfus, too, the day's business was of grave importance. Roger de Clinton abhorred time wasted, and was needed in Coventry, and it was his intention to make an end, one way or another, at this morning's chapter, and be off back to his restless and vulnerable city.

'Oh, yes, and I have brought and delivered to Canon Gerbert,' said Hugh, rising to take his leave, 'the latest report from Owain's borders. Earl Ranulf has come to terms for the time being, it suits Owain to keep the peace with him for a while. The earl will be back in Chester by tonight. No doubt the canon will be relieved to be able to continue his journey.'

'No doubt,' said the abbot. He did not smile, but even in two bare syllables there was a tone of satisfaction in his voice.

Elave came to his trial shaven, washed clean of his smoky disfigurement, and provided, by Brother Denis' good offices, with a clean shirt and a decent coat in exchange for his scorched and unsightly one. It was almost as if the community had grown so accustomed to him during his few day's stay, and so completely lost all inclination to regard him as in any way perilous or to be condemned, that they were united in wishing him to present the most acceptable appearance possible, and make the most favourable impression, in a benevolent conspiracy which had come into being quite spontaneously.

'I have been taking advice,' said the bishop briskly, opening the assembly, 'concerning the ordinary human record of this young man, from some who know him well and have had dealings with him, as well as what I have observed with my own eyes in this short while. And let no man present feel that the probity or otherwise of a man's common behaviour has nothing to do with such a charge as heresy. There is authority in scripture: By their fruits you may know them. A good tree cannot bring forth bad fruit, nor a bad tree good fruit. So far as anyone has been able to inform me, this man's fruits would seem to bear comparison with what most of us can show. I have heard of none that could be called rotten. Bear that in mind. It is relevant. As to the exact charges brought against him, that he has said certain things which go directly against the teachings of the Church . . . Let someone now rehearse them to me.'

Prior Robert had written them down, and delivered them with a neutral voice and impartial countenance, as if even he had felt how the very atmosphere within the enclave had changed towards the accused.

'My lord, in sum, there are four heads: first, that he does not believe that children who die unbaptised are doomed to reprobation. Second, as a reason for that, he does not believe in original sin, but holds that the state of newborn children is the state of Adam before his fall, a state of innocence. Third, that he holds that a man can, by his own acts, make his own way towards salvation, which is held by the Church to be a denial of divine grace. Fourth, that he rejects what Saint Augustine wrote of predestination, that the number of the elect is already chosen and cannot be changed, and all others are doomed to reprobation. For he said rather that he held with Origen, who wrote that in the end all men would be saved, since all things came from God, and to God they must return.'

'And those four heads are all the matter?' said the bishop thoughtfully.

'They are, my lord.'

'And how do you say, Elave? Have you been mis-reported in any of these counts?'

'No, my lord,' said Elave firmly. 'I hold by all of those. Though I never named this Origen, for I did not then know the name of the elder who wrote what I accepted and still believe.'

'Very well! Let us consider the first head, your defence of those infants who die unbaptised. You are not alone in having difficulty in accepting their damnation. In doubt, go back to Holy Writ. That cannot be wrong. Our Lord,' said the bishop, 'ordered that children should be allowed to come to him freely, for of such, he said, is the kingdom of heaven. To the best of my reading, he never asked first whether they were baptised or not before he took them up in his arms. Heaven he certainly allotted to them. But tell me, then, Elave, what value *do* you see in infant baptism, if it is not the sole way to salvation?'

'It is a welcome into the Church and into life, surely,' said Elave, uncertain as yet of his ground and of his judge, but hopeful. 'We come innocent, but such a membership and such a blessing is to help us keep our innocence.'

'To speak of innocence at birth is to bring us to the second count. It is part of the same thinking. You do not

234

believe that we come into the world already rotten with the sin of Adam?'

Pale, obstinate and unrelenting, Elave said: 'No, I do not believe it. It would be unjust. How can God be unjust? By the time we are grown we have enough to bear with our own sins.'

'Of all men,' agreed the bishop with a rueful smile, 'that is certainly true. Saint Augustine, who has been mentioned here, regarded the sin of Adam as perpetuated in all his heirs. It might be well to give a thought to what the sin of Adam truly was. Augustine held it to be the fleshly act between man and woman, and considered it the root and origin of all sin. There is here another disputable point. If this in every case is sin, how comes it that God instructed his first-made creatures to be fruitful and multiply and people the earth?'

'It is nevertheless a more blessed course to refrain,' said Canon Gerbert coldly but carefully, for Roger de Clinton was on his own ground, noble, and highly regarded.

'Neither the act nor abstention from the act is of itself either good or bad,' said the bishop amiably, 'but only in respect of its purpose, and the spirit in which it is undertaken. What was your third head, Father Prior?'

'The question of free will and divine grace,' said Robert. 'And namely, whether a man can of his free will choose right instead of wrong, and whether by so doing he can proceed one step towards his own salvation. Or whether nothing can avail of all he does, however virtuous, but only by divine grace.'

'As to that, Elave,' said the bishop, looking at the resolute face that fronted him with such intent and sombre eyes, 'you may speak your mind. I am not trying to trap you, I desire to know.'

'My lord,' said Elave, picking his way with deliberation, 'I do believe we have been given free will, and can and must use it to choose between right and wrong, if we are men and not beasts. Surely it is the least of what we owe, to try and make our way towards salvation by right action. I never denied divine grace. Surely it is the greatest grace that we are given this power to choose, and the strength to make right use of it. And see, my lord, if there is a last judgement, it will not and cannot be of God's grace, but of what every man has done with it, whether he buried his talent or turned it to good profit. It is for our own actions we shall answer, when the day comes.'

'So thinking,' said the bishop, eyeing him with interest. 'I see that you can hardly accept that the roll of the elect is already made up, and the rest of us are eternally lost. If that were true, why strive? And strive we do. It is native to man to have an aim, and labour towards it. And God he knows, better than any, that grace and truth and uprightness are as good aims as any. What else is salvation? It is no bad thing to feel obliged to earn it, and not wait to be given it as alms to a beggar, unearned.'

'These are mysteries for the wise to ponder, if anyone dare,' said Gerbert in chill disapproval, but somewhat abstractedly, too, for a part of his mind was already preoccupied with the journey on to Chester, and the subtle diplomacy he must have at his finger-ends when he got there. 'From one obscure even among the laity it is presumptuous.'

'It was presumptuous of Our Lord to argue with the doctors in the temple,' said the bishop, 'seeing he was human boy as well as God, and in both kinds true to that nature. But he did it. We doctors in the temple nowadays do well to recall how vulnerable we are.' And he sat back in his stall, and regarded Elave very earnestly for some minutes. 'My son,' he said then, 'I find no fault with you for venturing to use wits which, I'm sure you would say, are also the gift of God, and meant for use, not to be buried profitless. Only take care to remember that you are also subject to error, and vulnerable after your own kind as I after mine.'

'My lord,' said Elave, 'I have learned it all too well.'

'Not so well, I hope, as to bury your talent now. It is better to cut too deep a course than to stagnate and grow foul. One test only I require, and that is enough for me. If you believe, in all good faith, the words of the creed, in the sight of this assembly and of God, recite it for me now.'

Elave had begun to glow as brightly as the sun slanting across the floor of the chapter-house. Without further invitation, without an instant's thought, he began in a voice loud, clear and joyful: 'I believe in one God, the Father, the ruler of all men, the maker of all things visible and invisible . . .'

For this belonged in the back of his mind untouched since childhood, learned from his first priestly patron, whom he loved and who could do no wrong for him, and with whom he had chanted it regularly and happily for years without ever questioning what it meant, only feeling what it meant to the gentle teacher he adored and imitated. This was his faith for once not chiselled out for himself, but received, rather an incantation than a declaration of belief. After all his doubts and probings and rebellions, it was his innocence and orthodoxy that set the seal on his deliverance.

He was just ending, in triumph, knowing himself free and vindicated, when Hugh Beringar came quietly into the chapter-house, with a bundle wrapped in thick swathes of waxed cloth under his arm.

'We found him,' said Hugh, 'lodged under the bridge, caught up by the chain that used to moor a boat mill there, years ago. We have taken his body home. Girard knows everything we could tell him. With Jevan's end this whole matter can end. He owned to murder before he died. There is no need to publish to the world what would further injure and distress his kin.'

'None,' said Radulfus.

There were seven of them gathered together in

Brother Anselm's corner of the north walk, but Canon Gerbert was not among them. he had already shaken off the dust of this questionably orthodox abbey from his riding-boots, mounted a horse fully recovered from his lameness and eager for exercise, and set off for Chester, with his body servant and his grooms, and no doubt was already rehearsing what he would have to say to Earl Ranulf, and how much he could get from him without promising anything of substance in return. But the bishop, once having heard of what Hugh carried, and the vicissitudes through which it had passed, had the human curiosity to wait and see for himself the final outcome. Here with him were Anselm, Cadfael, Hugh, Abbot Radulfus, and Elave and Fortunata, silent, hand in hand though they dissembled the clasp reticently between their bodies in this august company. They were still a little dazed with too sudden and too harsh experience, and not yet fully awake to this equally abrupt and bewildering release from tension.

Hugh had delivered his report in few words. The less said now of that death, the better. Jevan of Lythwood was gone, taken from the Severn under the same arch of the same bridge where he had hidden his own dead man until nightfall. In time Fortunata would remember him as she had always known him, an ordinary uncle, kind if not demonstrative. Some day it would cease to matter that she still could not be certain whether he would indeed have killed her, as he had killed one witness already, rather than give up what in the end he had valued more than life. It was the last irony that Aldwin, according to Conan, had never managed to see what was within the box. Jevan had killed to no purpose.

'And this,' said Hugh, 'was still in his arms, lodged fast against the stone of the pier.' It lay now upon Anselm's work-table, still shedding a few drops of water as the wrappings were stripped away. 'It belongs, as you know, to this lady, and she has asked that it be opened here, before you, my lords, as witnesses knowledgeable in such works as may be found within.'

He was unfolding layer after layer as he spoke. The outermost, scorched and frayed into holes, had already been discarded, but Jevan had given his treasure every possible protection, and by the time the last folds were stripped away the box lay before them immaculate, untouched by fire or water, the ornate key still in the lock. The ivory lozenge stared up at them with immense Byzantine eyes from beneath the great round forehead that might have been drawn with compasses, before the rich hair was carved, and the beard, and the lines of age and thought. The coiling vines gleamed, refracting light from polished edges. Now at last they all hesitated to turn the key and open the lid.

It was Anselm who at length set hands to it and opened it. From both sides they leaned to gaze. Fortunata and Elave drew close, and Cadfael made room for them. Who had a better right?

The lid rose on the binding of purple dyed vellum, bordered with a rich tracery of leaves, flowers and tendrils in gold, and bearing in the centre, in a delicate framework of gold, a fellow to the ivory on the box. The same venerable face and majestic brow, the same compelling eyes gazing upon eternity, but this one was carved on a smaller scale, not a head but a half-length, and held a little harp in his hands.

With reverent care Anselm tilted the box, and supported the book on his palm as he slid it out on to the table.

'Not a saint,' he said, 'except that they often showed him with a halo. This is King David, and surely what we have here is a psalter.'

The purple vellum of the binding was stretched over thin boards, and the first gathering of the book, and the last, when Anselm opened it, were also of gold on purple. The rest of the leaves were of very fine, smooth finish and almost pure white. There was a frontispiece painting of the psalmist playing and singing, enthroned

239

like an emperor, and surrounded by musicians earthly and heavenly. The vibrant colours sprang ringing from the page, as brilliantly as the sounds the royal minstrel was plucking from his strings. Here was no powerful, massive Byzantine block colouring, classic and monumental, but sinuous, delicate, graceful shapes, as pliant and ethereal as the pattern of vines that surrounded the picture. Everything rippled and twined, and was elegantly elongated. Opposite, on a skin side smooth as silk, the title page was lined out in golden uncials. But on the following leaf, which was the dedication page, the penmanship changed to a neat, fluent, round hand.

'This is not eastern,' said the bishop, leaning to look more closely.

'No. It is Irish minuscule, the insular script.' Anselm's voice grew more reverent and awed as he turned page after page, into the ivory whiteness of the main part of the book, where the script had abandoned gold for a rich blue-black, and the numerals and initials flowered in exquisite colours, laced and bordered with all manner of meadow flowers, climbing roses, little herbers no bigger than a thumbnail, where birds sang in branches hardly thicker than a hair, and shy animals leaned out from the cover of blossoming bushes. Tiny, perfect women sat reading on turfed seats under bowers of eglantine. Golden fountains played into ivory basins, swans sailed on crystal rivers, minute ships ventured oceans the size of a tear.

In the last gathering of the book the leaves reassumed their imperial purple, the final exultant psalms were again inscribed in gold, and the psalter ended with a painted page in which an empyrean of hovering angels, a paradise of haloed saints, and a transfigured earth of redeemed souls all together obeyed the psalmist, and praised God in the firmament of his power, with every instrument of music known to man. And all the quivering wings, all the haloes, all the trumpets and psalteries and harps, the stringed instruments and organs, the timbrels and the loud cymbals were of burnished gold, and the denizens of heaven and paradise and earth alike were as sinuous and ethereal as the tendrils of rose and honeysuckle and vine that intertwined with them, and the sky above them as blue as the irises and periwinkles under their feet, until the tips of the angels' wings melted into a zenith all blinding gold, in which the ultimate mystery vanished from sight.

'This is a wonder!' said the bishop. 'Never have I seen such work. This is beyond price. Where can such a thing have been produced? Where was there art the match of this?'

Anselm turned back to the dedication page, and read aloud slowly from the golden Latin:

Made at the wish of Otto, King and Emperor, for the marriage of his beloved son, Otto, Prince of the Roman Empire, to the most Noble and Gracious Theofanu, Princess of Byzantium, this book is the gift of His Most Christian Grace to the Princess. Diarmaid, monk of Saint Gall, wrote and painted it.

'Irish script and an Irish name,' said the abbot. 'Gallus himself was Irish, and many of his race followed him there.'

'Including one,' said the bishop, 'who created this most precious and marvellous thing. But the box, surely, was made for it later, and by another Irish artist. Perhaps the same hand that made the ivory on the binding also made the second one for the casket. Perhaps she brought such an artist to the west in her train. It is a marriage of two cultures indeed, like the marriage it celebrated.'

'They were in Saint Gall,' said Anselm, scholar and historian, regarding with love but without greed the most beautiful and rare book he was ever likely to see. 'The same year the prince married they were there, son and father both. It is recorded in the chronicle. The young man was seventeen, and knew how to value manuscripts. He took several away with him from the library. Not all of them were ever returned. Is it any wonder that a man who loved books, once having set eyes on this, should covet it to the edge of madness?'

Cadfael, silent and apart, took his eyes from the pure, clear colours laid on, almost two hundred years since, by a steady hand and a loving mind, to watch Fortunata's face. She stood with Elave close and watchful at her shoulder, and Cadfael knew that the boy had her by the hand still in the shelter of their bodies, as fast as ever Jevan had held her by the arm when she was the only frail barrier he had against betrayal and ruin. She gazed and gazed at the beautiful thing William had sent her as dowry, and her eyes were hooded and her lips set in a pale, still face.

No fault of Diarmaid, the Irish monk of Saint Gall, who had poured his loveliest art into a gift of love, or at least a gift for marriage, the loftiest of the age, a mating of empires! No fault of his that this exquisite thing had brought about two deaths, and bereaved as well as endowed the bride to whom it was sent. Was it any wonder that such a perfect thing could corrupt a hitherto blameless lover of books to covet, steal and kill?

Fortunata looked up at last, and found the bishop's eyes upon her, across the table and its radiant burden.

'My child,' he said, 'you have here a most precious gift. If it pleases you to sell it, it will provide you with a rich dowry indeed, but take good advice before you part with it, and keep it safe. Abbot Radulfus here would surely hold it in trust for you, if you wish it, and see that you are properly counselled when you come to deal with a buyer. Though I must tell you that in truth it would be impossible to put a price on it fit for what is priceless.'

'My lord,' said Fortunata, 'I know what I want to do with it. I cannot keep it. It is beautiful, and I shall always remember it and be glad that I've seen it. But as long as it remains with me I shall find it a bitter reminder, and it will seem to me somehow spoiled and wronged. Nothing ugly should ever have touched it. I would rather that it should go with you. In your church treasury it will be pure again, and blessed.'

'I understand your revulsion,' said the bishop gently, 'after all that has happened, and I feel the justice of your grief for a thing of beauty and grace misused. But if that is truly what you wish, then you must accept what the library of my see can pay you for the book, though I must tell you I have not its worth to spend.'

'No!' Fortunata shook her head decidedly. 'Money has been paid for it once, money must not be paid for it again. If it has no price, no price must be given for it, but I may give it, and suffer no loss.'

Roger de Clinton, himself a man of decision, recognised as strong a resolution confronting him and, moreover, respected and approved it. But in conscience he reminded her considerately: 'The pilgrim who brought it half across the world, and sent it to you as a dowry, he also has a right to have his wishes honoured. And his wish was that this gift should be yours – no one's else.'

She acknowledged it with an inclination of her head, very seriously. 'But having given it, and made it mine, he would have held that it was mine, to give again if I pleased, and would never have grudged it. Especially,' said Fortunata firmly, 'to you and the Church.'

'But also he wished his gift to be used to ensure you a good marriage and a happy life,' said the bishop.

She looked back at him steadily and earnestly, with Elave's hand in hers, and Elave's face at her shoulder matching the look. 'That it has already done,' said Fortunata. 'The best of what he sent me I am keeping.'

By mid-afternoon they were all gone. Bishop de Clinton and his deacon, Serlo, were on their way back to Coventry, where one of Roger's predecessors in office had transferred the chief seat of his diocese, though it was still more often referred to as Lichfield than as Coventry, and both churches considered themselves as having cathedral status. Elave and Fortunata had returned together to the distracted household by Saint Alkmund's church, where now the body of the slayer lay on the same trestle bier in the same outhouse where his victim had lain, and Girard, who had buried Aldwin, must now prepare to bury Jevan. The great holes torn in the fabric of a close-knit household would gradually close and heal, but it would take time. Doubtless the women would pray just as earnestly for both the slayer and the slain.

With the bishop, carefully and reverently packed in his saddle-roll, went Princess Theofanu's psalter. How it had ever made its way back to the east, to some small monastery beyond Edessa, no one would ever know, and some day, perhaps two hundred years on, someone would marvel how it had travelled from Edessa to the library of Coventry, and that would also remain a mystery. Books are more durable than their authors, but at least the Irish monk Diarmaid had secured his own immortality.

Even the guest-hall was almost empty. The festival was over, and those who had lingered for a few days more were now finishing whatever business they had in Shrewsbury, and packing up to leave. The midsummer lull between Saint Winifred's translation and Saint Peter's fair provided convenient time for harvesting the abbey cornfields, beyond the vegetable gardens of the Gaye, where ears were already whitening towards ripeness. The seasons kept their even pace. Only men came and went, acted and refrained, untimely.

Brother Winfrid, content in his labours, was clipping the overgrown hedge of box, and whistling as he worked. Cadfael and Hugh sat silent and reflective on the bench against the north wall of the herb-garden, grown a little somnolent in the sun, and the lovely languor that comes after stress has spent itself. The colours of the roses in the distant beds became the colours of Diarmaid's rippling borders, and the white butterfly on the dim blue flower of fennel was changed into a little ship on an ocean no bigger than a pearl.

'I must go,' said Hugh for the third time, but made no move to go.

'I hope,' said Cadfael at last, stirring with a sigh, 'we have heard the last of the word heresy. If we must have episcopal visitations, may they all turn out as well. With another man it might have ended in anathema.' And he asked thoughtfully: 'Was she foolish to part with it? I have it in my eyes still. Almost I can imagine a man coveting it to death, his own or another's. The very colours could burn into the heart.'

'No,' said Hugh, 'she was not foolish, but very wise. How could she have ever have sold it? Who could pay for such a thing, short of kings? No, in enriching the diocese she enriches herself.'

'For that matter,' said Cadfael, after a long, contented silence, 'he did pay her a fair price for it. He gave Elave back to her, free and approved. I wouldn't say but she may have got the better of the bargain, after all.'

245

Eight and a half centuries have passed since Brother Cadfael walked the streets of Shrewsbury but you can still follow in his footsteps.

The Abbey of Saint Peter and Saint Paul and Shrewsbury Council have joined together to create a series of walks round this ancient town that will allow you, literally, to stand in the steps of Brother Cadfael. You can see the castle, the Meole Brook, St Giles' Church and many other locations that have survived from mediaeval times.

These walks have been created by the Abbey Restoration Project, which is dedicated to the upkeep of the Abbey of Saint Peter and Saint Paul and the excavation and preservation of the monastery ruins.

If you would like further details, or even to make a contribution to the horrendous cost of preservation, please contact:

> Shrewsbury Abbey Restoration Project,
> Project Office,
> 1 Holy Cross Houses,
> Abbey Foregate,
> Shrewsbury SY2 6BS